MY SCORCHING SUMMER DIARY

BY KELLY ann

Liz Rettig

CORGI BOOKS

MY SCORCHING SUMMER DIARY

A CORGI BOOK 978 0 552 56491 5

First Published in Great Britain by Corgi Books,
an imprint of Random House Children's Books
A Random House Group Company

Corgi edition published 2011

This Corgi edition published 2012

1 3 5 7 9 10 8 6 4 2

The Random House Group Limited supports The Forest Stewardship Council
(FSC®), the leading international forest certification organisation. Our books
carrying the FSC label are printed on FSC® certified paper. FSC is the only
forest certification scheme endorsed by the leading environmental organisations,
including Greenpeace. Our paper procurementpolicy can be found at
www.randomhouse.co.uk/environment

MIX
Paper from
responsible sources
FSC® C016897
www.fsc.org

Corgi Books are published by Random House Children's Books,
61–63 Uxbridge Road, London W5 5SA

www.totallyrandombooks.co.uk
www.randomhouse.co.uk

Addresses for companies within The Random House Group Limited
can be found at: www.randomhouse.co.uk/offices.htm

THE RANDOM HOUSE GROUP Limited Reg. No. 954009

A CIP catalogue record for this book is available from the British Library.

Printed and bound by CPI Group (UK) Ltd, Croydon, CR0 4YY

This novel is dedicated to my old school friends Anne Campbell, Marie Hand, Patricia McCabe and Pauline McAlavey. Thanks for your loyalty and all the laughs which brightened up my teenage years. Oh, and no worries, none of you is in the book, so your secrets are safe with me. Honestly!

With special thanks to my lovely niece Eileen Clarke. She is my 'first reader' and always gives me valuable (and frank!) feedback as well as encouragement.

I'm also hugely grateful to the talented team of people at RHCB who made all these books possible; especially Annie Eaton who suggested the theme of this novel, and editors Kelly Hurst and Lauren Buckland for their unfailing and patient support.

And finally, a huge thank you to the men in my life; my husband Paul, son Chris and agent Guy Rose, for putting up with me after all this time.

SATURDAY JULY 27TH

'Don't go to London, Kelly Ann,' Chris said. 'I've got a bad feeling about it.'

I frowned and closed the book I'd been leafing through. *The Complete Idiot's Guide to London.* 'Is it because I'm reading this? It's a present from Mum. Her idea of a laugh, I suppose. Don't worry, I'm not as totally stupid as she thinks I am. Nobody could be.'

He smiled. 'No, it's not that.'

I tossed the book on the floor and sidled closer to him on the sofa. 'So, have you had some kind of premonition then? I thought you medic students didn't believe in all that rubbish.'

'We don't.'

'Good, so you haven't had visions of me being strangled on a tube by a psychopath, then bits of my bloated body found weeks later floating in the Thames half eaten by crabs.'

'No. Much worse than that.'

'What!'

'I'm worried you're going to love London.'

'Well, what's wrong with that?' I asked, puzzled.

'You might love it so much you never want to come back to Glasgow. I don't want to lose you.'

I wound my arms around him and looked into the warm brown eyes of my gorgeous boyfriend. 'Of course I'll come back. It's just a six-week summer job.'

'You promise?'

'I promise,' I said and kissed him. I glanced at the clock and moved away from him reluctantly. 'You better go now. Liz and Stephanie are coming over.'

But he pulled me towards him and kissed me again; long and slow. 'You sure you don't want me to stay?'

I sighed. 'No, we're going to have a last girlie night before I go off to London. Facepacks, leg waxes and sexy vampire films. You'd hate it.'

He cupped my face in his hands and gazed at me. 'Kelly Ann, you know I love you?'

'Yeah, of course.'

'And I'd do anything for you. Even die for you if I had to.'

'Yeah, I know.'

'So do you think facepacks, leg waxes and stupid vampire films would put me off staying with you tonight?'

'No, I suppose n—'

'Definitely.' He stood up and smiled. 'I'm off.'

I threw a cushion at him as he headed for the door. He came back, swept me up into his arms so that my feet were lifted right off the floor and kissed me. 'Say hi to Liz and Stephanie for me. See you tomorrow.'

When he'd gone I finished off the last of my packing and washed my hair. Took ages to blow-dry and straighten it. My friend Stephanie was right – it had got too long, and I should have had it cut, but there was no time for that now. She'd also suggested highlights to brighten up the dark brown colour, but there was no way I could have afforded that. Maybe when I get my first week's wages I'll have them done in London.

Oh God, wages. Real earnings of my own instead of pocket money from parents. And London. In just two days I'd be in London. Felt my stomach twist with excitement. And fear. Hoped Chris's bad feeling really wasn't a premonition after all.

Liz arrived first with a huge tin of Cadbury's Roses for me. Probably feeling guilty – and so she should as she was supposed to be coming down to London with me but had cancelled at the last minute. In fact, it was all her idea in the first place. She'd found an agency that recruited hotel summer staff for London. This way, she said, we'd be able to stay in London all summer for nothing and even get paid. 'Think about it, Kelly Ann. We'd have our own place in the centre of London. And no parents around to tell us when to come home or complain about noise. There are thousands of cool clubs and bars to go to and we'd probably get to meet loads of famous people too. London's practically crawling with celebs.'

When I hesitated because I wasn't sure if I wanted to leave Chris, she got on at me. 'You mustn't be too co-dependent on a boyfriend, Kelly Ann. It's very bad for you psychologically, you know. And nothing puts guys off more than needy dependency.'

So we went to the recruiting agency together and celebrated with a pizza and a bottle of Asti Spumante when we passed the interview and were offered a job in a hotel right in the centre of London. But Liz backed out at the last minute when her boyfriend booked a surprise trip to New York for them both. Hmm.

Still, there was no point in falling out about it, and to be honest if I'd been offered a free trip to New York I suppose I might have done the same thing, so I just ushered her inside.

'We can watch the movies in the living room tonight, Liz. Mum and Dad are at Aunt Kate's and they've promised not to come back until midnight at the earliest.'

'Great.' Liz handed me the chocolates and settled down on the sofa facing the television. 'So, only two days to go until you're off to London. How are you feeling?'

'OK,' I said. 'Considering I have to go on my own now. *Without my friend.*'

'I sense you might be feeling some resentment towards me.'

'No, it's all right.'

'Also possibly experiencing feelings of rejection, abandonment and worthlessness?'

'I'm fine, Liz.'

'Don't worry,' she said, ignoring my admittedly not totally honest reassurances. 'We don't have time right now but we'll tackle these negative emotions of yours in a therapy session when you get back.'

Hmm, typical of Liz to suggest I was the one with a problem when *she* was the one who should be feeling guilty. One thing I wouldn't miss about Liz was her habit of psychoanalysing people all the time. God knows what she is going to be like next year when she starts studying psychology at uni. As for a therapy session with Liz, well, I'd rather be slowly skinned alive with a cheese-grater than endure that.

I decided to change the subject. 'Have a chocolate, Liz.'

'No thanks, I'm on a pre-holiday diet.'

'You've no need to diet,' I said dutifully. 'You look great.' It was true, actually. Although Liz is slightly plump, she is blonde and busty so loads of guys fancy her. Especially her boyfriend Julian, who adores her curves.

'Thanks. Well, I might have just one then,' Liz said.

We'd got through half the tin – Liz ate most of them – by the time Stephanie arrived. She handed me a very expensive bottle of wine, probably pinched from her mum's kitchen, which would taste OK once I added some lemonade to it to sweeten it up a bit. Stephanie is loaded, or her parents are anyway, which is the same thing really, so there had been zero chance of her coming with me if it meant taking such a menial job. Anyway, she is going off on holiday with her fiancé Dave next week after first cancelling her wedding plans last month when a hot bikini wax went wrong. Don't ask. She's only eighteen, though – a year older than me – so no one is really sure now whether a wedding will ever happen. Especially as, apart from shopping, lusting after fit guys has always been Stephanie's favourite pastime.

'Right, let's get your packing done first,' Stephanie said, heading up to my bedroom before I could stop her. 'Then we'll slap on our facepacks and watch the movies.'

I scrambled up after her and pointed to my suitcase and rucksack. 'Already done.'

'You're joking. Right? I mean, this wouldn't be enough for a weekend at a nudist camp.'

'It's fine, Stephanie. Anyway, I can't manage to lug more than one suitcase about London on my own.'

'Then you'll need a bigger suitcase! I'll get Mum to

bring one of mine over.' She unzipped my luggage and shook her head despairingly. Opened my wardrobe and drawers and started pulling stuff out. Oh God.

It was nearly two hours before we finally settled down to watch our favourite bits of the *Twilight* series movies. Great fun, but things turned ugly for a while when Liz and Stephanie argued furiously over who was the hottest star. Liz was definitely in Team Edward – 'just look at his profile when he kisses her'. Stephanie in Team Jacob – 'check out his six-pack'. Eventually they agreed that Edward's face on Jacob's body would be the ideal. I didn't fancy the idea – too much like Frankenstein for me – but shut up about it so we could watch the rest of the movies in peace before my parents got back.

Liz was the first to leave as she'd a busy day tomorrow shopping for her New York holiday. 'Good luck in London. Don't forget to tell me everything that happens. Every single detail. Including all your thoughts and feel-ings.'

Yeah, right. 'Will do.'

'Sorry I didn't go with you to London. If it wasn't such a negative emotion I would be feeling a bit guilty.'

Ha! At last. Knew she felt guilty. 'That's OK, Liz.'

She hugged me. 'Try not to make too much of a mess of things. I really will miss you.'

I blinked back a tear. Yeah, Liz could be a pain at times but we'd been friends for years and I knew she really cared about me. I was going to miss having such a good pal in London.

Stephanie left a bit later after adding yet more stuff to my luggage.

'Good luck in London. And remember to wear brown leather or suede accessories with your denims. Not black or, God forbid, navy.'

'Erm, I'm not sure I have any real leather or suede stuff.'

'And don't forget,' she continued, ignoring me, 'your purple camisole goes with the forest green skirt, not the lime one, which is in any case a crime against fashion and should be thrown out.'

'Hmm, yeah, I'm not particularly keen on that skirt now, either.'

'Why don't you get rid of it then?'

'I can't. It cost me nearly thirty quid – reduced from sixty in a sale. It's too expensive to throw out.'

Stephanie shook her head and sighed theatrically. 'I give up.' But then she hugged me. 'Try not to make a total arse of everything and let me know if there are a lot of fit guys at the hotel. I really will miss you.'

Oh God, I'd miss Stephanie too. Also, whose make-up and clothes would I borrow now?

My phone buzzed. A text from Chris. HOPE YOU HAD A GOOD NIGHT. LOVE YOU. XX.

My eyes welled up. What was I doing leaving all the people who love me to go stay in a place where I knew no one? Maybe this was all a horrible mistake. For a panicky moment I actually thought about cancelling the whole thing. But how stupid and pathetic would that look? I'd never be able to hold my head up again. No, it was too late now. No matter what happened, I had to go through with it. Anyway, maybe I'd have a brilliant time in London and show everyone just how independent and smart I really am. Instead of the useless idiot I suspect even people who like me probably think I am.

And there's another reason I just had to go through with it. I opened the text I got from my dance teacher, Mrs Davies, last week and read it again: SENT YOUR DEMO TO MARTYN DARLING TODAY. FINGERS CROSSED.

Martyn Darling. Only the most famous modern dance director in London! And Mrs Davies says he'll be auditioning for new talent at the end of August. There's nothing definite, of course, but if he likes my demo there's a chance he'll want to see me perform in person. Mrs Davies says I've to remember to practise my routines every day just in case.

Haven't told my parents as I know they think this 'dancing nonsense' is just a phase and I need to concentrate on getting a getting a good degree when I go to uni in September. Haven't told Chris either in case it makes him worry more that I won't come back from London.

Also haven't mentioned anything to Liz or Stephanie because they would tell everyone – or Liz would, anyway, as she couldn't keep a secret if her life depended on it. So I've just hugged this (maybe) fantastic news to myself for days now.

I closed my phone and crossed my fingers. Look out, London. Here I come!

MONDAY JULY 29TH

Even though I told my parents not to bother, Mum and Dad came along with me and Chris to the station. Parents also insisted on coming right onto the train with us to make sure I got on the right seat. Honestly, they must think I'm still seven, not seventeen.

'Mind and take care of yourself down there, Kelly Ann,' Dad said. 'There are a lot of dodgy characters in London.'

I rolled my eyes. 'Unlike Glasgow, where everyone is a total saint. Look, I'll be fine, Dad. I'm sure people will be just the same in London, except maybe a bit more polite.'

'And there's a heatwave down there just now,' Dad continued. 'Forecast is for a scorching summer. Be careful you don't get burned.'

'Dad, it's England, not the Sahara. I won't get burned.'

'And don't forget to eat properly,' Mum added. 'A packet of crisps and a cream egg for breakfast, lunch and dinner every day won't feed a growing girl. Don't want you coming home with scurvy.'

Hmm, this from a woman whose idea of a nutritious breakfast is black coffee and half a dozen Silk Cuts. Still, I just said, 'I'll be working and living in a hotel, Mum. Meals are included.'

'And remember – first sign of a cold, rub your chest with Vicks – it's the only thing that works with you. I've put some in your suitcase. And I hope you're not still wearing those thongs instead of proper knickers. Bloody things are practically designed to give you thrush—'

'Mum! For God's sake. I'll be fine.'

'Anyway, I've put some cream—'

'Mum!'

'Time we were going, Moira,' Dad said. 'Give the kids a chance to say goodbye properly.' He planted a kiss on my forehead. 'Bye, love. Take care, mind.'

Mum hugged me, then, blinking a tear away, hurriedly left. Probably dying for a fag.

Chris had said nothing during all this. Just held my hand silently the whole time. However, once they'd gone, he took a small gift-wrapped box out of his pocket and handed it to me. 'Go on, open it.'

Oh God, he'd got me a present and I hadn't got him anything. Wish he'd warned me. I unwrapped it to reveal a silver chain with a large cylindrical-shaped pendant. 'Oh, um, you shouldn't have, Chris.'

He smiled. 'Do you like it? I was going to get you a heart-shaped pendant with a photograph of the pair of us inside, but I thought that would be a bit cheesy. Instead, I got you this. Look.' He twisted the end of the pendant and tugged on a fine silver thread which hung from the base. A glass tube slid out with a piece of paper rolled inside. At first I thought it was a photo, but when Chris took it out and flattened it I saw it was a typed message. He asked me to read it out loud.

If you love someone let them go.
If they come back they are yours.
If they don't they never were.
All my love, Chris xx

'Of course I'll come back, Chris. It's just a summer job.'

He rolled the paper and put it back in the glass container, inserted the tube into the silver cylinder again, then gently clasped the chain around my neck and kissed me. 'Something to remember me by.' He smiled, then added in a kind of mock-serious tone, 'I hope you'll wear this close to your heart every day and think of me.'

'Of course I will. But I don't need anything to remind me of you. I'm hardly going to forget the most important person in my life in just a few weeks.'

The train was about to go, so Chris swept me into a bear hug then quickly scrambled to the door and jumped onto the platform. I stood by the window and waved until the train moved out of the station and Chris was completely out of sight. Then I sat down and pulled off the pendant. Now don't get me wrong, I love Chris. I really do. But not even for him was I going to have hanging from my neck something which looked exactly like a tampon.

The first hour of the journey was OK as I'd all four seats to myself, but a load of people got on at Carlisle, including an annoying nerd with too short trousers, white socks and BO who sat beside me and tried to chat me up. Even though I made it totally obvious I wasn't interested and pointedly concentrated on my magazines or puzzles, he wasn't put off. *Oh, that looked like an interesting story I was reading. And would I like some help finishing that Sudoku?* Even when I plugged in my iPod he talked on. Bloody relentless. In the end I closed my eyes and pretended to sleep for most of the way.

When we were just over an hour from Euston I needed the loo. Since I also wanted to look my best on arrival, I took my make-up bag with me and headed off to the toilets. A number of people had the same idea but I managed to squirm quickly past them and was first in the queue when a huge guy with an enormous beer belly exposed by his too-tight, too-short T-shirt came out of the toilet. I nipped in and slammed the door shut triumphantly behind me, then nearly passed out. The stench was overpowering and literally made my eyes water. There was no way I was doing my make-up in this, but I really needed to use the loo so I held my nose and, breathing through clenched teeth, sat down on the pan.

But it was warm from the previous disgusting occupant's fat arse and the thought made me spring up again. What to do? Carefully I placed loo paper around the seat, sat down and tried to pee quickly, hovering as much as possible for good measure, then scrambled up, grabbed my bag and gratefully twisted the door handle.

But nothing happened. Twisted it again, harder. Tried turning it the other way and pushing instead of pulling but the door still wouldn't open. The bloody lock must have jammed. Began to panic. How long would I be trapped here? Would I be able to keep breathing these noxious fumes through my mouth without poisoning myself? Oh God, maybe I'd have to push the emergency button, but the shame of being publicly rescued from a toilet was too much. No, if necessary I'd just have to spend the rest of my life going back and forth from London to Glasgow in a public convenience rather than risk that humiliation.

Tried again and again, twisting, pulling and pushing

frantically but still couldn't get it open. Someone rattled the door and I heard an impatient, 'Bloody hell, what are you doing in there?'

I mean, some people are so totally ignorant. You're not supposed to ask anyone what they are doing in a toilet. Especially not a complete stranger. It's private. But the rattling seemed to have sorted out the jammed lock problem because when I tried again the door opened, no problem.

I smiled in relief at the small queue outside, even though they were scowling at me. The man at the front, who smelled strongly of lager, brushed rudely past into the toilet. And came right out again. He looked at me in amazement. 'Christ, the place reeks to high heaven. Ye'd have thought a troop of soldiers wi' dysentery had just used it. No' a slip of a lassie like yourself. I'm no' using this shit hole.'

Everyone in the carriage was staring at us and I flushed scarlet. 'It wasn't me!'

But all I got in response were sceptical *well-she-would-say-that-wouldn't-she* kind of looks. I flushed even hotter, which probably made me look guilty rather than embarrassed and furious.

'It really wasn't me!' I insisted.

But it was hopeless. No one believed me so I was trapped for another hour with a whole carriage full of people who thought I was a minger. On the plus side the annoying nerd with the too-short trousers and BO stopped trying to chat me up. He'd a nerve.

Finally pulled into Euston station and my stomach twisted with excitement. This was London. Home to some of the most important people in the world: the Queen, the Prime Minister, famous actors, dancers, singers, WAGs. Everybody.

In fact, Stephanie told me the streets are practically crawling with celebrities so I'm sure to bump into loads. I've not to ask for autographs, though (totally uncool), just ignore them and treat them like normal people. Unless it's Johnny Depp, when I'm to rugby tackle him to the ground if necessary and give him Stephanie's mobile number. Hmm.

Liz agreed that there are lots of famous people in London but advised me not to ignore them. Instead, I should wave casually and say: 'Hi, how's it going? Sorry I've not called in a while but I've just been sooo busy.' That way she says they'll probably think they know me but feel embarrassed about forgetting my name and chat to me anyway. However, she says if I see Robert Pattinson I've to forget all that, rugby tackle him to the ground if necessary and give him Liz's mobile number.

Not sure I'll be taking Liz or Stephanie's advice about celebs but I know they are right about London being a magnet for famous, talented people. And now I'm going to live and work here. Be a part of it. Had a weird feeling that this summer in London was going to change my life for ever.

A message came over the tannoy to remind passengers it would be a good idea to take their belongings with them when leaving the train. Really useful advice. I mean, if I hadn't heard that announcement, I was thinking of just leaving the lot here. Honestly, just how stupid do rail companies think we are?

I hauled my luggage from the rack with the help of a burly backpacker who took pity on me after I'd tried and failed to budge the thing. I really shouldn't have taken Stephanie's advice and should have left at least some of my possessions at home. For example, I probably didn't need the heated rollers (a present from Aunt Kate that I never use as I always straighten my hair) or the bulky foot spa, but Stephanie convinced me to take everything 'in case of emergencies'. What kind of emergency might require me to curl my hair and give myself a luxury pedicure she didn't specify, so I'm stuck with a suitcase the size of a wardrobe to manoeuvre around London.

Even though it was nearly seven o'clock it was still rush hour and the station was heaving. Have never seen so many people hurrying about determinedly in so many different directions in my life. Everyone seemed to have important, exciting things to do somewhere else that they were on the verge of being late for.

I wondered where they were all going and what

fantastic, interesting things they'd got planned. This had to be the most amazing city in the world. A place where anything was possible. Where you could do and be anything you wanted. Only problem was, everyone was so busy, no one seemed to have time to help me find my way to the southbound Northern line (a really stupid name if you ask me), although to be fair most people I asked didn't speak English. Still, if I'd been in Glasgow, I know by now someone would have stopped and taken me where I wanted to go even if it was out their way. But here you had to fend for yourself.

Managed to find the correct platform eventually and fight my way onto a train, but changing for the Circle line was a nightmare. I found the platform OK but couldn't get onto it at first as the entrance was blocked with people. When I finally managed to push my way in, I was at the back of rows of commuters at least twelve deep. Don't think it is always quite as busy as this, as I heard some people muttering about trains being delayed due to someone trying to top themselves by jumping on the line. They weren't very sympathetic about it. 'Bloody inconsiderate' was the kindest comment I heard. Maybe London wasn't going to be quite as fantastic as I'd thought.

Wasn't able to get on the first three trains but managed to squeeze myself and my suitcase onto the fourth, although my body was pressed onto the slightly curved doors, arching my back uncomfortably, and my nose was flattened on the glass, making breathing difficult. At the next stop I was thrown out, along with my luggage, onto the platform by a surge of people getting off.

Eventually I managed to get on another train, but this time I made sure I battled my way inside enough to hook my arm round a metal support so I couldn't be pushed out again. It wasn't very comfortable, though, with people squeezed up against me, close enough to snog if we'd wanted. In fact, I thought I felt someone's hands rubbing my bum, but when I twisted round to look it was a respectable businessman in a pinstripe suit so I must have been mistaken.

Or maybe not. Missed my stop as I was jammed in and no one would move to let me out but remembered it was a Circle line, so rather than attempt to get off at the next station and get a train back, I decided just to stay on until the train made its way round to my stop again. After a while the number of passengers thinned out and there was plenty of standing room, but the respectable businessman stayed glued to my bum like a barnacle to a rock, except not as immobile.

'Excuse me, but would you mind removing your hands from my bum,' I said, loud enough for the whole carriage to hear.

He reddened, muttered something about all Scottish people being rude and obnoxious, then shuffled off at the next stop.

Finally managed to bag a seat and tuck my suitcase in a luggage storage space by the door so I could relax at last. Tried chatting with the girl sitting next to me who looked about my age. Told her I had just come down from Glasgow on the train and that I was going to work in London for the summer. Asked her where she lived and if she was still at school or working, but she basically ignored me. Even cringed away as though I was diseased or something. Too late I remembered that you're not supposed to talk to anyone in London or they would think you were a nutter. A bit later, when a seat became vacant on the far side of the carriage, I'd expected her to move away from me, but she didn't. Probably English people think it's rude to pointedly change seats like that even if they are convinced they are sitting beside a psychopath who could slit their throat any moment. It was going to take me a while to get used to London. Wondered how long it would take to circle the Circle line. Not long, I hoped, as I was bored with travel and just wanted to get to the hotel.

Ten minutes later we were still nowhere near my destination so I decided to try some puzzles to pass the time as I'd got no peace to do them on the train from Glasgow. After a couple of easy ones I was engrossed in a really difficult Sudoku but managed to get it out eventually. Yeah! So much for Mr Simmons thinking I'd never be any good at maths.

Bollocks. Was so absorbed in the bloody Sudoku I'd gone past my stop again. At this rate I'd never get to the hotel. What to do? The doors were about to close so I had to make a quick decision. Better get off and make my way back. It didn't look as busy now, and anyway I wasn't going to risk going full circle and missing my stop again. Dived off just in time and was feeling pleased with myself until I realized I'd left my luggage on the train. Oh God.

The tube train person at the ticket office wasn't very sympathetic. Said I'd need to contact lost property in the morning, but I'd be lucky if my case wasn't destroyed as a suspected bomb, and leaving my luggage on the train was a really stupid thing to do. Thanks for that. As if I didn't know already that leaving my luggage on the train was a really stupid thing to do.

At least I had my bag with money and phone. Also, the hotel supplies us with uniforms so I'd be OK for a day or so until hopefully I could collect my stuff at lost property.

When I finally got to the hotel it was a bit of a disappointment. For a start it wasn't two minutes from the tube station – more like ten – and it looked much smaller than the website and brochure suggested. But it was nearly ten o'clock and I was exhausted, so I was grateful to have finally arrived. I pushed through the revolving doors to the brightly lit reception and gave my name to the girl at the desk.

'Please take a seat. I'll let our manageress, Mrs Frost, know you've arrived,' she said briskly.

I slumped onto a horrible overstuffed chintzy armchair near the entrance and closed my eyes. Must have dozed off for a second as next thing I knew a sour-faced stout woman was looming over me. 'You're almost three hours later than scheduled,' she said. 'I hope this won't be indicative of your timekeeping when you're working here.'

I stood up quickly and stifled a yawn. 'Course not. I mean, I won't need to get a train from Glasgow every day for a start, and anyway—'

'Because punctuality is very important to me.'

'Yeah, me too.'

'Still, this isn't a good beginning,' she huffed. 'First impressions are very important, you know. You never get a second chance to make a first impression.'

Hmm. You don't want to know my impression of you – grumpy old bag. But I hung my head and just said, 'Yeah, I know.'

'And you've no luggage with you?'

'It's, erm, arriving separately. I like to travel light.'

Well, there was no way I was telling her I'd left it on the tube. Didn't want her thinking I was stupid as well as unpunctual.

'I see,' she said dubiously. She gestured to the girl at the reception desk. 'This is Joy. She will be your line manager while you're here and should be able to fill you in on what is expected of you.'

Bloody hell, line manager! She looked just a year or two older than me. Still, it would be better than having to deal with the old witch. Hopefully I would make a better impression on someone young like me.

'Hi,' I said, all friendly, and smiled.

'Hi, I'll show you your room now. We can talk on the way.'

She hadn't smiled back but maybe she was intimidated by the dragon too. As soon as we were out of sight of the manageress I whispered conspiratorially, 'Miserable old bag. Suits her name. She must be a nightmare to work for.'

'She's my mum.'

Oh God. I could only hope that she didn't really get on with her mum and was just being loyal.

'We're very close,' she added.

Of course. They would be. Just my bloody luck.

We continued along the corridor in silence until we came to the lifts when, to my surprise, instead of going up, we went down to basement level and came out onto a dimly lit corridor.

'Are you sure we're going the right way?' I asked.

She looked at me contemptuously. 'Yes.'

'What's that rumbling noise?' I asked.

She pointed to a door on the right-hand side. 'This is the launderette. It's open twenty-four hours a day and is used by guests and staff for personal items, but there is a fee, of course.'

'For guests, you mean.'

'For everyone.'

'Right.'

'And this,' she said, pointing to a door next to the launderette, 'is your room.'

'Room' was a bit of an exaggeration. Large box or small changing cubicle was more like it. There was a single narrow bed which took up the entire length of it, and only enough space beside it for a small table and lamp. My 'wardrobe' was a metal rail bolted diagonally in one corner beneath which was a triangular wooden shelf. Harry Potter's cupboard under the stairs had more space than this.

'Are you sure this is—'

'Yes.'

'But I thought. I mean, I looked at the rooms on your website and I thought—'

'You didn't think you were going to get a guest room, did you? Oh my God.' She laughed. 'You did, didn't you? Wait till I tell everyone this one. Oh my God, that's the funniest thing.'

'Of course not. I'm not that stupid.' I stretched my face into a smile. 'I mean, how naïve do you think I am? I was just wondering about, erm, drawers, that's all. I'll need some drawers to put my stuff.'

'You don't have any stuff,' she said, and nearly wet herself laughing again.

My smile was starting to hurt my cheeks but I kept it in place. 'When I get my luggage.'

She stopped laughing and gave a good impression of her mother's sour expression. Maybe it was in the genes. 'You've got hangers.'

'For socks and pants?'

'Look, if all you're going to do is complain I don't think you're going to fit in here at all.' She shook her head to emphasize the point. 'Don't you know how lucky you are to have free accommodation in the centre of London? There are people who would sell their own mother for this.'

Particularly if she was a miserable old bag like yours, I thought, but kept my mouth shut as she continued, 'Bathroom is at the end of the corridor on the opposite side. Towels are not supplied. Breakfast is served from seven until ten.' She handed me a wad of papers. 'Here is your duty roster. Make sure you read it tonight.'

Then she was gone. Joy, my arse. I hope the rest of the hotel staff weren't like her. Or her mother.

I'd promised to text everyone as soon as I'd 'got settled' at the hotel, so I did. But what to say? *Yeah, you were all right about me. I've made a total mess of everything. Turned up late, lost my luggage, got groped by a pervert and now I'm living in a converted cupboard*? Texted: GOT HERE OK.

ACCOMMODATION COSY. MET LOTS OF NEW PEOPLE. SOME VERY FRIENDLY. KELLY ANN XX

Well, it was all kind of true. I did manage to get here. The accommodation was definitely not over-spacious, plus BO boy and the pervert businessman had been very friendly in a way. Too depressed and exhausted to do anything else, I kicked off my shoes and crawled under the covers. But I couldn't sleep for the constant noise of the washing machine and dryers next door. Especially the loud spin cycles. For God's sake. Had people nothing better to do in London at night than laundry?

Tried to take my mind off things by thinking about home. Oh God, how I missed Chris. And my friends. And yeah, never thought I'd say this, but I really, really wanted my mum. Have never felt so homesick in my life. And I've only been away for twelve hours. But there was no going back now. It would just prove to everyone that I'm the pathetic idiot they thought I was all along. No, I was going to stay, no matter what.

TUESDAY JULY 30TH

Was woken by someone banging on my door. Couldn't believe it. Felt like I'd only been asleep half an hour. Probably some drunk.

'Leavemealoneandgoaway.'

But they didn't. Instead, Joy's shrill voice shrieked, 'Kelly Ann, why aren't you up yet? Breakfast starts at seven.'

'I'm not hungry. Think I'll skip it.'

'You're not *eating* breakfast – you've to help prepare and serve it. It's your job. Remember?'

I checked the time on my mobile. 'For God's sake. It's only five-thirty. The middle of the night. Go away.'

I snuggled under the duvet and put a pillow over my head but it didn't drown out the sound of her banging on my door again and yelling, 'Kelly Ann, didn't you read your duty roster? You're on early shift this morning. Starts at five forty-five. C'mon, we'll never get all the breakfasts prepared on time if you don't get up now. I've left your uniform outside your door.'

Oh God.

The uniform was hideous. A white puffed-sleeved blouse, flared pink skirt with frilly apron and a stupid lacy mobcap. There was no way I was wearing the mobcap. No way.

The chef has told me I have to wear the mobcap. Health and safety. Tried to argue with him. I mean, how many people wear a hat when they are cooking in the kitchen? That's right, no one. And the whole nation hasn't come down with typhoid or botulism, has it?

But he wouldn't listen. Just wiped his greasy hands on his apron, jabbed a nicotine-stained finger at my head, then told me to put the hat on and clean some pots which had been soaking overnight.

Have never seen pots as big as these in my life. If they had been clean I could have had a bath in them. Fortunately a muscular young Polish guy with an unpronounceable name saw me nearly disappear into the huge vat and took pity on me. 'You go put cereal and juice out and I will scrub her.'

The next four hours passed in a blur. The kitchen was noisy, hot and steamy while the restaurant was full of happy, relaxed holidaymakers having a fabulous time. I rushed out of the hellish kitchens with cooked English breakfasts, and scurried back with the greasy remains, over and over again until finally the last guest left. Two other waitresses – Theresa, a curvy Irish girl with long wavy light red hair, and Suzie, a pretty Chinese girl with a slight cockney accent – had been doing the same thing. They seemed OK, but apart from exchanging names we'd had no time to talk, other than stuff like 'three cooked breakfasts for table three and hold the baked beans'.

Theresa plonked three mugs of tea on the kitchen counter and we collapsed into folding chairs Suzie brought from the function room. I tossed my mobcap on the table but caught a glimpse of my hair reflected in the aluminium surfaces, all frizzed by the steamy kitchen, and put the cap on again. Took a sip of tea and sighed contentedly.

'Why are you all sitting down?' Joy hissed.

'Because the floor's too dirty to lie on,' Theresa hissed right back.

'Then wash it. You know the rules. No one stops for tea until everything has been cleaned up after serving.'

Joy turned her back on us and marched off. We got up reluctantly and started cleaning, but not before Suzie made a rude sign to Joy's retreating back. Think I'm going to like Theresa and Suzie.

Just twenty minutes' break then it was time to prepare lunches, served from twelve until three. I mean, for God's sake, do people in London do nothing but eat all the time? But I got some good news about my suitcase. It's been handed in and not blown up, so if I can get to lost luggage before six I can pick it up along with a humiliating lecture about my carelessness.

The luggage and lecture will have to wait until tomorrow as we didn't finish cleaning up until five, then the manageress told me I'd have to go and do my Health and Safety training, along with Theresa, who is to have a refresher course because of her failure to comply with regulations last week. Apparently she'd been caught smoking in the kitchen during her break by the chef, who'd told on her.

'Bloody nerve of the man,' Theresa grumbled on our way to the Health and Safety officer's base. 'Smokes fifty a day at least, mostly in the toilet, and never washes his hands afterwards. The Pole told me.' .

'You can't pronounce his name either, then?'

'No,' Theresa laughed. 'A pity because he's not bad-looking. But it would be too awkward, though, dating a guy and just having to call him darling all the time. Especially if you're introducing him to your mates.'

I giggled. 'Might be worth trying to learn it if you fancy him enough.'

'Not really – he's not my type. Anyway, he's got a gorgeous girlfriend who could model for *Cosmo* without a scrap of make-up on her. Polish, of course – they're all bloody beautiful. It's not fair. Immigration should do something about it and send all the females home. How are ordinary girls supposed to compete with them?'

I nodded sympathetically. It was true. Don't think I've ever seen a Polish girl who wasn't at least stunning.

The Safety Officer and First Aid base proved to be a small room under the stairs with no windows, one light bulb, two plastic chairs and a sink. A young guy in a smart suit and tie introduced himself as David Sidebottom without laughing. Though he pronounced it Sidybot*tam*, with the emphasis on the last syllable, which made it even more difficult for me and Theresa to stifle our giggles.

He handed us clipboards and pens and suggested we make notes of important points but assured us he would also provide us with printed summaries at the end as backup.

He spent the next forty-five minutes telling us really interesting and important stuff, like knives were sharp and should be used to cut food, not slice our fingers off, that bare electric wires might give us a shock if we touched them, and that boiling water was very hot and could scald us if we threw it over ourselves or our colleagues.

Theresa yawned and checked her watch again but he didn't take the hint.

'You've not taken any notes yet, girls,' he said sternly like a primary school teacher talking to ten-year-olds. Bloody nerve – he wasn't that much older than us.

Theresa pointed to her head. 'Got it all in here.'

'So what was I just saying?' he asked.

'That we hadn't taken any notes.'

'Before that.'

'You were saying if we discover a fire we should try and put it out.'

Sidebottom nodded. 'Good. And if you can't put it out?'

Theresa nibbled the end of her pen, pretending to be deep in thought. 'Jeezus, I'm not sure. Throw a few bits of wood and some lighter fluid on it to get a good blaze going, then put my feet up with a nice mug of tea?'

I giggled but Sidebottom frowned at me. 'Health and

Safety is no laughing matter. Now, both of you, please write this down. *If you can't put the fire out you should raise the alarm then make your way to the nearest fire exit and gather at your designated assembly point.'*

Finally satisfied, he released us, along with a fat wad of Health and Safety bumpf, from possibly the longest fifty-three minutes and fourteen seconds of my life.

'What did you write?' Theresa asked.

I passed her my one scribbled note. *David Sidebottom is a pompous prat.*

She grinned and passed mine back along with her own. *David Sidebottom is a tiny-tadgered tosser.*

'I think you and I are going to get along just fine, Kelly Ann,' she said. 'Want to come out with Suzie and me tonight? We're going to a new wine bar that's opened just up the road.'

'Great.'

We exchanged mobile numbers, then Theresa said, 'OK, I'm just off out to get some fags. See you at the entrance around seven.'

Was so happy I could have floated back to my room. Here I was in London for just one day and already I'd made a friend and would be going to a cool, sophisticated wine bar in the very centre of the capital. But what would I wear? I suppose my jeans would be OK, but the T-shirt and blouse I'd slept in would be a bit tacky. Maybe it would be OK if I left off the T-shirt and ironed the blouse.

Yeah. But I'd no clean pants, and even though no one would see them I didn't want to go out for my first night in London with minging knickers. If I hurried I might have time to give them a quick wash then pop them in a dryer at the launderette.

I started to run along the corridor to my room but bumped into Joy coming in the opposite direction and landed on my arse. She had managed to keep her balance and helped me up while collecting the Health and Safety papers which had scattered on the floor, which was nice of her. Maybe she'd forgiven me for the stuff I said about her mum. Perhaps she would become my friend too eventually.

She glanced at the papers and quipped, 'I think you need to study these more carefully.' But then she spotted the handwritten comments about Sidebottom and scowled. 'What's this supposed to mean?'

I flushed. 'Look, I know Health and Safety is really important and all that but, no offence, the guy was really boring.'

'I don't think David is boring at all. He's a very interesting person, in fact. And I do find this offensive.'

A horrible thought occurred to me. 'I'm really sorry. It was just a joke. He's not a relative of yours or something?'

'No, he's not.'

I heaved a sigh of relief. 'Thank God.'

'He's my boyfriend.'

'Oh.'

Don't think Joy and I are going to be friends after all. But I didn't have time to dwell on it if I wanted to get my knickers washed and dried for seven o'clock.

Washed them in the bathroom sink and dashed into the launderette. Although there was just one woman there, two of the enormous dryers were in use, but there was one free. I opened the cavernous door, read the instructions and frowned. Bloody hell, a quid just to dry a pair of pants.

The woman, a middle-aged mumsy-looking person, came up alongside me and started to unload her laundry. She glanced at me and smiled. 'Is that all you've got, dear?'

'Yeah.'

'Well, my washing is dry but I'm sure there must be twenty minutes or so left on this machine. Why don't you pop your wash in mine when I'm done?'

Maybe this was going to be my lucky night after all. 'Thanks.'

After I'd put my pants in to dry, I hurried off to my room and collected two lovely white fluffy hotel towels that I'd borrowed this afternoon – well, not exactly borrowed as I'd swiped them off a trolley in the corridor, but I would give them back once I collected my lost luggage. Maybe. Then I scurried across the corridor to shower.

Fortunately there was a hairdryer attached to the wall in the bathroom so I was able to blow-dry my hair straight afterwards. Only problem was that it wasn't very powerful or hot – in fact, about as effective as someone blowing gently through a straw onto my scalp – so it was nearly seven o'clock by the time I was done.

Still wearing just a towel, I put my head through the laundry-room door to check it was empty, then tiptoed quickly in and grabbed my knickers from the dryer. My wringing wet knickers from the dryer. Shit. Looked like there hadn't been much time left in the machine after all.

What to do? Wear wet knickers and hope they would dry off eventually with body heat? Not very comfortable and they'd probably make a damp patch on my jeans like I'd wet myself. Wear no knickers? Possibly, but that was a bit minging and wouldn't make me feel very confident or comfortable for my first night out in London. Maybe I could ask Theresa or Suzie if I could borrow a pair. Hmm. They might think it odd someone they've only just met asking to wear their knickers.

It was then I noticed the dryer next to mine had stopped, but no one had come to collect the laundry. The owner wouldn't notice if just one pair of knickers was missing, would they? And it wouldn't be stealing. I'd wash them tomorrow and hand them in to lost property or something.

I took a look inside. Jeans and shirts. Socks and boxers.

A guy's wash. Just my luck. But then boxers weren't that different from pants, were they? I pulled out a blue pair and examined them. Way too big for me, but my jeans would keep them up. Yeah, they'd do. I grabbed them, turned round, and came to face to face with a really nice-looking guy with blond hair and a golden tan who looked at me curiously then pointed to the boxers and said in an American accent, 'Hey, I believe those are mine.'

Oh my God, what could I say? Probably anything other than what I did. 'No, they're not.'

'Yeah, I really think they are,' he countered. 'I just watched you take them from my laundry.'

'No, I didn't,' I persisted inanely.

He folded his arms. 'Look, maybe we should just call the cops. Let them sort this out.'

Oh my God. He was going to call the police. I'd be arrested for stealing men's underwear. The story would definitely be in the papers. Probably on the internet too. I'd be a laughing stock in London and Glasgow. I couldn't stay here or go home. There was no way I could live with this embarrassment. I'd just have to top myself. How had it come to this after only two days away?

'I'm really sorry, please don't call the police,' I begged. 'If you do, I'll throw myself in front of a tube train. I really will. And OK, I know you probably don't care what happens to me because I took your boxers, but think of the other people. All those innocent commuters who'll be late because of people having to scrape my body off the tracks. Please, please don't do this.'

He unwound his arms. Spread his palms face up towards me. 'Whoa, hey, calm down. I was only kidding about the cops; it's just a pair of boxers. But I'm curious. Look, I'll do a deal with you. You tell me why you wanted my underpants and I won't take this any further. Might even let you keep them.'

Relief and gratitude flooded through me. I explained about my travelling to London for a job, my missing luggage, my wet knickers and my plan to borrow, rather than steal, his boxers for the wine bar tonight. Luckily he seemed to find the whole thing funny rather than annoying and even let me keep the boxers. Maybe tonight was going to be all right after all.

The wine bar had bare brick walls, polished wooden floors and lots of mirrors. Really classy. Theresa ordered three wines but the barman asked for my ID before he'd serve us, which was a bit embarrassing. And worrying, because mine was still fake although I only had a few months to go before I'd have a real one. However, he accepted it, no bother.

Couldn't believe the price of the wine! There was no way any normal person could get drunk here, but maybe that was a good thing. I didn't want to do anything too stupid in front of my new friends. The wine tasted awful too. Not sweet and fizzy the way I like it, but so dry and sophisticated it was like drinking Jif lemon juice and it made the inside of my cheeks practically stick together. After the first sip, the only way I could drink it was to pour the lot straight down my throat in one go so I couldn't taste it.

'Jeezus,' Theresa said admiringly. 'Must be true what they say about Glasgow people and booze. And here I thought we Irish liked our alcohol.'

'Better slow down, though, until we find some guys to buy our drinks,' Suzie advised. 'What about those three standing at the bar? I think I overheard them talking about working in the City. Probably loaded.'

I shook my head. 'Sorry, I've got a boyfriend back home.'

Theresa shrugged. 'So what? We're just talking about a bit of a chat while they buy us a few drinks. Where's the harm?'

'Well, I don't know,' I said anxiously. 'Look, I'll get the next one, OK.'

'Cheers,' they chorused.

We chatted for a bit and I found out quite a lot about (hopefully) my new friends. Both of them were twenty, so I said I was nineteen. They'd gone to uni two years ago and lived away from home ever since. They said they didn't think they'd ever want to live with parents again. I said, 'Me too.' Then they told me that they both preferred to date older guys, Theresa because she found them more interesting and Suzie because older blokes had more money to pay for nights out. I agreed with both of them and said my boyfriend Chris back home was a doctor (rather than a medical student).

Felt bad about lying, but there was no way I wanted them to think I was too young and naive to be their friend. Anyway, that was the great thing about being so far away from home – I could be anyone I wanted to be and no one would ever find out.

When we'd finished the second round Theresa and Suzie wanted to go outside for a cigarette, so not wanting to be stuck on my own, I went with them. Suzie opened a pack of Silk Cut and held it out to me. 'Want one?'

I was about to say, *No thanks, I don't smoke*, but hesitated. What if they thought I sounded priggish or boring? Maybe even disapproving? I *do* hate smoking but one cigarette wouldn't matter, would it?

'Thanks, Suzie.'

It was absolutely vile. Managed not to choke or splutter, probably because of all the secondary smoke I'm used to at home, but I felt slightly nauseous and dizzy. Forced myself to finish most of it, then went off to the loo to get a drink of water and sit down. How can my mum smoke so many of these things? Why would anyone want to?

When I returned, Suzie and Theresa were back in the bar talking to the three guys they'd fancied earlier, so

I'd no choice but to join them. The tallest one bought us all drinks but it was soon clear he was mostly interested in Theresa and all but ignored me and Suzie. Suzie didn't mind as she was busy chatting up the nicest-looking one, which left me with Jeff, who seemed OK and didn't abandon me when I told him right away I'd a boyfriend in Scotland. He even bought me a double vodka and Coke, refusing my offer to pay for it, which is just as well as it was even more expensive than the wine.

Spotted the American guy whose boxers I'd stolen. He saw me too and smiled over, but I pretended not to notice. There was no way I wanted to risk him coming over and maybe chatting about my laundry theft. Even so, a minute later, when I heard the group of Australian guys he was with burst out laughing at something he'd said, I worried he might have told them about my underwear, and flushed scarlet. Wished we could leave, but Theresa and Suzie were obviously enjoying themselves so I knew I'd have to wait.

Around eleven my friends finally decided to head off. The guys offered to walk back to the hotel with us. I wasn't keen on the idea, but Theresa and Suzie said yes so we set off in pairs. I felt a bit sorry for Jeff really as his mates had their arms wrapped around the girls they'd got off with, and would probably get a snog at some point, whereas he might as well be escorting his aunt home. Still, I *had* told him I'd a boyfriend from the start so he couldn't really complain.

Everybody but us started kissing on and off on the way home so I was glad when Jeff said he needed to nip into the twenty-four hour chemist to get some Alka-Seltzer. With any luck, if we browsed for a bit, we could lose our amorous companions and not feel so awkward.

Was surprised when Jeff bought condoms as well as Alka-Seltzer. Although I was a bit embarrassed he'd shopped for something like that with me there, it did make me feel less sorry for him as I supposed he must have a girlfriend.

Even though it was late, there was a small queue, so by the time he was served the others had gone. When we got near the hotel I stopped at the corner away from the main entrance so Joy, who was on reception tonight, wouldn't see us. Theresa and Suzie had warned me she was always trying to stick her nose into the staff's business then telling her mum everything.

'Thanks for walking back with me, Jeff,' I said. ''Night.'

'Hey, wait a minute. Don't I get a kiss?'

'Sorry, but I told you I've got a boyfriend.'

I turned to go but he caught my arm. 'Yeah, but he's, like, four hundred miles away.' He smiled. 'I'm right here.'

'Sorry, but I can't.'

He put his face close to mine. 'Just one kiss,' he wheedled. 'I bought you drinks all night.'

This was true and I did feel a bit guilty, to be honest, but there was no way I was going to betray Chris over a few vodka and Cokes, no matter how expensive.

'I really am sorry, it's just that—'

Didn't get to finish what I was going to say as Jeff shoved me against the wall and clamped his beery mouth over mine. I tried to struggle free, but he had me pinned tight and I couldn't even shout for help or swear at him due to his trying to work his tongue through my clenched teeth. The more I tried to push him away the harder he squashed me to the wall so I could hardly breathe. But I really started to panic when his hands began to rove under the waistband of my jeans. Oh my God, what if he found out I was wearing boxers? Would he think I was some sort of weirdo?

Suddenly the crushing pressure stopped and Jeff was yanked off me. An American voice said, 'I'm pretty sure you heard the girl say no.'

The laundry guy! Never thought I'd be glad to see him again, but I was.

Jeff looked for a moment as though he was going to argue but then thought the better of it. 'You're welcome to her. No tits, anyway.' Then he stomped off.

Bloody nerve. And depressing too as I was wearing my new gel super-cleavage bra, which had cost a fortune.

Maybe Stephanie is right and guys *can* feel the difference.

'You OK?' he asked.

'Yeah. And, erm, thanks.'

'Mark.'

'What?'

'My name's Mark.'

I smiled. 'Thanks, Mark.'

'You're welcome, Kelly Ann.'

'How do you know my name?'

'You told me you started work here. I asked around. Hope you don't mind.' He smiled teasingly. 'Just curious to know who was wearing my underwear tonight.'

I flushed. 'You're not going to forget about that, are you?'

He grinned. 'Nope.'

Couldn't blame him, I suppose. We walked into reception together.

'Hotel bar is still open. Can I buy you a drink? Might help you relax after that jerk hitting on you like that.'

'No thanks. I've got an early start.'

'OK, cool. Goodnight, Kelly Ann.'

''Night, Mark.'

'See you tomorrow?'

'Maybe. I mean, yeah, I hope so.'

And I did. Mark was nice. In fact, although he didn't look anything like Chris, and had a cute American accent instead of Chris's low-pitched Glasgow voice, he somehow reminded me of him. He was kind and protective, but sort of teasing and funny at the same time. Just like Chris. God, how I missed him.

When I got back to my large cupboard I checked my mobile and immediately felt guilty. There were several texts from Mum, Liz and Stephanie that I hadn't got round to reading, never mind answering. And four from Chris plus a missed call tonight which I'd probably failed to notice because of the noise in the pub. It was too late to call Chris as I knew he was doing night shifts this week at the hospital, where he works as a porter (for experience as much as money) and he always switches his mobile off when he's working.

Texted everyone back but got no answer then I undressed, put the light out and crawled into bed, but not before taking Chris's present out of my bag and putting it on. I clasped the pendant to my chest and thought of his message:

If you love someone let them go.
If they come back, they're yours.
If not they never were.

'I'm yours, Chris,' I whispered. 'And I always will be.'

Was interrupted by a loud rap at my door followed by Theresa saying, 'Kelly Ann, who are you talking to? Have you got someone in there?'

'No. No one.'

'You sure? I thought I heard you talking to someone?'

'No.'

'Good. Open the door. Me and Suzie have got a bottle of vodka to share.'

'It's nearly twelve,' I groaned. 'And we have to be up before six.'

'Rubbish. The night's a baby.'

I put the light on, stumbled out of bed and opened the door a crack to find Suzie and Theresa grinning at me. Theresa waved a bottle of vodka. 'Mr Smirnoff would like to come in.'

I smiled and opened the door fully. Theresa peered into my room. 'Bloody hell, are you even able to turn around in here? If you were a dog you could get the RSPCA on to them. C'mon, get dressed and we'll go to our room. It's not much, but it's better than this.'

'OK. Just give me a minute.' I moved to close the door but Suzie stopped me. She peered at my pendant. 'Why have you got a silver tampon slung round your neck?'

I clutched the pendant to hide it. 'Erm, well, it's—'

'And why, for feck's sake,' Theresa interrupted, 'are you wearing boxers?'

I flushed. 'It's a long story. The thing is—'

'Or, to be more exact, why *were* you wearing boxers?' Theresa said as my over-large pants started to slide towards the floor.

Fortunately I managed to grab them in time and shut the door. I quickly got dressed and followed Theresa and

Suzie upstairs to the room they shared. It was much bigger than mine and had an ensuite bathroom, but it was still quite cramped for two people. Suzie's half was very neat, with all her things stacked tidily on shelves or put away out of sight. Theresa's stuff was all over the place – bras and knickers on the floor, make-up overflowing from a lipstick-stained bag on the bed, and what looked like two weeks' worth of dirty laundry mouldering in a corner of the room. The only items neatly stacked were her books, which were kept in a bookcase I'm guessing she must have bought herself.

I plonked myself down on Suzie's bed and peered at the titles. Novels and poetry by classical writers like the ones we were forced to study in English, but since she'd brought them with her in the summer, she must actually like reading that kind of stuff for fun.

She saw me looking at them. 'You like reading? Want to borrow something?'

'Yeah, I do sometimes, but these look a bit heavy going.'

'You think?' Theresa said. 'They're not, really. I mean, Barrett and Browning's poetry. So romantic. And D. H. Lawrence.' She giggled. 'Very sexy. You should try them.'

'Maybe.'

'Or you could try one of these,' Suzie said, lifting the duvet overhanging Theresa's bed to reveal a load of cheesy Mills and Boon books on the floor underneath. She rolled her eyes. 'So romantic.'

Theresa blushed. 'Well, yeah, it's important to read modern stuff too sometimes. You know, for comparison. Anyway,' she continued quickly, handing us each a large glass of vodka and Coke, 'what were those guys like tonight? Totally naff, right? Mine was brainless. Dumb as soup and boring as a repeat of last week's weather forecast. And guess what?

'What?' I asked.

'Told me he loved my long red hair.'

I frowned, puzzled. 'But you really do have nice red—'

'When it's obvious you're a strawberry blonde,' Suzie interrupted, flashing me a warning look. She took a swig of her drink. 'Mine was crap too. Told me he worked in "the City" so I'm thinking he's loaded, but I found out he works for the council, call centre stuff, and earns about as much as we do. What about yours, Kelly Ann?'

'Sleazer.'

We had a laugh then, slagging off all guys for being totally useless and pathetic or lying tossers, every single one of them. Great fun. Of course, mentally I excluded my lovely boyfriend Chris, but it would have spoiled the atmosphere to actually say so. Also, I really think the Polish guy is nice, but when Theresa said he was OK but reminded her of Frankenstein without the bolts, I sniggered along with her. It would have been kind of standoffish and spoilsport to do anything else.

Must have been after three in the morning when I finally left Theresa and Suzie's place to go back to my hobbit room, but I didn't feel tired. Just happy and excited to have made new friends already.

Texted everyone in Glasgow to tell them what a fabulous time I was having but no one texted me back. Texted a few more times but again no reply. Probably jealous. And no wonder. Living in London was going to be brilliant.

WEDNESDAY JULY 31ST

Suzie knocked on my door telling me it was time to get up or I'd be late.

She sounded grumpy and tired but I felt fine. Not hungover at all, in fact. This was fantastic. Maybe I'd grown out of hangovers. Yay, finally.

When I got to the kitchens I noticed that Theresa and Suzie looked really rough. Obviously they couldn't handle their booze the way I could. I felt wonderful. So great, in fact, the first thing I did was to go and hug the Polish guy, who was scrubbing the enormous pots.

'Thanks so much for doing this for me,' I said, giving him another squeeze. 'I love you so much I'm going to make a point of learning to pronounce your name.'

Saw the chef staring at me. Grouchy old tyrant. But to

be fair he was a good cook, if not particularly hygienic, so if you died of food poisoning at least you'd have had a tasty last meal. The thought made me smile but the chef didn't smile back. Instead he scowled at me and pointed to my head. 'Where's your hat?'

I pulled the mobcap from my pocket. 'Oops, forgot.' I put it on and squinted down to see my reflection on the counter. 'Don't think it's really me, though.' I looked up at him again, noticed his tall chef hat. 'I bet yours would suit me better. Want to swop?' Without waiting for a reply I pulled his hat off and plopped mine on his head instead.

Oh my God, he looked so funny in the mobcap. Ha ha. Especially since his face had gone all purply red with fury, which made him look even more hilarious. He-he-he. I put his chef hat on and twisted quickly out of his reach as he tried to grab it from me. 'Catch me if you can,' I giggled as I danced around the kitchen, dodging his attempts to grab me.

'Kelly Ann, for feck's sake,' Theresa shouted. 'What do you think—'

Didn't hear what she said after that as I slipped on a greasy bit of floor and landed on my arse. Looked up to see the chef looming over me, still wearing the mobcap, and I collapsed into helpless laughter.

Theresa came up behind me, hauled me to my feet and dragged me away from the chef. She kept her arm around my waist, put her mouth close to my ear and hissed, 'You're still drunk, you eejit.'

'Dwunk?' I slurred.

Suzie came up on the other side of me and grabbed my arm firmly. 'As a skunk,' she whispered.

The chef was still glaring at me. Suzie eyeballed him and said, 'We'd better report this serious Health and Safety violation.'

'What violation?' he growled.

'Kelly Ann has slipped on a pool of grease you dropped on the floor. This hazard was not dealt with right away, nor were warning notices posted. It's our duty to report it.'

'Wait! I mean, it's just a minor incident, girls. No point in overreacting. She's all right, isn't she?'

Suzie shook her head doubtfully. 'I don't know. She looks traumatized. Maybe she's concussed too. What do you think, Theresa?'

'I think what she needs most is rest to get over the shock. Maybe the rest of the day off and she'll be right as rain.'

'Get her out of here,' the chef growled.

Theresa and Suzie marched me to my room. I'd left the door open by mistake, but it wasn't as though there was anything much to steal.

Theresa pushed me in and wagged a finger at me. 'Stay in bed until you sober up, for God's sake.'

Actually bed suddenly seemed like a wonderful idea. My drunken euphoria had disappeared and now all I wanted was sleep. I kicked off my shoes, shrugged out of my hideous uniform and crawled under the duvet.

It was nearly 2 p.m. when I woke and wished I'd died in my sleep. My whole body ached like someone had set about me with a baseball bat. My tongue stuck to the roof of my mouth and felt dirty and furry, as though I'd been licking a rodent's nest. I squinted open gummy eyelids but the light burned into my corneas. Closed them again and groaned. My stomach churned and I'd an acid tobacco taste in the back of my throat. Remembered now that I'd had at least another five or six cigarettes last night and learned to blow smoke rings through my nostrils while singing 'Puff the Magic Dragon' and giggling like a demented poltergeist. Oh God. Why had I done it? Vowed there and then that I'd never drink or smoke ever again.

I pulled the duvet over my head and tried to block out the pain and the embarrassing memories but my stomach roiled and I knew I was going to be sick. Very soon.

I rolled off the bed and stood up. Felt the barf rise up to my throat and knew I'd no time to get dressed. After a quick peek to make sure no one was in the corridor I stumbled to the bathroom, pushed open the door and lurched for the toilet. Kneeling in front of the pan like some weird toilet worshipper, I clutched onto the sides and threw up. Several times.

If someone had offered to shoot me there and then I'd have accepted gratefully. No one did, so, too weak to do anything else, I lay face down on the floor and pressed my cheek onto the cool tiles.

Don't know how long I stayed sprawled there, and it's possible I dozed off, because the next thing I was aware of was a flustered woman's voice saying, 'Oh dear, I'm terribly sorry, I thought the bathroom was unoccupied.'

I opened one eye and saw a smartly dressed fortyish woman standing by the opened door. ''S OK,' I said.

Mercifully she closed the door with her on the other side of it, as even under these embarrassing circumstances, I couldn't have sprung to my feet if my life had depended on it.

'Are you all right?' she asked from behind the door. 'I mean, erm, should I call you an ambulance?'

Oh God, paramedics bursting in and finding me in this state, then being publicly carted out in an ambulance! I had to stop her.

'I'm totally fine, thanks all the same,' I said as brightly as I could from the floor.

'Oh, good. Right, well, sorry for disturbing you.'

Heard her heels heading off down the corridor towards the launderette and gave a sigh of relief. Say what you like about English people, but they're very polite – unless on a tube – and they mind their own business. Anyone else who stumbled on a half-naked girl sprawled on the floor like a murder victim would have had asked loads of nosy questions. But not an English person, thank God.

Still, at least I wasn't wearing boxers, which might have freaked her out a bit. Having said that, the thongs Suzie lent me when she found out about my underwear crisis must have left me a bit exposed.

I crawled to the sink, hauled myself up and slopped water into my parched mouth, but somehow this did nothing to slake my raging thirst. Of course not. What I needed was the fizzy orange elixir, Irn Bru, the only known cure for hangover dehydration.

Forced my weak, sickly body along the corridor to my room and pulled on jeans plus a LONDON ROCKS T-shirt also lent to me by Suzie. Then I trudged upstairs in search of the drink dispenser machine on the first floor. Damn. Only Coke or Sprite. Knew there was no Irn Bru in the kitchens either. What kind of country was this? How could they allow the sale of alcohol when people couldn't buy Irn Bru afterwards?

Bought a Coke and glugged it down. Not as good as Irn Bru but fizzy and sweet so it helped a bit. Got another one and turned to go back to my room with it when I heard a voice say, 'Oh, Kelly Ann, this is lucky. I was just going to look for you.'

Sidebottom. Not my idea of luck exactly.

'The thing is,' he continued, 'you haven't got your security badge yet and this is your second day with us. We have to get this sorted straight away. I'll need to take a photo of you first. If you'd just come with me now it will only take a minute.'

'Oh, right, but, erm, I'll need to freshen up a bit first. Put some make-up on.'

'That won't be necessary.' He smiled. 'It's not a fashion shoot, you know. Mrs Frost wants it done right away.'

Brilliant.

Ten minutes later Sidebottom handed me my new badge with instructions to wear it at all times whilst in the hotel, then walked off with a satisfied smirk. I glanced at it. My bed-head hair looked like an abandoned crow's nest and my shrunken eyes were as red as a devil's. But it was the insane grin – '*Say cheese, Kelly Ann*' – and Coke-stained lips and chin that really made me look like an escapee from a high-security mental institution.

Tossed the badge in the bin and trudged off to my room. Crawled back into my sweaty bed without bothering to undress, and tried to fall back to sleep but was interrupted by my mobile buzzing. A new text message. Correction. Lots of new unread text messages. Must have been while I was sleeping.

A quick scan. Most of them started with WTF except

for my dentist, home library and my old school office numbers. Oh God, must have hit TEXT ALL button. What had I said? Stephanie's reply copied the messages.

I AM SOOOO HIPPY. LONDON SOCKS! HAVE MAD SO MANY GRATE FIENDS. GOT COT STEALING BOXERS BUT COPS NOT WRUNG. YAY!! AMERICA COCKS TOO!!!! GET PANTS SOON IF NOT BLOWN UP. HA HE.

Oh God.

Pulled the duvet over my head and prayed for unconsciousness. No such luck. Mobile rang but I ignored it. Went to voicemail and Mum's voice ranting, 'Pick up the phone, I know you're bloody there. Sodding thing is always stuck to you like a giant wart.'

I picked it up and she immediately went off on a megamoan. Only two days in London and I'd turned into a thieving cross-dresser, probably on drugs too. And how was she to tell everyone her daughter had turned into some pervert transsexual?

'Transvestite, Mum, and I'm not. I'd just run out of clean pants,' I interrupted.

'I'll give you transvestite all right,' she fumed.

Not quite sure what she meant by that but guessed she didn't appreciate my point. She ranted on for another ten minutes or so while I held the phone at arm's length.

Fortunately got interrupted by someone knocking on my door. Probably Suzie or Theresa on their break, come to see how I was. 'Sorry, Mum,' I said. 'Got to go, there's someone here.'

Was about to open the door but hesitated. Maybe it wasn't one of my friends. What if it was Mrs Frost or her sour-faced daughter come to tell me off for not being at work?

'Who is it?'

'Januariusz.'

'Who?'

'Januariusz Grzeszczuk.' He paused. 'The Pole. You can call me Yan.'

'Oh God, I'm so sorry about this morning. Don't worry, it's not that I fancy you or anything. I don't mean you're ugly, of course. Definitely not. But I've got a boyfriend, even though he's in Scotland right now. I really miss him. But that doesn't mean I'm so desperate I'd go about accosting innocent guys while they're working. It's just that I'm really grateful about the pots. But, erm, not so grateful that I'd—'

'Kelly Ann, my English is not so good. Excuse me, but I cannot follow when you speak so fast.'

Hmm, probably just as well. 'Sorry.'

'Theresa say you must get luggage today. She say I help you.'

Thought about it. The last thing I wanted to do was battle my way round London's Underground to Baker Street, where the lost property office was, with a humungous hangover, then trudge back again with an equally humungous suitcase. Negotiating this with a big muscular Pole who probably knows his way around London would be easier than doing it by myself.

I opened the door. 'Yeah, thanks. Just give me half an hour to shower and get ready.'

He shook his head apologetically. 'Sorry. We must go now. It close soon.'

Right, so a trip round London looking and probably smelling like a tramp. Brilliant. I pulled on my shoes, grabbed my bag and headed out. Caught a glimpse of Mark just as I was leaving the hotel. He spotted me too and waved over, but I pretended I hadn't noticed him and hurried out. Didn't want him to see me looking so awful. Don't know why really as I hadn't been that bothered about Yan seeing me in this state. Hmm.

With Yan's help I got to lost property, no bother. He didn't talk much on the way, partly because his English wasn't very good, and partly because he's quite shy, I think. I wasn't in the mood for chatting either because of my hangover and the fact that I kept hiccupping – probably due to having swilled down two cans of Coke in about ten seconds.

I did think he was really nice, though: he gave up his seat in the tube twice because a woman was standing. And they weren't even pregnant or old. Not that they were very grateful. One even scowled at him suspiciously, as though he were some kind of freak, and refused to sit down, so Yan's place was nabbed by a young Australian guy standing next to her.

'Thanks, mate!' he said, grinning at Yan.

I think Yan was annoyed, but at least, unlike the two women, the guy had said thanks.

When we got to the lost property office Yan waited outside while I collected my luggage along with a fine (administration costs, yeah, right) and a lecture on my carelessness. It's so annoying. Why is it, even when you've finally left school and home, people still think they can tell you off like you're a ten-year-old?

Finally released, I wheeled the suitcase away. Or tried to, anyway, but one of the wheels must have got damaged and kept listing to the left, so I ended up almost going round full circle back to the lost luggage desk. The man at the desk didn't even try to help me. Just laughed and called for a colleague to watch me too.

And they are supposed to be serving the public. Huh. Thank God Yan was here. He'd be able to lug the suitcase, no bother, and would never laugh at a girl in distress. He really was lovely. A sort of big, gentle giant.

Managed to get to the door eventually and looked around for Yan. Couldn't see him and was beginning to worry, when suddenly he jumped out in front of me growling like a monster and flailing his arms.

'Aaaaaaaaaaaaaaaaaarggggggg,' I screamed. Or something like that. I let go of my suitcase and ran for it, but he chased after me. Oh my God, Yan was obviously a homicidal maniac. Probably had to flee Poland after a series of motiveless murders of young women and was the most wanted criminal in Europe. But surely he didn't plan to strangle me in broad daylight in front of crowds of people? Then again, if he was really mental, maybe he wouldn't care.

I kept running but he was gaining on me. Some people glanced at me in surprise as I raced past but quickly looked away again. No one stopped to ask me why I was in such a hurry or if I was OK. Maybe they thought we were both running for a train or something. Or more likely they thought it was nosy to question someone they didn't know. I could only hope that London people wouldn't think it was too rude to interfere when he started to throttle me.

I would soon find out as Yan had caught up and grabbed my arm. There was nothing else for it – I'd have to scream for help no matter how embarrassing it might be. 'Fire,' I shrieked. 'Fire! Fire!'

No one except Yan took any notice of me whatsoever. So much for the notion that shouting 'fire' would attract more attention than 'help' or 'rape'.

Yan's kind, puzzled face looked down at me. 'Kelly Ann, I am sorry I scare you too much. I just mean a little scare to cure your hics. But' – he looked around – 'where is this fire?'

Oh God. I was too breathless to answer for a while, but really, a six-foot-three seventeen-stone-of-solid-muscle Pole jumping out at you is no way a little scare. We made our way back to the lost property office, where I again reclaimed my suitcase, along with another longer lecture on leaving unattended baggage near a station.

Yan bought me a kebab on the way back and kept apologizing all the time, but I wasn't mad any more. I wasn't murdered, my hiccups were gone and, best of all, I now owned more than one pair of knickers. Also my hangover was slowly disappearing. But I wasn't going to forget how bad I'd felt. There was no way I'd ever drink alcohol again. Ever.

Bumped into Theresa going out just as we were coming into the hotel. 'Hi, Kelly Ann, just out to get some fags for tonight. We're off to McGinty's at seven so you've only half an hour to get ready. Better get a move on.'

'Oh, I think I'll skip it tonight, Theresa.' I pointed to the suitcase Yan was carrying. 'Got some unpacking to do.'

'Rubbish – get your pulling gear on. Irish pub. Drinks half price and live music as well. It'll be a laugh.'

She turned to Yan. 'Thanks for helping Kelly Ann get her stuff. I was worried she'd get lost otherwise. She's a right eejit and a half.' She gave him a hug and dashed off.

Well, I suppose there wasn't much point staying in on my own. Of course, I'd just drink soft drinks all night, listen to music and have a bit of a chat. There would be no harm in that, after all. Would there?

We had to travel quite a way to get to the pub in Kilburn, and at first I thought it wasn't worth the bother as it wasn't nearly as nice as the wine bar we'd been to last night. It was an Irish pub and it also had a special Irish theme night, which meant that everything was covered in green plastic and the pissed-off bar staff had to wear stupid leprechaun costumes complete, with beards. Even the females. Maybe my mobcap wasn't so bad after all.

But it was obviously popular – probably because of the cheap drinks: 'happy hour' two-for-one offers were on sale from noon until midnight – and was so crowded we had to stand. There were a lot of people with Irish accents around, but the band playing hip hop in the corner were black and quite good – the folk group had apparently cancelled at the last minute.

After a few vodka and Cokes (well, there was no point in just having soft drinks as they were almost as dear as alcoholic ones) I began to feel better, but Theresa seemed oddly nervous and angsty. Her eyes kept roving round the room, obviously looking for someone, and twice she went to the loo to re-apply her make-up.

'What's up with Theresa?' I asked Suzie when she had disappeared for the third time.

'Liam hasn't turned up yet. He should have been here an hour ago.'

'Is he Theresa's boyfriend? I didn't know she had one.'

Suzie shrugged. 'On and off. More off than on. Theresa's mad about him.'

'He must be really hot if Theresa fancies him so much. What's he like?'

Suzie glanced towards the door. 'See for yourself. That's him now.'

I looked over. He was tall and slim with dark, untidy hair, pale skin and a serious expression. Not bad-looking, but nothing special. He glanced over at Suzie and nodded, but went straight to the bar and didn't come over, which I thought was a bit off given that he knows her.

Saw Theresa making her way towards us, but when she spotted Liam she veered over to him and mouthed, 'See you later,' to us.

He didn't kiss her or anything, just leaned lazily by the bar and smiled, so maybe they were in a kind of 'off again' phase. Didn't buy her a drink, either. Instead, she bought another fluorescent green cocktail for herself (which she'd assured Suzie and me tasted better than it looked but we hadn't wanted to risk it) and a Guinness for him. Bloody hell. She must be keen. It was weird, though. Theresa seemed the kind of tough take-no-shit-from-anyone type like my friend Stephanie back home. Couldn't understand why she'd let any guy treat her like this.

'So what's so great about Liam?' I asked.

Suzie shrugged. 'He's supposed to be a painter and poet. Theresa's got a thing about arty types.'

'Supposed to be?'

She rolled her eyes. 'Never sold a painting. Never had a line published. Always broke.' She looked over at Theresa, who was gazing at Liam with rapt attention. 'Don't think I can watch this any more. Let's go out and have a fag.'

Felt guilty about always taking cigarettes from my new friends and didn't want them to think I was a cadger, so I bought a pack from the shop across the road.

We lit up and leaned against the pub wall companionably. I blew the smoke right out of my mouth without inhaling as I really didn't want to start smoking properly and also hoped I wouldn't feel sick that way. Also managed to drop the cigarette on the ground behind me halfway through smoking without Suzie noticing. But when she saw I was finished, she immediately offered me another and I'd to do the same thing again. Felt bad about wasting so much money as cigarettes cost a fortune. It was like setting light to fivers! However, a tramp saw what I was up to and snapped up the long fag ends from the pavement gratefully as we headed back inside. It was good to know I wasn't being too wasteful, but then again I was probably also encouraging the tramp to be unhealthy. Seemed I was going to feel guilty no matter what.

Spent most of the rest of the night chatting to Suzie as she didn't seem to fancy anyone there. Lots of guys seemed to fancy her, though, even though she's not blonde. Asked her about it.

'Yeah,' Suzie said. 'It's 'cos I'm Chinese. Some guys have got this stupid idea that we're nicer than other girls and will look after them or something.' She laughed. '*As if.*'

'Why would they think that?'

She shrugged, took another swig of her vodka and Coke. 'No idea. Anyway, they can dream on. Unless they're loaded. Hmm, even then, don't think I could be bothered.'

I didn't think it likely that was the reason, but it turned out she was right. About some of them, anyway. Just as we were thinking about going, a drunk English guy lurched up to us and started talking to Suzie.

'Hello, darling, haven't seen you in here before.'

'Hi,' Suzie said in a bored voice.

'Hope you don't mind me telling you this, but I've a real thing for Japanese girls. I think you're all gorgeous.'

'I'm Chinese.'

'Same thing, innit.'

'No, it's not.'

'I mean, all you Oriental chicks, you know how to treat a guy. None of this women's lib rubbish. Bunch of dykes, if you ask me.'

'I didn't ask.'

'But Oriental girls, they look after their man. Give him massages and that with their bare feet.'

'That's Thai girls.'

'Same thing. I bet you could massage a guy like that. Stand on his back and knead his tired muscles with your little feet.'

'Yeah, I suppose I could. Would you like me to give you a massage like that?'

He grinned stupidly, hardly believing his luck. 'Yeah. Anytime. Your place or mine?'

'Chinese girls do it a bit differently, though.'

He shrugged. 'No worries.'

Suzie looked at her feet. 'We keep our stilettos on.'

Idiot was too drunk to realize Suzie was winding him up and kept trying to hit on her, so it was a relief when Theresa came over and said we should get going. Liam had already gone off home with his flatmate apparently, so I thought she might be disappointed, but instead she looked really happy.

'We're going to meet up on Saturday for dinner at his place,' Theresa confided on our way to the tube. 'Just the two of us.'

'Cool,' I said.

'Yeah, great,' Suzie added unconvincingly. 'Cheap too.'

'And guess what?' Theresa went on, oblivious to Suzie's tone.

'What?' we chorused.

'He's written a poem about me! I'll show you it once we're on the train.'

The poem was written on a beer mat. Suzie and I read it together while Theresa smiled dreamily.

The Girl Who Bought Me Guinness

Black as night white as foam. Satin smooth
Guinness
I thirst. I thirst but . . .
Nothing.
My thirst burns.
It rages
In deep darkness and despair

But then she comes. The laughing girl with
Guinness
I lust. I lust. But . . .
Not yet
Then I drink
I slurp
And my thirst is quenched, slaked, gone

The raging fires have been doused by
Guinness.

I swill, I swill. But . . .
For love
Not thirst now
I thank
The girl who bought me Guinness.

'So, what do you think?' Theresa asked eagerly.

I couldn't think of anything to say so I kept quiet and let Suzie answer.

'It doesn't rhyme.'

'It's not supposed to.'

'Or scan.'

'Modern poets aren't bound by convention these days.'

'It's crap.'

'No, it isn't. It's amazing. Deep. And anyway, it's a poem about me and he's used the L word for the first time.'

'Lust?' Suzie said.

'Love.'

'I think you'll find he was referring to a pint of Guinness. Not you.'

Theresa turned to me. 'What did you think of the poem, Kelly Ann?'

'Erm, very interesting.'

Suzie laughed. 'See, she thinks it's crap too.'

'I didn't say—' I protested.

But Suzie and Theresa weren't listening to me any more, just arguing among themselves about Liam and the poem.

In a strange way it made me feel a bit lonely and out of things. Unlike Suzie, I didn't know Theresa well enough to say what I really thought. Suzie, though, could give her honest opinion. Theresa would never actually fall out with her about it. Hmm, or maybe not.

'Right, that's it. I'm never talking to you again,' Theresa spat at Suzie.

'Suits me,' Suzie said.

Oh God.

But Theresa couldn't keep her promise to shut up, so they ended up slagging each other off the whole way back. Once we got to the hotel I hurried off to my tiny room gratefully. Yeah, it may be a bit lonely and cramped but at least I'd have peace.

Was glad I'd brought Gerry, the furry toy giraffe I've had since I was a kid. Hadn't actually slept with him since I was four – OK, all right, fourteen – but tonight I got undressed, pulled on an old comfy T-shirt and snuggled into bed with Gerry. Had almost dropped off when I heard a knock at the door. 'Can I come in, Kelly Ann?' Suzie sobbed. 'Theresa's still bitching at me.'

I opened the door to find Suzie, red-eyed and tearful, dressed in pyjamas and dressing gown. 'Can I sleep here tonight?'

'Oh God, Suzie, I'm sorry. There's no room.'

She came in anyway. 'I'd rather be squashed in here than spend another second with her. She's really freaking me out.' She looked over at my bed. Spotted Gerry. 'There's plenty of room if you ditch the giraffe.' She tossed Gerry aside and got under the duvet. 'C'mon, Kelly Ann, it's nearly one o'clock. We need to be up in four hours.'

Looked like I wasn't going to be lonely tonight after all.

THURSDAY AUGUST 1ST

When I woke up I had my arms wrapped around Suzie, which was a bit embarrassing, especially as she was already wide awake.

'I'm glad you told me you had a boyfriend back home, Kelly Ann. Otherwise I might have been a bit worried about you last night.'

I flushed and hurriedly got up. By the time I'd showered she'd already gone to her own room to get ready.

I hoped she and Theresa would have made up before the shift started, but no such luck, and I spent the morning as go-between.

Theresa: 'Kelly Ann, please tell Suzie table numbers three and four need to be cleared.'

Suzie: 'Please tell Theresa to clear them herself. She's not my boss.'

Theresa: 'Please tell Suzie *those* are her tables and there's no way I'm picking up after her lazy arse.'

Suzie: 'Please tell Theresa she has the memory of a goldfish and Pot Noodles for brains. Otherwise she'd know numbers one to six are *her* tables.'

Oh God.

But around lunch time Theresa must have got fed up with fighting.

'Look, Suzie,' she said, 'I suppose there's no point in us falling out over a guy. Even one as talented and deep as Liam.'

'OK,' Suzie agreed stiffly.

'So, we're, erm, friends again?' Theresa asked.

'Suppose so. I mean, yeah, you're right. No point in falling out over a guy.'

'Good. So you wouldn't mind me borrowing your plum sparkly eye shadow on Saturday then?'

'OK.'

'And your black lacy camisole?'

'Won't it be a bit tight for you?'

Theresa grinned. 'That's the whole point.'

'Well, OK then, if I can borrow your pale blue leather Gucci bag.'

'Christ, that was an eighteenth birthday present from my mum. Cost a fortune.'

'I'm just borrowing it.'

'Well, all right then. Liam doesn't approve of conspicuous materialism, anyway. Just don't lose it, for feck's sake.'

SATURDAY AUGUST 3RD

Everyone got paid today except me. Knew I wouldn't get anything until next Saturday because we all get paid a week in arrears. Couldn't help feeling a bit depressed about it, because even though I know I'll get the money eventually, it still felt like I was working for nothing.

But at least Theresa and Suzie were getting on again, and as part of the reconciliation Theresa got us an invite to a party in Hackney tonight. Some friends of her older cousin have moved into a new flat there and are having a kind of housewarming party but they were short of girls. I suggested we get a taxi so we wouldn't get lost, but Suzie said she knows the area like the back of her hand as she used to work in her dad's Chinese takeaway there, so we'd just get a bus – it would be cheaper and we'd find the place, no bother.

Turned out Suzie didn't know the place as well as she thought, or the directions Theresa had given us must have been wrong, as we spent over half an hour trying to find it. Suzie finally owned up to being lost and texted then called Theresa but got no reply. We stopped and asked a

71

woman with a grocery bag, thinking she'd be from around here, but she didn't have a clue and hurried on.

The next two we tried didn't even speak English.

'God, does no one actually live in Hackney?' I asked, exasperated.

'Probably not if they can help it,' Suzie said. 'Most of it is a bit dodgy.'

Hmm, like the guy who'd seen us asking directions and had just approached us. He had muscular tattooed arms, thick as beer barrels, and a black wool hat pulled so low down over his forehead that it nearly touched a bent squat nose which looked as though it had been broken several times.

'Got a problem, girls?' he asked.

There was no way we were going to talk to someone like that. 'No, we're fine, thanks,' we chorused.

'Oh, right, sorry to bother you. Just thought I over-heard you say you were looking for Bellevue Avenue. Wanting directions, like. But I must have been mistaken. My apologies.' He gave us a wave and moved off. 'You have a nice evening then.'

Suzie and I looked at each other, both shamefaced. Obviously he was a perfectly nice man just trying to be helpful and we'd jumped to conclusions about him just because of his appearance. It was totally wrong. Prejudiced, even.

'Wait,' I called to his retreating back. He stopped,

turned round and approached us. 'Actually, you're right, we are a bit lost. Do you know how we can get to Bellevue?'

'Do I? My old nan happens to live in the street along from it. Just been to see her tonight, in fact. She gets a bit lonely on her own since Gramps died so I try to stop by as often as I can. Keep her company like.'

'That's nice of you,' I said, feeling even worse about misjudging him.

'It's no bother. Not easy, getting on, you know. Shockin' how some people neglect their old relatives. Not me. Couldn't live with myself if I did that. Anyhow, Bellevue you said . . .'

He gave us directions, telling us it was just about ten minutes' walk, but even though we followed them exactly, twenty minutes later we still hadn't found the place and finally ended up in a scary industrial estate with nothing but closed warehouses and workshops.

'This can't be it,' Suzie said. 'Maybe we should just go back the way we came.'

'Yeah, in a minute, though, my feet are killing me in these high heels and I think I've got a stone in my shoe.'

Suzie waited while I took off my right shoe and shook a piece of gravel out. I leaned against a wall to steady myself and rubbed my foot.

I heard him before I saw him. ''Ello, girls. Lost again?'

I looked up to see him coming out from behind a

rundown factory just ten feet away and ambling towards us. Had he been following us? Why hadn't we seen him? Or had he known we'd end up here?

'You lot are useless with directions, ain't you?' he went on. 'Never mind, darlin's. Tell you what, I'll take you there myself if you like. Make sure you get there safe and sound like.'

He was standing right in front of us now, looking all casual and relaxed. Unlike us.

'Erm, no thanks, we're fine,' Suzie said, scowling.

'No problem. Understood. Quite right too. You don't want to be going nowhere wif a strange man, do ya? Thing is, though, I was just wondering if you could do me a favour. Since Ah'v been so helpful like. You wouldn't happen to 'av some spare cash on ya, would ya? Thing is, I'm a bit short.'

'Sorry, no, we don't have any money,' I said.

'Now you're telling me porkies, ain't ya,' he said with a nasty smile. 'Two young ladies like yourselves don't go for a Saturday night out with no cash on you, do you? Stands to reason.' He eyeballed Suzie. 'C'mon, love, let's see what's in that bag of yours.'

Suzie glared at him. 'Back off, creep, or you're gonna get hurt. I'm a martial arts expert. Black belt fifth Dan. These hands are licensed.' She held them out in front of her, angled like hatchets, and chopped the air. 'Better run now or I'm warning you, I'll show no mercy.'

Oh, thank God. Suzie was a kung fu fighter like in the movies. We were safe.

But he just laughed, swatted her hands away and removed her bag from her shoulder.

Suzie gave me an apologetic it-was-worth-a-try look. Brilliant.

He scooped the contents of her bag into his pocket, then tossed it on the ground. Huh, shows you how much *he* knows about bags. Suzie gratefully grabbed it. At least she wouldn't have to face Theresa's fury later.

'Now you, love,' our mugger said.

Thought about it. At least my mobile was in the hotel room charging – I'd forgotten to take it – and there was only a tenner in my purse, but still there was other stuff too. Like the dance director's business card Mrs Davies gave me before I left and my concealer which I planned to re-apply at the party as I'd a couple of spots on my forehead. Also my Elizabeth Arden bronzer, which Stephanie gave me as a present before coming to London and cost a fortune. There was a lot of rubbish in my bag too; like the half-eaten Curly Wurly, a piece of chewed gum wrapped in tissue, and a lipstick which I've lost the top for so it was covered in hairs from my hairbrush. Not sure why I minded a scummy criminal thief knowing I was so messy, but I did. However, the most embarrassing thing of all was the spare pants I've decided to always carry since my knickers crisis and the just-in-case tampon. No, there was no way I could hand over all this!

Smashed my high heel down hard on the bridge of his nose. There was a really satisfying cracking noise, then he bent over and shrieked, clutching his face as blood leaked out through his fingers.

He held his hands out in front of him, gazing in disbelief for a second at his crimson palms, then swore and lurched for me. I whacked the heel fast twice more on the same spot. It was funny to hear someone so squat and muscular give out such a high-pitched scream, but I didn't have time to dwell on it. As he reeled, blinded by pain and blood, I took off my other shoe and hissed at Suzie, 'C'mon, run!'

'Just a sec!' She scrabbled in his pocket and stuffed the contents into her bag. 'OK, let's go!'

We ran back in the direction we'd come, not stopping to look behind us until we were totally out of breath. We needn't have worried, though. He hadn't attempted to follow us. Probably had to go and get his broken nose seen to instead.

'That was really impressive, Kelly Ann,' Suzie panted. 'You were brilliant.'

I shrugged. 'Yeah, well, a smack right on the bridge of the nose is really the most painful place to get hit. Except for a guy's you-know-whats, but a lot of them are prepared for that.'

'How do you know that? Have you trained in martial arts?'

'No.'

'Then where did you learn to do that?'

I shrugged. 'I'm from Glasgow.'

She seemed to accept this. Took out her mobile. Checked her texts. 'I've got one from Theresa. Said she gave us the wrong address by mistake. Typical. I definitely do know where this is. Only five minutes from here.'

'But shouldn't we go to the police? Tell them about our mugger?'

'Suppose. But that might take ages and we're late enough as it is. They'd probably never catch him, any-way.' She searched through her bag and frowned.

'Something wrong?' I asked.

'Not really. It's just that I seem to have thirty quid more than I thought I had. Must have been his.'

'So he wasn't short of money! A liar as well as a thief!'

She looked at me strangely. 'A dishonest mugger. Who'd have thought it?'

'We'll have to go to the police now, though. We can't keep the money. That would be stealing, wouldn't it?'

'And tell them what? You broke his nose and I nicked his cash?'

Had to admit she had a point.

* * *

The party wasn't what I was used to. Everyone was older – in their twenties – and neither of us knew anyone. It was packed, though, so whoever was giving it must have been popular or maybe it was full of gate crashers. The kitchen seemed to be the place with the most people, so Suzie and I settled ourselves there even though I had to sit on the sink as it was the only space left.

We got talking to a couple of guys who said they lived in a squat nearby and busked for a living, which I thought was quite exciting, but I knew Suzie would just consider them broke. They were a good laugh, though, so we were chatting away quite happily until an over-bleached blonde girl sidled up to the guy talking to me and said, 'Haven't you got me my vodka and Coke yet, Steve? You've been gone half an hour.' She gave me a hard stare. 'Don't think I know you.'

'I'm Kelly Ann.'

'She's from Glasgow,' Steve added. 'Great music scene up there.'

'How come you're down here then?' She peered at my face closely. 'Aren't you a bit young to be in London on your own. You look like you're still at school. You a runaway or something.'

'I'm nineteen.'

'Yeah, right.'

'Nineteen and a quarter actually—'

'Oooh. Nineteen and a quarter,' she trilled sarcastically.

Steve nudged her and frowned. 'Cut it out.'

'And I'm not at school. I'm at Glasgow Uni,' I insisted.

'You are?' she said more politely, but her raised eyebrows were still sceptical.

'For a year, actually, doing English Literature and Theatre Studies.'

'Cool,' she said, all fake friendly. 'Hey, I've got a friend at Glasgow Uni doing English as it happens.'

Shit, she would have. 'Oh, erm, that's interesting.'

'Yeah. She's going to drop out, though. Can't stand the weather and the stupid foul-mouthed neds up there.'

'There's nothing wrong with our weather. Or our foul-mouthed neds,' I protested loyally.

'Didn't mind the uni, though. Said the lecturers were great. Especially Professor Campbell.'

'Oh yeah, he's good,' I said.

'She,' my blonde tormentor corrected.

'I meant she. Of course.'

'And Doctor Kilburn. A real laugh. Everyone wants to be in his tutorials.'

'God, yeah, he's brilliant. Great sense of humour.'

'Yeah, especially as he doesn't exist. I just made both of them up. You've never been to university, have you?'

There was a horrible silence. A horrible, long silence. Honestly, there is nothing so humiliating as being caught out in a lie – except maybe being caught naked in the street because you'd forgot to put your clothes on, but how likely is that?

Suzie broke the silence first. 'Of course she has. Are you calling my friend a liar?'

'That's exactly what I'm calling her.'

Steve shrugged. 'So what if she never went to uni? I went for a couple of weeks and packed it in. Couldn't hack it. Anyway, I wanted to concentrate on my music. Arts course was just a waste of time and money for me.' He turned to me. 'That what happened to you? Did you drop out too?'

'Yeah, actually I did. Same sort of reason really. Wanted to focus on my dance career.'

The blonde wasn't buying any of it. 'Yeah, right. Course you did. What dance career?'

'Part of the reason I'm in London, actually. My agent has arranged a meeting for me with a dance company director next month because he wants me to join his troupe. I mean, up to now I've been performing in Scottish theatres mainly, but he's saying it's time to move on. Hit the London scene. Maybe even do a tour in the US and Europe.'

'Oh yeah? In your dreams. You don't expect anyone to believe this rubbish, do you?'

'So what's this then?' I said, rooting in my bag and taking out the gold-embossed business card Mrs Davies had given me. 'Martyn Darling. He's only the head of one of the most important dance companies in London. And they're well known in New York too. Got a tour in Europe lined up as well.'

I babbled on some more, trying to remember what my dance teacher had told me about him and his famous troupe, plus adding some more made-up stuff of my own for good measure. I could see that Steve and Suzie were impressed and even the blonde was wavering but she wasn't going to give in.

'Still don't believe it,' she huffed.

Suzie scowled at her. 'More believable than your blonde hair. Isn't it time you did your roots? They're blacker than mine. Pint of Guinness is so not a good look, you know.'

Things got a bit awkward after that, but fortunately Steve, like most guys, wasn't keen to get involved in a girls' cat fight and managed to persuade her to move off with him.

When they'd gone Suzie said, 'That's amazing about the dance company. I mean, I know you told us you'd like to be a professional dancer one day, but I'd no idea you'd actually done performances and were maybe going to join a famous company. Why didn't you tell us?'

Good question. 'Oh, erm, I didn't want you or Theresa to think I was too up myself or special or anything.'

She nodded. 'Yeah, I suppose we might have been a bit kind of overawed at first, but you should have told us, anyway. Don't know how you managed to keep it a secret. I couldn't. I'd be telling everyone.'

I flushed. 'It's not that important really. I mean, I'm not famous or anything.'

'But you might be. You're a dancer with an offer of getting involved with a big dance company. It's pretty awesome. Wait till I tell Theresa.'

Oh God, I wished she wouldn't but it was too late now. I didn't mind lying to the blonde, or anyone else at the party for that matter, but Suzie and Theresa were my friends now. Still, if the director has time to look at my demo, and if he likes it, then he might agree to meet me. Then if I did really well at the audition, and if he thought I'd got exceptional talent, and was better than all the other properly trained dancers at the audition, then there was a chance he might sign me up. Then it wouldn't really be a lie at all, would it?

Hmm. Had to admit there were an awful lot of ifs.

When we left the kitchen and wandered into the sitting room, news about me being a professional dancer had spread and some people, including the sceptical bleached blonde, asked me to show what I could do. But I didn't want to launch into a dramatic dance performance at a party and there wasn't room, anyway. Everybody understood when I explained this, except for the blonde.

'Yeah, right,' she said loudly, her voice dripping sarcasm.

'I'm sure that's the reason she doesn't want to perform now. Nothing to do with the fact she can't dance. Pathetic.'

Bloody nerve. I marched right up and eyeballed her. 'Are you calling me a liar?' I asked furiously.

'That's exactly what I'm calling you.'

'So you think I can't dance?'

'I'm saying you're no more a dancer than I am.'

'Right. Can you do this then?' I slid down slowly to the floor in a perfect 180-degree side split. Well, almost a perfect side split, as my chinos were really tight. But good enough to impress the small crowd around us who'd seen me.

A ripple of applause broke out and people moved back a bit to allow me to change position to a forward split. 'And this,' I said triumphantly.

More applause. Louder this time. Encouraged, I got up, gracefully moving to the music in the background and asked, 'Anyone want to see me do a jump split?'

They did. I checked the ceiling. Yeah, an old-fashioned flat, so quite high. There would be plenty of vertical space. Everyone in the room was watching me now (except for a couple in the corner, who were snogging, and a guy who'd passed out behind a sofa) and had formed a circle around me. I asked them to move further back and give me more room, then, taking a small run, I leaped as high as I could in the air and landed in a forward split with my arms gracefully extended towards the ceiling.

Huge applause broke out around me, including whistles and calls for more. Yay! I got up and bowed deeply several times to my appreciative audience. This was brilliant. Was about to launch into a full dance, improvising to the music, but Suzie came up behind me and hissed, 'That's enough. Time to go.'

'Not yet. This is great fun.' I twisted round to see her, but she moved so she was still behind me and whispered, 'You've split your chinos up the back.'

Oh God.

Fortunately Suzie had brought a cardigan, which she wrapped round my bum so I'd be able to travel back to the hotel without exposing myself. We decided to use our mugger's money to get a taxi. It turned out not to be enough, though, even with our own cash added, and after a bit of an argument with the driver it was decided Suzie would stay with him as a kind of hostage while I found an ATM. Tosser kept his meter running too, so I was rushing back breathless when I barrelled into Mark, who was standing just outside the hotel door.

'Sorry,' he said, holding my elbow to steady me.

Was suddenly very aware that this was the first time he'd touched me and that his hand lingered for a fraction longer than it really needed to.

'It's OK, my fault really – I wasn't looking where I was going. I do that a lot.'

'No problem.' He smiled. 'I was hoping to bump into you again actually.'

He really had a gorgeous smile. 'You were?'

'Kelly Ann,' Suzie shrieked. 'The meter's running.'

'Sorry, got to go.'

Was still fifty pence short of the fare. This time Suzie went off to get more money and I stayed as hostage (was this even legal?) while the meter ticked away. Bloody driver had the nerve to complain when we didn't leave him a tip too.

Mark was still in the foyer, talking to a tall, sporty-looking American girl with long tanned legs and swingy fair hair. He waved over at me, but I ignored him and stomped off to my room, feeling annoyed somehow, which was totally stupid. Mark wasn't my boyfriend, after all. He'd every right to talk to any girl he wanted. What was wrong with me?

Maybe I was just missing Chris. Yeah, God, I missed my boyfriend so much. If only he were here with me, everything would be so much better.

Pushed my bedroom door open and scanned the tiny space. Hmm, Chris wasn't the only thing I missed about home. My bedroom for a start. A proper bedroom with drawers, real windows and space to turn right round in without bumping into anything. And I missed my parents too. So OK, they could be sarcastic and annoying at times, but at least they cared about me, unlike Frost Face and her daughter.

But even more than my parents I missed my friends – especially Stephanie and Liz, who knew all about me but liked me anyway. I never had to lie to impress them. They liked me just as I was. God, I missed them. Wondered what they were up to now.

Wished I was still on Facebook and could see what everyone was doing, but I'd had to come off it last month because of Mum, who'd finally got into modern technology and went online. Of course, she immediately insisted on friending me on Facebook, 'because a mother is the best friend a girl could have'. Soon she was posting embarrassing comments and pictures, then trying to friend all my friends. Within a week practically everyone had blocked me (including Chris – I insisted) and I had probably the saddest teenage profile online, with only four friends: my mum, my sister, my Aunt Kate and Mr Pickles (a pal's cat). When Mr Pickles blocked me too I gave up and closed my account.

I sighed, looked at the time. One-thirty in the morning, so probably too late to call anyone. Checked my mobile for messages. Nothing new from Stephanie and Liz, probably because I now realized guiltily that I'd forgotten to answer the last couple of messages from them. Loads of texts from Mum. Most likely the usual. Was I remembering to lock my doors at night – there were a lot of dodgy characters in London – and she hoped I wasn't spending all my wages on fags and booze ha ha.

I ignored them and opened two from Chris.

MISS YOU. LOVE YOU. XX

NIGHT DARLING. XX

There was also a voice message from him – a missed call while I was at the party. Probably didn't hear it over the din. It was just a short one saying he'd try and call me tomorrow, but I played it over and over while I got ready for bed.

I crawled under my duvet, still listening to Chris's voice and, on impulse, kissed my mobile, hoping it would feel a bit like Chris was here. It felt nothing like it. Snogging a tiny smooth plastic box is absolutely no substitute for the real thing.

Was about to switch off my mobile when I noticed it – a message from my dance teacher, Mrs Davies. Could it be about the director? Or maybe it was just a polite how-are-you-getting-on text. Then again, it could be a sorry-but-he's-not-interested message. Only one way to find out.

With trembling fingers I opened it and read: GOOD NEWS. MARTYN SAYS HE LIKES UR DEMO. WILL ARRANGE AUDITION. HE WILL CONTACT YOU SOON. U R PRACTISING EVERY DAY? AT LEAST 2 HRS?

Can't believe it. A top dance director wants to see me! I leaped up and danced on the bed. Hit my head on the ceiling, but who cares? I was too excited to feel pain. I was going to be famous.

Of course, like Mrs Davies says, I'll have to practise every day, which I definitely hadn't been doing, but how would I find the time? And I'd need to do more than two hours now. At least three. I suppose I could get up three hours early, but given I don't usually get to bed until really late, and have to start so early, that would mean I'd only have a few hours' sleep. In fact, sometimes it would mean getting up before I got to bed.

No, all these late nights would have to stop. And I'd need to get totally fit too, which would mean eating proper stuff like vegetables and salad. Not greasy bacon butties and leftover lasagne for breakfast like yesterday. Or chocolate gateau and chips the day before. Also, from now on, I will drink only spring water and fruit juice. Absolutely no alcohol. As for cigarettes – never again, even if I don't inhale. Starting right now.

Was interrupted by a knock on my door and the sound of Suzie and Theresa giggling outside. There was no point in ignoring it. Both of them knew I was here. Opened the door and Theresa danced in, hips swaying, holding a bottle of fizzy wine and some paper cups.

'What's all this I hear about you being a professional dancer with a top director head-hunting you and all?'

Suzie followed her in. 'It's true, isn't it, Kelly Ann? Tell her. She thinks I'm having her on.'

I flushed. 'Yeah, well, sort of. I mean, I'm only just starting. I'm not famous or anything.'

Theresa plonked herself on my bed and started to pour the wine. 'But you probably will be one day. Like Liam.'

'So, erm, what happened with Liam tonight?' I said, hoping to stop any more questions about my dancing career lies.

Theresa's smile disappeared. 'He had to go someplace right after dinner. Meet some other artist or something. It was really important.'

Suzie rolled her eyes. 'Oh yeah, right. Don't suppose he told you who this artist was?'

'Yeah, of course he did. Just can't remember the name, that's all.'

'So probably not anyone famous then,' Suzie said sarcastically. 'Like Dali or Picasso.'

Theresa bristled. 'Obviously not, since they're dead. I don't imagine they'd be much company.'

They glared at each other and I thought for a moment they were going to fall out again, but suddenly Theresa's shoulders slumped and she sighed. 'I know what you're thinking and you're right. I'm an eejit chasing after Liam. He's not really interested in me. Totally out of my league.'

'He's not out of your league,' Suzie and I chorused loyally.

Theresa smiled. 'But I *am* an eejit sitting here on my own on a Saturday night when I could have been out with my mates getting rat-arsed.' She handed a paper cup of wine to me and Suzie, took one herself and slugged it down. 'Got a lot of catching up to do.'

'Isn't it a bit late?' I said desperately.

'Rubbish,' Theresa said, taking out a packet of Silk Cuts and offering them round. 'The night's a baby.'

Oh God.

MONDAY AUGUST 5TH

Frost Face told us she would be 'observing' us today, as apparently there have been complaints from customers about service staff efficiency and 'attitude'. God, 'attitude' – you'd think we were all still at school. When am I ever going to feel like an adult if people keep talking to me like this?

So anyway, a whole day of being spied on by our boss. Great. I hope no one complains about me when she's there.

No such luck. At breakfast the woman from table five waved me over.

'This tea is cold. Please take it back and bring me another pot.'

'It's not cold.'

'Yes it is – please replace it,' she insisted, raising her voice.

'Shh,' I hissed, turning to check if Frost had noticed anything. Good, not yet. 'Be quiet or people might hear you.'

'I will not be quiet! Now please replace this cold tea.'

'Look,' I whispered urgently. 'OK, the tea is cool now but it wasn't my fault. It was hot when I brought it out, but you went off to put your make-up on when the guy from room seventeen came down, so it was cold by the time you got back.'

'I beg your pardon. I did no such thing.'

'Yeah, you did. Don't blame you. He's gorgeous, isn't he? Theresa says she thinks he's a male model. But there was no point in your doing your face, you're way too old for him, and anyway—'

'This is outrageous. I've never been so insulted in all my life.'

Hmm. *Why not?* I felt like saying, but didn't as I know it's important to be tactful with customers even when you don't feel like it.

'Sorry, didn't mean you were *way* too old but, well, he must be at least fifteen years younger than you – maybe even twenty. Not that your age matters, of course, as he's gay. Or I think so, anyway, as he shares his room with another guy and they asked for a double bed.'

'Would you keep your voice down!' she yelled.

That was it. Frost heard and came over. 'What seems

to be the trouble, madam?' She said with an obsequious smile.

'She says her tea is cold but it was hot when I gave it to her,' I butted in quickly.

Frost gave me a look that would have frozen Niagara Falls but carried on talking sweetly to the customer. 'We're very sorry, madam. Let me take this cold tea away and bring you a fresh pot immediately.'

'It was cold from the start.'

'Of course it was, madam. You're quite right. We'll get this sorted out for you at once.'

She motioned for me to follow her into the kitchen. 'You stay here. I will attend to this customer myself, then I'd like a word with you.'

Once she got back she rounded on me right away in front of everyone. Theresa and Suzie threw me sympathetic looks while Yan busied himself washing pots at the sink and pretended not to notice – I suppose so I wouldn't be so embarrassed – but I couldn't help feeling humiliated.

'Kelly Ann, what is the first, most important rule of customer care?'

'Hmm, I'm not sure. Always make sure they pay their bill?'

'No.'

'Always give them the correct change and don't get annoyed when you don't get a tip even when you know they are loaded and just being totally mean?'

'No.'

Oh God, maybe the woman complained about my comments on her fancying the guy in room seventeen. 'Don't tell them they are too old to be hitting on guys half their age?'

'What!! I hope you would never say anything of the sort!'

'Course not,' I said, forcing myself to look her straight in the eye. 'You don't think I'd be that stupid, do you?'

'Thank God,' she said, moving to sit down on the kitchen stool behind her just as Theresa silently whipped it away so that Frost fell on her arse with her legs in the air.

Hadn't realized that she wore magic kickers to pull her tummy and thighs in. Don't know why she bothered, because with a face that could sour yoghurt it hardly mattered if you looked a bit fat as well. Or maybe the too-tight pants gave her that constantly pained disapproving expression. No, they wouldn't make her a sarcastic, nasty, mean person either. Think Frost was just born that way.

I tried to help her up but she brushed me away, scrambled awkwardly to her feet and scanned the kitchen suspiciously. By this time Theresa was busy stacking salt cellars onto a tray and humming innocently, but Frost's eyes homed in on her anyway. Theresa was definitely nearest to the stool and she couldn't quite keep the smirk from her face.

'So, Mrs Frost,' I said quickly, hoping to divert her, 'what *is* the most important rule of customer care?'

It worked. Frost wagged her finger at me and began, all pompous. 'Ah yes, the most important rule of customer care is this: *The customer is always right.*'

'Can't always be right,' I said.

'Always, Kelly Ann.'

'But what if—'

'No ifs, no buts, no exceptions. The customer is *always* right. Remember that and you can't go far wrong. So, Kelly Ann, tell me, what is the most important rule of customer care?'

Oh my God, she wanted me to repeat it like some primary school kid. Really hated her so much. Wish I could have dunked her know-it-all face in syrup and then pushed it into a hive of giant African killer wasps. Or at least stuck my tongue out at her and told her to shove her job. But I repeated it, like she'd asked, my face burning beetroot with embarrassment. How pathetic was that. Vowed one day she'd pay for this.

TUESDAY AUGUST 6TH

Didn't have to wait that long. Next morning she was there again, spying on us. Or I should say spying on *me*, as her beady eye was on me all the time.

Things went OK until this Essex guy from last night's stag party came in. He was dressed in rumpled, beer- and curry-stained clothes that he'd probably slept in and his devil-red eyes were screwed almost shut against the light. But he ordered a full cooked breakfast with extra fried bread, then slumped head down on the table.

When I brought him his order, he raised his head and squinted at me. 'You wouldn't happen to have a beer to go with that, sweetheart? Hair of the dog, like. The only real cure, you know.'

'I'm sorry, sir, we're not allowed to sell alcohol before ten o'clock, and anyway, only Joy our cocktail waitress and Nigel our wine waiter can serve you.'

'Oh, c'mon, love. Be reasonable. It's just a beer. Rules are made to be broken, ain't they?'

Saw Frost frowning at me from across the room. In two seconds she'd be over telling me off again for not doing what a customer wanted.

'Of course, sir. You're quite right, I'll bring your order directly.'

Two minutes later I was back with a bottle of Carlsberg I found in the fridge and handed it to him.

'Thanks, love. You're a life-saver.'

'No problem, sir, my pleasure,' I said, smiling.

But my smile disappeared when Frost marched over and glared at me. She said nothing to me, instead focusing on the customer. 'I'm sorry, sir, but we're not licensed to sell alcohol before ten o'clock.'

Ignoring her, he took a swig of his beer and burped. 'God, I needed that.'

'I don't think you understand,' Frost fumed. 'I'm the manageress of this establishment and I must insist you adhere to our rules.'

He shovelled some egg and sausage into his mouth and chewed it slowly. 'Grouchy old battle axe, ain't she?' he said to me.

'Yes, sir,' I said. 'If you say so.'

She glared at both of us. 'How dare you!'

'Well, he's a customer and you said—'

'We'll discuss this later,' she hissed. She turned her most officious stony gaze on the customer, who was now calmly drinking his beer again. 'Right, that's it. I must insist you leave the premises immediately.'

'Don't get your knickers in a twist. I'm going.' He stood up, pushed the chair back and slapped some bacon between two bits of fried bread. He picked up his beer, slugged the rest of it down and put the bottle back on the table. 'Wouldn't stay another day in this fleapit if you paid me to.'

'You're quite right, sir,' I said. 'I couldn't agree more.' I eyed Frost, all innocently. 'Because the customer is always right. Always. No ifs, no buts, no exceptions.'

WEDNESDAY AUGUST 7TH

Despite Theresa and Suzie's worries that Frost would have it in for me now, I've been promoted by the chef today – sort of – probably because his sous chef got hacked off and quit yesterday. Anyway, this is the first time he has allowed me to help prepare food instead of just serving or cleaning up.

I'm supposed to make the Marie Rose sauce for the shrimps. It's not that difficult really. I just have to squeeze plastic bottles of Hellman's mayonnaise into one enormous glass bowl, and plastic bottles of Heinz tomato ketchup into another, then mix them up. Correction. The chef has just told me *he* is to mix them up as this difficult, important job can't be delegated to the likes of me. Bloody nerve – I'd have thought a proper chef in a hotel would have made his own sauce from scratch, not relied on stuff anyone can buy in the supermarket, but apparently not. As Theresa said, waving a large cucumber in the direction of the retreating chef's back, 'Don't think he's going to get the Michelin star for this.'

After a few minutes I was getting annoyed with the whole thing, especially as the bottles made stupid farting noises when they got to the end, which made even Yan laugh. Hmm, suppose even serious, polite Polish blokes are just guys after all.

Was beginning to envy Theresa, who was chopping up

salad stuff, and even Suzie, who was skinning chicken bits, but at least I finished before them and was able to sneak a mug of tea when the chef disappeared to the loo with a newspaper and a packet of fags. Theresa and Suzie saw me and pulled a face so I made some for them too and they joined me.

'He'll be a while,' Theresa said confidently. 'He's taken the sports page and his fags with him.'

But she spoke too soon. He burst into the kitchen a minute later and started bawling at us.

'Leave you lot alone for two bloody seconds and this is what I find. Hasn't anyone got any work to do around here? The world doesn't owe you a living, you know.'

He marched over to the nearest counter, picked up a cleaver and began chopping up a leg of lamb a lot more energetically than than was strictly necessary.

We all got the message and jumped up quickly to do as he asked. As Suzie said, 'You don't argue with a man whose team has lost and who's waving a meat cleaver.'

We were hurrying back and forth to set tables for lunch when the chef yelled at me to bring him the sauce bowls. 'And hurry up about it – we haven't got all day!'

I grabbed the tomato ketchup bowl and raced over, but before I could get to him the door to the dining room flew open and flipped the bowl of sauce all over my face and head, then it shattered on the floor. Brilliant.

'Jeezus, I'm sorry, Kelly Ann,' Theresa said. 'I barged

through there like an idiot. Didn't realize you were on the other side. Are you OK?'

I didn't answer. Too busy trying to wipe the stuff off my face with my hands, but all I succeeded in doing was smearing the sauce over a larger area, including my chest and skirt.

'Oh my God,' Suzie said. 'You look like Carrie!'

'Who's she?' I asked, still trying to wipe myself clean; with zero success.

'You know, the girl in the film? Remember the bit at the end of the prom when she's covered in a bucket of pigs' blood.'

'Thanks, Suzie. That really helps.'

'Sorry.' Suzie grabbed some paper towels from a roller and started dabbing at my skirt. 'Let me help you.'

'Never mind that,' the chef bawled. 'Get that mess cleared up off the floor. And that bowl is coming off your pay.'

Charming. And to think I used to moan about teachers being heartless, uncaring sods. Maybe Mum was right when she told me that when I got out into the real world I'd think my teachers were 'sodding fairy godmothers' by comparison. Though the thought of my sour-faced maths teacher Mr Simmons being anyone's fairy godmother was a bit much.

Theresa went off to get a dustpan and mop while Suzie and I tried to pick the biggest bits of glass off the floor and put them into the broken glass and crockery bin. Hadn't even realized that I'd cut myself until Theresa returned and said, 'Kelly Ann, I think that's real blood oozing from your thumb.'

Looked at it. It was the same colour as the ketchup but runnier and definitely increasing all the time.

The chef came over. 'What is it now?' He looked at the cut and handed me a kitchen towel. 'That's all we bloody need! Wrap this around it, keep your arm up and get off to First Aid.'

'I'll go with her,' Theresa said.

'She'll be OK on her own. It's just a scratch. You stay here and clean the rest of this mess up.'

I hurried off. Had really wanted to clean myself up a bit first, but the chef and Theresa said I had to go straight to First Aid. Probably about the only thing they have ever agreed upon. Problem was I had to pass the reception desk to get there but I was in luck. There was no one in the lobby – just Joy, who was on duty at the desk but was working on the computer and didn't notice me. I raced past, banged on Sidebottom's door and went right in without waiting for his imperious 'Enter'.

'I've had an accident,' I said.

Or started to say, because before I'd finished he'd passed out and collapsed at my feet.

Bloody hell. Some first-aid officer. Despite having to hold onto my towel and keep my arm up, after a bit of shoving and hauling I managed to manoeuvre him into the recovery position – sort of sprawled on his tummy but head to the side, like my boyfriend Chris had once shown me – and waited for him to come round. I peered down at him, bringing my face close to his to see if he was breathing OK.

After a few seconds I heard him groan.

'David, are you all right?' I asked.

He opened his eyes, stared at my tomatoey face, then passed out again. Knew I should have cleaned up first.

There was no way I could hang about much longer without our psycho chef going mental at me when I returned late, especially as I would need to shower and change before I got back, so I looked around the room for a first-aid kit. Nothing. Saw a cupboard beside the door and rummaged through it. Hmm. Some magazines, DVDs and a pack of condoms. Yuk. Wondered if Joy knew about this. I slammed the cupboard door shut, which caused a metal box from a shelf above it to fall on my head. Ah, the first-aid box. Fantastic. It's what my old English teacher might have called ironic but I call bloody sore and annoying.

I peeled off the bloody towel and noticed that I'd stopped bleeding as, though the cut was long, it wasn't very deep. A strong plaster would do.

I wiped the cut with disinfectant and stuck on a plaster, then I wrote up the details in the accident incident book.

Heard Sidebottom moan and stir so I quickly sneaked out before he could see me and probably faint again.

This time Joy wasn't at the reception desk – most likely nipped out to the toilet as that's the only thing that could persuade her to leave her post – but a group of German tourists with loads of luggage were coming through the doors. They saw me and gawped. I didn't feel like going into a long explanation so just said, 'If you ring the bell someone will be with you in a minute.'

But they turned and practically ran out of the doors with their suitcases wheeling crazily behind them. In a way, that's good as there won't be as many guests for breakfast and lunch tomorrow. But on the other hand, they looked quite well off so I suppose we might have lost some good tips. Oh well.

I frowned and stomped off along the corridor heading for my room. Was just passing the lift when I spotted Mark – the good-looking American guy whose underwear I'd stolen on my first day – coming out of it with his suitcase and rucksack.

I turned back. 'Oh, you're leaving!' My voice sounded surprised and disappointed even to me, which was totally stupid. I mean, it's a hotel for God's sake. People don't stay in hotels for ever. What was the matter with me?

'I'm checking out, yeah. So, erm, what does the other guy look like?' he said, smiling.

I blushed. 'Oh, I wasn't fighting. This is just tomato ketchup.'

'Yeah, I heard. I asked your Irish friend where you were and she told me about your ketchup accident.' His expression turned serious again. 'But you got a cut too. You OK?'

'Yeah, it's not deep or anything. I'll live. So, erm, why were you asking about me?'

'I wanted to see you before I checked out. We never did get around to meeting up and—'

'You wanted to say goodbye. That's nice.' I held out my hand to shake his but he just looked at it. Blushing, I withdrew my tomatoey palm and wiped it on my skirt. 'Sorry.'

'I was about to say we never got around to meeting up, so I wondered if you'd like to do something on your day off.'

'In America? It's a bit out of my way.'

He smiled. 'I'm checking out. Not going home. Law school doesn't start again until mid-September so I've plenty of time. But the hotel is a bit expensive to stay long-term, no matter how great the staff are.'

'So you're staying in London?' I said, sounding far more pleased than I ought to.

'Yeah, Earl's Court. Some Australian guys rent an apartment there. One of them left yesterday so there's a room spare until they find a permanent replacement.'

'Cool.'

'So when's your day off? Sunday, isn't it? Theresa told me.'

'Yeah, but I'm not sure. I mean, I've got a boyfriend back home and—'

'Me too,' Mark interrupted. 'I just thought, well, since we're both new in town it might be nice to explore it together.'

'Oh,' I said, flushing. 'I didn't realize. I mean, I suppose I should have known. All those pink shirts in your laundry and the highlights in your hair.'

'Whoa, hey, wait a minute. I'm not gay. I meant I've got a girlfriend back home. Her name's Cindy.'

'Oh.'

'The pink shirts were a laundry accident,' he explained. 'Put them in the wash with red boxers. And my hair is sun–bleached, not peroxide. I'm from California – it's always sunny there.'

'Oh God, sorry.'

'No problem. So, what about it? Want to meet up? Do the tourist stuff together maybe?'

'Well . . . I don't know—'

'Just as friends. I mean, we've both got commitments, right? It will be just like I'm gay except I've no fashion sense, so clothes shopping is out.'

'OK, maybe then. I'll think about it.'

'Look, why don't I give you my cell number and you can call me if you want.'

'OK.'

He shrugged off his rucksack and extracted a stubby pen from an outside pocket, along with a notepad purloined from our hotel. He tore off a page, then instead of handing it to me – given my saucy palms – he tucked it underneath the puffed sleeve of my left arm. The action seemed oddly intimate and tender – maybe because of the slow, gentle way it was done, or perhaps because his eyes never left my face the whole time. Found myself holding my breath in anticipation of something. Not sure what.

But then he grinned and swung his rucksack back over his shoulders and the moment was gone. Maybe I just imagined it anyway.

He patted my arm where the note was. 'Hey, don't lose it!'

I smiled back. 'I won't.'

'Bye, Kelly Ann.'

'Bye.'

I walked off to shower feeling somehow happy and excited. It would be nice to have a guy friend in London. Caught sight of my sauce-stained face grinning back at me like a mental person. Well, one thing was for sure, he couldn't have been asking to see me because he fancied me. It was all completely platonic so there was no need to worry on that score.

But as the day went on I started to feel a bit uneasy

about Mark. Kind of guilty really, as though I was somehow being disloyal to my boyfriend. Decided to call Chris when my shift finished and, after we'd chatted for a bit, I'd tell him about my plans do touristy stuff in London with a nice American guy I'd met. A nice American guy who'd a girlfriend back home so, like me, was just looking for someone to see the sights with. Then everything would be totally above board. Completely innocent.

'Hi, Chris, how are you?'

'Hi, Kelly Ann.'

We hadn't spoken on the phone for nearly a week now – kept missing each other and leaving texts instead – so the sound of his low, gentle voice full of love caught me off-guard and I felt a sudden stab of longing. 'God, I miss you so much,' I said.

'Miss you too, darling. How was your day?'

Didn't feel like going into the whole tomato ketchup fiasco right then so just said, 'You first. What have you been up to?'

'OK. Well, it was my day off so I went to the pub this afternoon with Gary. Wish I hadn't bothered – ended up getting into a brawl.'

'Oh my God, what happened?'

'Well, you know Gary, always getting into trouble over girls. This time he was chatting up some blonde assuming she was free, but it turned out she wasn't, so her boyfriend and his pals turned on him. He tried to apologize but they weren't having it. Jumped him when we went outside. There were three of them all laying into him so I had to get involved as well.'

'Are you OK?'

'Yeah. Gary and I are fine. I'll probably have a black eye tomorrow but nothing serious. The other guys came off worse.'

'I should hope so!' I said, furious at the thought of anyone trying to hurt Chris even though I knew he could take care of himself. 'Hope you battered them to a bloody pulp. They deserve it.'

Chris laughed. 'Well, we inflicted quite a number of contusions, abrasions and other soft tissue injuries on our opponents, but they'll live.'

'Good for you.'

'Kelly Ann,' he sighed, 'my aim in life is to treat injuries, not cause them.'

'Suppose,' I conceded. 'Well, as long as you're OK. What are you up to now?'

'Reading a book.'

'What's it called?'

'You wouldn't be interested.'

'Try me.'

'It's a medical textbook. I'm reading about tapeworm infections.'

'You're right,' I laughed. 'I'm definitely not interested.'

'Did you know the longest tapeworm pulled out of a human body measured thirty-seven feet?'

'Aargh. I *told* you I wasn't interested. So, erm, what are you doing tomorrow?'

'I'm working during the day but Gary has persuaded me to get him an invite to a student nurse party at the hospital tomorrow night. Don't worry, I'll go with him and make sure he doesn't hit on anyone with a boyfriend this time. As far as I know, all the girls at this do are single anyway.'

'Oh,' I said, my voice tight.

Chris picked up on it immediately. 'You're not jealous?' he teased.

'Course not.'

'Good. Because you've absolutely no reason to be. No one compares to you. Not even close. I love you, Kelly Ann.'

'Oh God, I love you too. Wish I could be there with you right now. Miss you so much.'

'Wish you were here too, darling. Curled up in my lap like you used to be.'

'Mmm, yeah,' I breathed. 'That would be soooo nice.'

'I could wrap my arms around you,' he whispered, his voice soft and low, 'and press my lips to your warm skin, then . . .'

'And then?' I smiled, feeling all kind of tingly with anticipation.

'We could read about intestinal tapeworm infections together.'

'Idiot!' I laughed.

But suddenly Chris turned all serious again. Telling me how much he loved and missed me. And how wonderful it was going to be when we were together again. By the time I hung up I was feeling all warm and fuzzy, as though I'd been wrapped in a cocoon of Chris's love. In fact, it wasn't until I was getting ready for bed that I realized I hadn't mentioned Mark at all.

THURSDAY AUGUST 8TH

Realized I hadn't been in touch with Stephanie and Liz for ages despite getting loads of texts and emails from them. But they were both on holiday while I was working full-time so it wasn't my fault that I'd been a lot busier. Sent them both long emails today anyway, filling them in on everything I'd been doing. Well, not everything exactly. Don't get me wrong, Liz and Stephanie are great, but it was kind of nice sometimes for them not to know absolutely every single thing I was up to. Especially Liz.

They emailed me back soon after.

Email from Stephanie:

Holiday a disaster. No topless bathing allowed at our hotel pool so after the first week I'd white boobs! I ask you – and they call this a five-star hotel. Tried to find a sun bed solarium but was told there were none on the whole island. When I complained, they pointed out that the Caribbean islands were practically the sunniest islands on the planet, so had sunshine all year round and therefore there was no market for them – or some bollocks like that. Resorted to fake tanning my boobs but the shade is subtly different. Total nightmare.

Talking of nightmares, they canNOT be serious about your hotel uniform. Surely there's some law against forcing you to wear a dirndl skirt and puff sleeves – never mind a mobcap etc. Must be against your human rights – Geneva Convention or something. Why don't you ask that American law student you met? A pity he's so ugly – although I suppose, like you say, at least you won't be tempted to cheat on Chris. But really, playing away isn't really cheating, is it?

Your Pole sounds quite fit – can you email me a pic? Must get hot in those kitchens during the summer so hopefully you can persuade him to take his shirt off. Don't know if I ever told you about the Polish assistant plumber I went out with before I met Dave? All muscle – biceps like barrels and thighs as thick as tree trunks.

Mmm. Hardly spoke a word of English – but we didn't do much talking.

Don't forget the pic!!

Stephanie x

PS: Try not to make a total arse of things in London.

Email from Liz:

Having a brilliant time. So many neurotic people in New York – it's a psychologist's paradise. Although Julian objected when I tried to counsel our McDonald's waiter regarding his self-harming problem. Said the guy was probably telling the truth about nicking himself shaving by accident and all he needed was a band-aid, not therapy.

Now, I love Julian – or should I say we have a very healthy, reciprocal relationship based on mutual positive regard – but he knows nothing about psychology or he'd realize that there are NO SUCH THINGS AS ACCIDENTS. It's totally obvious that the poor waiter's so-called accident is due to the self-loathing of a damaged psyche. Thankfully I was able to see through his denials as a typical defence mechanism and offer him some therapy.

Our burgers got cold, though.

What's all this about the American law student? I mean, come on, if you're telling me he's totally unfanciable it's just so obvious he's hot as hell and you're trying to repress your feelings. Doomed, of course – the sex drive is the most important, powerful urge we have. Libido will out!

Email back and tell me everything, including all your thoughts and feelings, so we can work through them together.

Liz x

PS: Try not to make a total arse of everything in London.

I smiled to myself as I read them. God it was great to hear from my friends again even if they are both a bit nuts. Felt bad about not being entirely honest with them about Mark, but I'd hoped it would stop them jumping to totally the wrong conclusions about our relationship. Hasn't worked with Liz, though.

But I'm not that pleased about their PS notes. It's pretty obvious they *do* think I'm going to make a total arse of things here. Hoped I'd prove them wrong. But to be on the safe side decided it was best to keep my London life a secret from them as much as possible. Then at least they'd never know. When you've got a friend as nosy as Liz it was the only way.

'*Guess what?*' *Theresa said excitedly.*

Suzie sighed and rolled her eyes. 'Oh God, it's not Liam again, is it?'

Theresa frowned, but then decided to ignore Suzie's unenthusiastic response. 'Yeah, and guess what?'

'He's emigrating to Australia?' Suzie asked hopefully. 'Or joined a Trappist monk community in Bosnia and taken a vow of silence so we'll never hear from him again? He's contracted a fatal disease and has only six more weeks—'

'He's giving a poetry reading tonight and wants me to come along.'

'Cool,' I said politely.

'Yeah, and guess what?' Theresa continued.

'For God's sake!' Suzie said. 'Just get on with it.'

'He says to bring as many friends as I like.'

'No way,' Suzie said.

'Please come,' Theresa pleaded. 'Liam's really keen for me to invite you and tickets are less than a tenner.'

'We have to pay? You've got to be joking.'

'Even poets need money to live,' Theresa said. 'And there will be other poets there. Not just Liam.'

'You mean proper poets? Ones with actual talent?'

'Stop it, Suzie,' Theresa said. 'C'mon, if you two don't come it will look like I've no friends. You'll come, won't you, Kelly Ann?'

'Only if Suzie does,' I said.

'Suzie, please, as a favour to me!' Theresa begged.

'Oh, all right then. But just for a little while. I'm not staying for the whole thing if it's as awful as I expect it is.'

'OK.'

'So me and Kelly Ann can just sneak out halfway through if we get bored?' Suzie said.

'Yeah, but you'll probably love it.'

Hmm. The tickets were £9.99, so under a tenner, I suppose, but only just. The recital was held in a large dusty church hall with seating for over four hundred people. There were three poets including Liam. With the exception of the sole female poet's gran, we were the only audience. So much for sneaking out unnoticed.

The first 'poet' was a guy with a huge beer belly and a long greasy ponytail which reached to his waist (perhaps to make up for the fact that he had gone almost bald at the front). His poem was called 'Why Won't Hot Girls Date Me?' and was basically about the fact that girls who looked like Keira Knightley and Angelina Jolie kept knocking him back when he tried to chat them up. He droned on for nearly twenty minutes, staring at each of us in turn as though looking for an answer. The temptation to tell him was so hard to resist I had to put my hand over my mouth.

Next was an earnest-looking girl with glasses who

read us a poem entitled 'Darkness of Despair'. Hard to say whether she was any good or not, as by the time she'd got halfway through her talk on death, disease and the ultimate utter futility and hopelessness of everything, I'd just about lost the will to live. She seemed really happy at the end of her recital, though. Maybe making everyone else as miserable as she was somehow cheered her up.

Finally it was Liam's turn. He strolled out onto the stage confidently and introduced himself briefly. 'Ladies and gentlemen, my name is Liam and my poem is called "The Sound of Silence".'

For Theresa's sake I tried to fix an interested expression on my face and waited for him to start. And waited. And waited. Five minutes later we were still waiting as Liam stayed perfectly still and totally silent on the stage. The only sounds we heard were the faint snoring of the poet's gran and me blowing my nose halfway through – which was embarrassing, but dust had got up my nostrils so what else could I do?

A long minute later, Liam spoke. 'Ladies and gentlemen, "The Sound of Silence".' Then he bowed.

I mean, for God's sake. Yet the two other performers applauded loudly and went up on the stage to congratulate him. 'Brilliant!' 'Genius!'

After a puzzled pause Theresa also applauded enthusiastically. She turned to us, her eyes shining. 'He's amazing, isn't he? So original.'

We looked at each other. It was hopeless. 'Yeah, amazing,' we agreed.

Afterwards we all went off to a pub next to the church. The guy with the ponytail tried to chat up the gorgeous-looking Polish barmaid with no success. Another verse to add to his poem, I suppose. Theresa bought a beer for Liam and he chatted with her while he drank it, then ignored her in favour of the earnest female poet, who kept telling him how fantastic his performance was. How he'd 'framed and shaped the concept of silence'. Rubbish like that. And how publishers were sure to be interested in his work.

Yeah, right. What would they print? Blank pages of framed silence?

Eventually Theresa trailed back to the hotel with us, totally dejected. 'Don't think Liam will ever commit to going out with me properly. It's hopeless, isn't it?' she asked.

Suzie and I made sympathetic noises, but I heard Suzie mutter under her breath, 'With any luck.'

SATURDAY AUGUST 10TH

My very first wage slip. A proper formal-looking envelope – an official minty green colour – with my name printed on. At last I'm no longer a child receiving pocket money from parents but a grown-up employee with a salary which will be paid into my new bank account.

'Well, are you going to open the thing or just stand there and admire it?' Theresa said, ripping open her own wage slip. 'I'd check it carefully if I were you. Sly sods have underpaid me twice already.'

She scrutinized her own and sighed. 'It's right, unfortunately. And they haven't forgotten to subtract last week's sub from it.'

Suzie had already checked hers and stuffed it into her pocket. 'The only way I could earn less than this would be if I were trafficked.'

Personally I thought they were being a bit moany. Say what you like about this place but the pay was pretty good for kitchen work. Way over the minimum wage that I'd expected.

Carefully I tore along the perforated edges, unfolded the envelope and smoothed out the paper. Didn't mention it to Theresa, but I would probably frame it and keep it. I gazed at it lovingly for a moment, not really reading the detail, just savouring the knowledge that I was now an independent wage-earning adult. At last, for this summer at least, I would not have to rely on parents. Just as well too. I only had 7p left from the money they'd given me to 'tide me over' for the first couple of weeks away.

A whole week's wages – probably more money than

I'd ever owned even at Christmas or birthdays. I checked the amount now.

Bloody hell – it was less than I expected. A lot less. There had to be some mistake.

The number of hours was right, I think, and the rate. But what were these deductions about? Subsidized accommodation fee. Subsidized? I thought it was free. And *accommodation* for that matter – they had to be joking. Much too big a word for such a tiny space. And food? Now OK, we didn't starve in here, but we never got to choose what we ate. Just whatever was left over after meals were served. In other words, what guests hadn't wanted, and would have been binned anyway. But the thing that made me maddest was the uniform. It wasn't even subsidized – we had to actually buy the hideous outfit at full cost. Bloody hell, it was like asking you to pay for the bullet for your own execution. There was no way I was standing for this.

'It's not fair,' I said.

Theresa glanced over at me. 'Oh, you've just found out about the deductions?'

Suzie looked at me ruefully. 'You got scammed too? Don't feel bad, I'm supposed to be a business student and I fell for it as well.'

'Yeah.' Theresa nodded. 'We've all been eejits and a half. Should have known those rates were too good to be true.'

I scowled. 'I'm not putting up with this. I'm gonna see Frost Face now. Make her pay me properly.'

Suzie and Theresa tried to talk me out of it, but I was determined. This wasn't about money. It was about PRINCIPLE! Well, OK, PRINCIPLE *and* MONEY. Whatever, she wasn't getting away with it.

'You did read your contract of employment, didn't you?' Mrs Frost asked with a smile about as friendly as a crocodile's.

'Of course I did.'

'Then you'll be aware that uniform, food and accommodation costs would be deducted?'

'No, I didn't see anything about that.'

'Perhaps you didn't read it carefully enough. It's quite clearly stated.' She took a sheaf of papers from a file and handed it to me. 'Here's a copy of your contract. I think you'll find the relevant terms in clause sixteen, paragraph c, subsections five, six and seven.'

I rifled through the papers but couldn't find anything. With a sigh she took the contract from me and pointed to a bit about halfway down the second last page. I peered at it. Bloody hell, no wonder I hadn't noticed it. You'd have needed a microscope to read type that size.

'Always read the small print, Kelly Ann,' she said.

'It's not fair,' I moaned, then flushed, knowing I must have sounded like a sulky kid.

'Well, you could always leave us if you feel that strongly.'

'Well, erm, I didn't say I was going to but–'

'Of course, if you did so, that would be breach of contract.'

This sounded kind of serious. 'Would it?' I asked nervously.

She nodded.

'But, I mean, it's a free country, isn't it? You can't keep me here if I don't want to stay. That would be kidnap. Well, false imprisonment, anyway. I know my rights.'

'Of course we wouldn't keep you against your will if you're not happy here, Kelly Ann. But you would be required to pay your full six-week accommodation costs up front, plus a fee for early release. About six hundred pounds in total.'

'Oh.'

'So, are you resigning your position then?'

'No, it's fine. I never said I wanted to leave.'

'So, you're happy here?'

'Nnyeah,' I said, forcing my lips to form the word.

'Good, good. Excellent. Because a happy staff is a helpful staff. That's always been my motto.'

Hmm. Felt more homicidal than helpful, but what could I do? Maybe Mum was right and my schooldays were going to be the happiest time of my life. The thought depressed me. It was like you've just been released from prison and are celebrating your freedom when you're told you're being sent to a forced labour camp with no chance of parole.

I trudged back to the kitchen, where Suzie and Theresa were waiting for me.

'Because a happy staff is a helpful staff,' they chorused.

I scowled. 'You got the same rubbish?'

'Yeah,' Theresa said. She picked up a meat skewer. 'Wanted to impale her with this and roast her on a giant spit when she said that, but what can you do?'

Suzie grinned. 'Yeah. Same. Only I'd have preferred to dice her into little pieces and stir-fry her.'

'Or put her through a mincer headfirst and make her into meat pies,' I suggested, laughing. 'Then feed them to mean customers who don't leave any tips.'

They both went all quiet and frowned at me.

'That's a bit off,' Theresa said.

'Yeah,' Suzie agreed. 'I think you've taken this too far.'

I flushed. 'Oh God, I didn't mean it. I'm not a psycho. It was just a joke. I mean, you both said stuff you didn't really—'

Was interrupted by gales of laughter from Theresa and Suzie.

'We really got you there, didn't we,' Suzie giggled.

'Your face, Kelly Ann!' Theresa guffawed. 'Honestly, you should have seen yourself.'

'Yeah, right, OK, very funny,' I said, aiming for a weak smile and failing.

Theresa wrapped an arm round my shoulder. 'Sorry, Kelly Ann, just couldn't resist. But look, it's payday, why don't we all go out tonight and celebrate? Go mad and blow the lot maybe.'

'Yeah, good idea,' Suzie said. 'Why don't we have a Chinese first then hit the pubs.'

I glanced at my wage slip again. 'Don't know if I can afford it. Anyway, no offence, Suzie, but I'm not that keen on Chinese.'

'Racist!' Suzie laughed. 'But don't worry, this will be proper Chinese. Not that rubbish you've probably been eating. And it will be cheap too. My dad's cousin is a friend of the owner. C'mon, you'll love it!'

The restaurant was in Chinatown, which is near Soho, and Suzie was dead right about the food. Delicious, and nothing like the rubbish takeaways I'd had before. Theresa and I both had trouble using the chopsticks, though, and ended up just spearing bits of meat and kind of shovelling noodles and rice into our mouths, dropping more than we ate. Suzie had no bother, of course, and I couldn't help admiring how easily and neatly she used the chopsticks. Was even more impressed when she talked to our waiter in rapid, fluent Chinese.

'That's amazing,' I said when he'd left to get us the rice wine Theresa fancied trying.

'What?' Suzie asked.

'The way you can speak Chinese like that.'

Suzie looked at me strangely. 'You may not have noticed this before, Kelly Ann, but I *am* Chinese, actually.'

'Yeah, I know, but, well, you usually speak English and Chinese sounds so complicated.'

'Not if you're Chinese. And it's Cantonese I speak. There are a lot of Chinese languages, you know.'

I flushed, realizing how ignorant I must have sounded. 'Anyway,' I said, 'what were you talking to him about? You can't just have been ordering Theresa's rice wine. Not unless Cantonese is even more difficult than I thought.'

Suzie laughed. 'No, it doesn't take five minutes to order one drink. He was hitting on me. Asked me out. This is the third time now – every time I've come here. You'd think he'd take the hint.'

I glanced over at him. He was tall for a Chinese guy and really quite muscular and toned. Looked more like one of the fighters you get in kung fu films than a waiter. Plus he'd a nice face and smile. 'Seems all right to me. Why don't you like him?'

'Not my type.'

'Why not?' I persisted.

Suzie shrugged. 'Chinese.'

'Racist,' Theresa laughed.

'You don't really mean that, Suzie,' I said, shocked.

'No, of course I don't mean it. It's just, well, you're probably going to think me a snob but I don't want to go out with a waiter.'

'Of course I don't think you're a snob,' I lied.

'Of course you're a snob,' Theresa said, laughing. 'Shame on you.'

'God, I know,' Suzie said. 'I do feel bad. But the thing is, my mum and dad spent their whole life slaving in a hot kitchen trying to make their takeaway business pay and never even got a holiday. It's not going to happen to me. And I'm not going to fall for any guy who wants to live like that either.'

'So,' I said, 'you're looking for someone rich?'

Suzie grinned. 'Rich would be nice. A business tycoon or something. But I'd settle for well off. Like a doctor, maybe. God, you're so lucky going out with one already, Kelly Ann. Must be nice he can take you to classy places when you're living on a student loan.'

I flushed. 'He's not that well off. Not loaded like a consultant or anything.'

'Still,' Suzie sighed. 'It's pretty cool. How did you meet him?'

Hmm, how had I met Chris really? When I was just a young kid I'd been riding my bike in the playground and was showing off by taking my hand off the handlebars then throwing Maltesers one by one into the air and catching them in my mouth. A small crowd had gathered to watch me, including a group of boys who cheered me on. But then I crashed into a wall, my Maltesers went flying and I landed in a puddle.

Even though my knees and nose were bleeding, when I started to cry, all the boys just laughed at me. Except for Chris. He helped me up and asked if I was OK, then cleaned the blood off my nose with his shirt sleeve. Probably some snot too, as I'd been crying, but he never let on. Later he gave me half his Milky Way to make up for losing the Maltesers. We've been friends ever since but didn't realize we fancied each other for another ten years. Well, *I* never realized it, anyway – I think Chris had always loved me somehow. I smiled at the memory now.

God, how I missed him.

'So,' Suzie prompted impatiently. 'How did you meet him then? It can't have been at uni as he was already a doctor by then, you said.'

Did I? Oh God, it was getting difficult to remember all my lies.

In the end I made up some story about how I'd sprained my ankle while rehearsing a particularly difficult dance routine and falling off the stage. I'd been rushed to A&E (because we thought at first it was broken) where this gorgeous young registrar had fallen for me immediately and we'd been inseparable since.

'It was love at first sight,' I said, warming to my story.

'Oh God, that's so romantic,' Theresa sighed. 'Like Romeo and Juliet but without all the tragic stuff. I suppose he must be suffering now with your being apart and all.'

Suzie shrugged. 'He'll probably come down and see you then. For a weekend, maybe. It would be great to meet him.'

'Oh God, I hope not,' I blurted.

'Sorry?' Suzie asked, puzzled. 'Why would you not want him to visit?

'I mean, erm, well, he's got lives to save. He couldn't leave his patients to die just to see me. No matter how crazy in love he is.'

Fortunately our waiter came back before they could ask any more questions and talk turned to where we'd be heading off to after. Eventually it was agreed we'd go to a club – not in Soho, thank God; too dear or too sleazy or both.

With Theresa and Suzie beside me I got into the club, no bother, with my fake ID. The place was so dark you could hardly see anybody and the music so loud it was impossible to be heard. Just like the clubs in Glasgow really, except there were even more different nationalities and races here: European, Australian, American as well as African, Asian and Arab. Come to think of it, I don't think I've met a proper Londoner since I came here except maybe for Suzie as she's lived around London since she was two years old.

There were an awful lot of guys and not many girls so we had a great time dancing non-stop when we wanted and people offering to buy us drinks when we didn't. I turned down the drink offers as I didn't want to feel guilty for not snogging anyone like last time, but Suzie and Theresa had no worries like that and got fairly smashed. Eventually they got off with two guys, and at the end of the night we all piled out of the club and walked to the taxi rank together. On the way I was surprised to see policemen handing out lollipops for free.

'Why do they do that?' I asked after helping myself to a cherry-flavoured one.

Suzie shrugged. 'I think it's meant to stop people getting into fights when they're drunk.'

'Does it work?'

'Sometimes, maybe. I think it's supposed to soothe you. Like sucking a baby's dummy.'

'Yeah, that could work,' I said.

But not always. As we reached the taxi rank I spotted two girls grappling on the pavement; gouging, punching and tearing each other's hair out by the roots. Four policemen were needed to pull them apart and the girls were hauled off, still arguing. 'The orange lollipop was mine!' one of them screamed. 'You stole it!'

'No, it bloody wasn't. Yours was the raspberry and you bloody well know it!'

Hmm.

We didn't have too long to wait for a taxi but the journey seemed a lot longer. It was a bit embarrassing sitting there like a prim maiden aunt as everyone else was snogging the face off each other. Especially when the taxi driver glanced over his shoulder at me and remarked, 'No luck tonight then, love? Never mind, your day will come.'

Decided to text a few people just to show I wasn't watching couples kissing, like I was jealous, or a pervert or something. Got no answer from Chris, Liz or Stephanie. Not surprising really as it was after two in the morning, but I felt kind of rejected anyway. Scrolled down my list of contacts looking for someone else to text when I came to Mark. Should I? Well, why not? What harm could it do?

HOW R U?

Got a text back almost right away.

GOOD U?

I hesitated. Mark would probably assume I wanted to meet up now since I'd contacted him, but was this really what I wanted to do? Even though it would just be as friends and totally platonic it seemed wrong somehow. Almost like cheating. Was just about to turn off my mobile without answering when it rang. Mark.

'Hi, Kelly Ann. Glad you got in touch. How are you doing?' He sounded relaxed and kind of optimistic, the way a lot of Americans do. Totally laid back and chilled, in fact. Suddenly all my worries about meeting up with him vanished. He was just a nice guy. Friendly. What was the problem?

'Yeah, I'm fine thanks. Where are you? Sounds a bit noisy.'

'Guys sharing my apartment decided to have a kegger. Australians. Jeezus, these guys can drink a lot of beer.'

'GET YOUR HANDS OUT OF MY BRA OR I'LL KNOCK YOUR HEAD OFF. TWO DOUBLE VODKAS DOESN'T MEAN YOU'VE BOUGHT MY FLAMING BODY!!'

'That wasn't me,' I said quickly.

'I gathered as much,' Mark said. 'Sounds like your Irish friend Theresa. Is everything OK?'

'Yeah, it's fine. We're in a taxi. The driver's just stopped and is throwing the guy out.'

'Cool.'

'Hmm, well, actually he's throwing us all out,' I said, scrambling from the taxi. 'It's OK, though. We're nearly at the hotel and the sleazer's already made himself scarce.'

I chatted with Mark the whole way back and for a while after settling back in my room. He was just so easy to talk to. Interesting and funny, with lots of stories to tell about his flatmates in Earl's Court and his student pals back home. We agreed to meet up tomorrow on my day off and do touristy stuff together. I hung up smiling and started to get ready for bed but my mobile buzzed again.

'Hi, Kelly Ann. How are you? I've been trying to call you for ages after I got your text but your phone's been busy.'

Chris. His deep, warm Scottish voice enveloped me like a hug. Oh God, how I missed him.

'I'm OK but, oh God, it seems ages since I've heard from you. I've got loads to tell you. Guess what? I got paid today. A proper pay cheque into my bank, but not as much as I'd hoped . . .'

I babbled on, telling him everything that had been happening to me. Well, not everything exactly. I didn't tell him about my audition because that was a secret. Didn't mention Mark either – not that it was a secret – it just didn't seem important any more. I loved Chris, and no audition, and definitely no other guy, could alter that fact. Nothing could ever change me.

After I'd given Chris all my news, I stopped at last, realizing I'd totally hogged the conversation. 'Oh God, I've been chattering on. How are you? What's been happening? God, I've missed you like crazy.'

There was a long pause, then finally Chris said a bit stiffly, 'Yeah, I'm fine. Miss you too.'

'What's the matter? Is something wrong?'

'No, of course not.'

'There's definitely something,' I insisted.

'No, it's cool.'

'Chris, tell me! What is it?'

'OK, it's nothing really, I suppose. It's just that, well, you sound funny.'

'What do you mean funny?'

'Well, kind of English. You've got an English accent already.'

'No, I haven't.'

'Yeah, you have. Definitely. When you first came on the phone I didn't recognize you. It's no big deal, I suppose. It's just that I hadn't expected you to change so quickly.' He forced a laugh. 'I hope my old Kelly Ann is still there somewhere.'

'Don't be stupid, of course I am. I haven't changed at all. Not really.'

But when I hung up I wondered. Sometimes I felt like a different person now. Like the person I pretended to be with my new friends. Older. More experienced. More successful. Better. What would happen when I went back home? Would I go back to being me again? Did I want that? Did I even want to go back home? This job was crap but London was exciting, buzzy. A place where anything might happen – and lots of things did. A place where dreams might just have a chance of coming true.

I looked at my alarm clock. Three a.m. God, another late night. But tomorrow was Sunday and my day off. I'd arranged to meet Mark at eleven o'clock so I wouldn't have to get up until ten. A whole four and a half hours later than normal. Bliss.

Woke at 5:30 a.m. exactly. Pulled the duvet over my head and prepared to sink back into blissful sleep... 5:45 a.m. and still awake. Lay on my stomach and put a pillow over my head. Gave myself a talking to: *Don't be stupid! This will be your last chance of a lie-in for a week. Go to sleep!!*

But it was hopeless. The bloody place had programmed me to be awake by 5:30 and my brain refused to let my knackered body sleep.

By 6:30 I'd given in. I got up, showered and dressed. Tidied my room. Put a wash on using the false coin tokens Theresa and Suzie had told me about. Now what? My mobile buzzed. This was early.

It was Mrs Davies. She'd just spoken to Martyn Darling and he'd told her he 'loved' my demo. Loved it! My audition was on September 2nd at 3 p.m. at North London Contemporary Dance Studios. It was definite. Real. Oh my God. Oh my God.

She warned me not to get my hopes up. Told me that I'd be up against lots of competition – experienced dancers who'd already performed professionally; people who'd trained intensively in dance schools for years. It was an achievement just to get an audition. Even if I wasn't successful, the experience would be valuable. But I hardly listened after she'd told me I'd got the audition. Martyn

Darling, famous dance company director, definitely wanted to see me dance. Me! Kelly Ann. And in just three weeks' time. Three weeks!

Oh my God, only three weeks to practise! I needed to start now. Wanted to. But where? Definitely not in this room where a leprechaun would struggle to find space.

I peeked out at the corridor. A bit narrow, but long and deserted. It would have to do. Put on my leotard, switched on my dance music and started to warm up, keeping an eye out for any guests who might wander down to the laundry room.

It was Mrs Davies who warned me about the importance of warm-ups to avoid injuries and make sure you were ready to do your best. I haven't been with her long but from the very first moment she saw me dance she said I was 'a natural' and trained me one-to-one intensively afterwards practically every day. As well as once being a professional dancer, she is a choreographer and she helped turn the dance moves I'd copied from musicals and pop videos into an original proper routine which she turned into a DVD clip. I owed her so much. Hoped I wouldn't let her down.

At first my routine, which was perfect last month, felt leaden and awkward. Oh God, Mrs Davies was right – I needed to practise every day or I'd be rubbish. Well, it wasn't exactly what she said but near enough. Why, oh why, hadn't I done it?

Well, to be fair, slaving for over nine hours a day in a boiling kitchen didn't leave me with much time or energy for dance practice. Especially when I was also trying to fit in with new people and make friends. Also, what was the point of living right in the centre of just about the most amazing capital on the planet if I never went out the door? But, oh God, this audition could be the most important day in my whole life. I had to be totally prepared for it. Just had to.

Decided to start my routine from the beginning again. This time I was better, and by the time I was halfway through, it was all coming back. I closed my eyes and forgot about everything else. Just threw myself into the music and movement, spiralling and leaping along the corridor before finally ending in a dramatic side fall to the floor.

At Sidebottom's feet.

He wasn't exactly an appreciative audience. I wasn't allowed to dance in the corridor. Health and Safety regulations, blah blah. Hotel wasn't insured, blah blah blah. Wouldn't report me this time but any further contraventions and blah blah blah bloody blah.

Now, I'm not that fond of Frost Face's daughter, but for God's sake, what on earth did she see in this sad tosser?

I'd almost totally tuned out by the time he said, 'It's a pity really. You're not a bad dancer.'

'Thanks a lot,' I said sarcastically.

'Yeah, well, anyway, just to let you know, there's going to be a fire drill this week.'

'When?'

'I can't tell you that,' he said, all pompous. 'Makes it a more authentic exercise if you can't predict when it will be.'

'So why did you tell me it was this week then?' I asked, genuinely curious.

'I have my reasons,' he blustered.

'Yeah, right.' *God, he really was that thick.*

After giving me another warning about dancing in the corridor, he shuffled off and I contented myself by making a rude energetic, gesture to his retreating back. Unfortunately I spotted Joy a little too late coming out of the lift towards him. I quickly changed my hand gesture to a friendly wave and darted into my room.

So, if I couldn't practise here, where would I do it? I couldn't afford to go to a proper dance studio. I'd have to find somewhere, but where? And there were other problems too. What if I *did* pass the audition and was selected to join the dance company? I'd have to live in London properly, which would be amazing, but what would my parents say? I suppose if I was getting paid to dance they would take me seriously and realize I'd been right all along. Hopefully, anyway. But what about Chris? I'd miss him so much and he'd be gutted. Maybe he could move to London with me? But he'd four more years of medicine to do and wanted to be a doctor just as much as I wanted to dance. Maybe even more so.

It was all going to be so difficult. But perhaps there was nothing to worry about, anyway. Started to think about the rest of what Mrs Davies had said. I'd be competing against proper professional dancers who'd trained for years. What chance did I really have? I'd probably just make an idiot of myself. Maybe I shouldn't go. But if I gave up this incredible opportunity, what then? I could spend the rest of my life regretting it.

Thank God I'd arranged to meet Mark today. I needed something to take my mind off this for a while or I'd go mental. Exploring London with a nice, friendly and, OK, very good-looking American guy would do exactly that.

I'd arranged to meet him at Tower Hill station since I've always wanted to see the Tower of London. It's really expensive but I've always fancied going there because of the Crown Jewels collection. It's also the place where loads of famous people like Anne Boleyn, and some other wives Henry the Eighth fell out with, waited to get their heads chopped off or worse.

And there *was* worse. The beefeater tour guide there told us that common folk just got hanged, which took longer, while others, like Scottish freedom fighter William Wallace (*Braveheart* hero) were hung, drawn and quartered if they'd really annoyed important people a lot.

Had always wondered what drawing and quartering actually meant. Wish I hadn't asked. According to our guide, they cut William Wallace up, burned his entrails then posted bits of his body on spikes to teach us savage Scots a lesson about rebelling against civilized English people.

Hmm, seemed totally over the top to me but I'm glad English people are so much nicer and kinder now. Well, just so long as you don't try to skip the queue for the toilets, as I learned a bit later on in the tour. Definitely not a good idea to piss them off like that even if you are desperate.

The Crown Jewels were amazing. Precious stones the size of golf balls and so big, in fact, they looked totally fake. Saw some women looking at their engagement rings kind of disappointedly, but honestly I'm really not jealous of the Queen. Don't think I'd like to wear a heavy crown and carry a diamond-encrusted sceptre. Anyway, where would I wear it? I'd look pretty stupid turning up at a party or club with all that stuff. No, even if she offered me a loan of her jewels for free I'd probably knock her back. Not that it's likely, I suppose.

When we finally left the Tower, Mark suggested we have a look at the Tower Bridge exhibition, but we would have had to pay another entrance fee so I told Mark that I wanted to wander around free places as I needed to make my wages last all week. He offered to 'loan' me some money, no problems and no worries about when I repaid him, but I refused. So, OK, maybe he was just being generous like most Americans seem to be – they were by far the best tippers in the hotel – but I needed to make it plain we were just two friends having a day out together. Not a couple on a first date where a guy might want to impress by buying me stuff.

It was a nice afternoon. Warm and dry, if a bit overcast, so we decided against going to indoor places like museums. Instead we got the tube to Embankment, where we bought some fruit, sandwiches and Coke and had a picnic lunch in St James's Park, from where you can see Buckingham Palace.

'So this is where the Queen lives?' Mark said. 'Nice pad. Want to go see it after?'

I shrugged. 'Not really – it's too expensive, and any-way, I don't think the Queen is at home right now so we probably wouldn't see her.'

'Where is she then?'

'Balmoral, probably. That's in Scotland.'

Mark smiled. 'So you've missed each other then? That's a shame.'

'Yeah – bet she's gutted.' I laughed. 'Obviously, if she'd been here she'd have offered to take me on a personal guided tour of the whole palace.'

'Not the whole palace,' he said. 'Probably best not to

show you round the laundry rooms in case you tried to nick royal underpants.'

'Yuk! That's gross. I'll have you know I'm very particular about whose underwear I steal.'

He grinned. 'You are?'

'Yeah, I only nick boxers from really hot young American guys.'

Oh God, as soon as I said it I wanted to snatch the words back. But of course I couldn't. Why, oh why, did I have to say anything so stupid? He probably thought I was hitting on him. I flushed beetroot.

'I'll take that as a compliment. Probably the weirdest one I've had in a while but kind of nice, anyway.'

'I was just joking. I mean, I don't fancy you or anything. Not that you're ugly, of course you're not, just, well, not my type. And even if you were my type – which you're definitely not – I've already got a boyfriend. And you've got a girlfriend. So I'd never, well, snog you, or make a pass or anything. You don't need to worry.'

'I wasn't worried.'

'Oh.'

There was an awkward silence for a bit. Mark's smile had gone and he looked all serious and kind of depressed really. Maybe he was thinking about his girlfriend back home and missing her.

I busied myself clearing up the remains of our lunch and putting it in a bin. When I got back Mark was still sitting on the grass in the sun, which had just come out, looking thoughtful.

'So,' I said, 'maybe I should head back now. It's been a really nice day, thanks.'

He squinted up at me. 'You got something important you need to do?'

'No, but—'

He smiled. 'So, there's lots more of London to see, isn't there?'

'Yeah,' I said happily. 'Lots.'

We strolled over to Hyde Park next as Mark has heard it's famous as a place for ordinary people to get up and make speeches about things they think are important. Don't know about the 'ordinary people' bit – most of the speakers at Hyde Park Corner seemed weird to me as they ranted on about anything from how the Prime Minister is really a secret CIA agent to we've all been invaded by aliens in flying saucers but our government won't tell us about it in case it caused a panic.

Still, it was a bit of a laugh and I was quite enjoying it until we joined a small crowd around some old guy who called himself 'the preacher', who was going on about the end of the world next week. Apparently, righteous people like him were going to be raptured up to Heaven and be blissfully happy, but sinners like us would all die a horrible death and then be tortured in Hell for all eternity.

Nice. Why is it these religious nutters really love the

idea of loads of people suffering torments? Not very Christian, if you ask me.

I was getting bored with his ravings, and we were just about to wander off and get an ice cream when the old guy pointed to us and screamed, 'Stop, fornicators! Come back and repent your sins or you will burn in the ever-lasting fires of Hell!'

Bloody nerve. I was furious, and embarrassed too, as everyone was staring at us. 'We're not fornicators,' I shouted back. 'We're just friends.'

'Liar,' he screamed. 'Repent your sins or die.'

'I am *not* a liar! Mark and I haven't even snogged, never mind shagged.'

One of the audience – an old lady with a grey bun wearing a floral dress and sensible shoes – waded in to support us. Wished she hadn't bothered. 'You leave that nice young couple alone,' she said. 'Their sex life has nothing to do with you. Why shouldn't they grab a bit of happiness while they can. You're only young once.'

A murmur of agreement rose up in the crowd.

'For God's sake,' I said, exasperated. 'We don't have a sex life!'

'Thou shalt not take the name of the Lord our God in vain,' the speaker shrieked.

'Jeezus,' Mark murmured in my ear, 'this old guy's a total fruitcake. Let's go.'

I nodded and we started to make our way out past the

crowd (which had grown a bit since the preacher started to yell at us). But before we got to the edge of it he'd got down off his soap box and was right behind us, screaming more rubbish. This was too much. I wasn't going to be chased away by this idiot. We turned round to confront him.

'Leave this to me,' Mark whispered. 'We get a lot of religious nuts in California so I know how to deal with them.'

'Sinner,' the preacher nearly spat in Mark's face. 'Renounce the Devil, turn from the path of evil this day and be saved.'

Mark fixed him with a brilliant smile. 'I'm happy you've found joy in your religion. Thank you so much for sharing.'

Totally confused by Mark's laid-back friendliness, the preacher was actually silent for a moment. Unsure how to deal with Mark's meaninglessly nice comment, he rounded on me instead.

'Jezebel!' he screamed in my face.

'My name's Kelly Ann,' I said, puzzled.

'You are a Jezebel,' he repeated.

'What's that supposed to mean?' I asked, though I was sure it wasn't anything nice.

I was right. The old lady in the floral dress filled me in. 'Slut,' she said cheerfully.

Right, that was it. I wasn't going to be called a slut in

public by anyone, never mind a total stranger. I jabbed a finger at the preacher's eye, forcing him back, then balled my hands into fists. 'Push off, perve, or I'll knock your teeth down your throat.'

They were probably false ones, but even so he got the message and scurried back behind his box. A ripple of applause broke out, which was a bit embarrassing but kind of nice.

'Let's go,' I said.

'Sure,' Mark agreed. 'That was very impressive, Kelly Ann,' he added.

I grinned. 'Well, we get quite a lot of religious nutters in Glasgow too, so I know how to handle them.'

It was nice touring London with Mark. Despite Suzie and Theresa's warnings that Mark definitely fancied me (why else would a guy want to spend a whole day with a girl?) he made no attempt to hit on me. In fact, the only time we touched was when he took my hand to guide me across a busy road. And nearly got us both killed. 'Sorry, Kelly Ann. Must keep reminding myself cars drive on the left here.'

And also later, when a couple of Japanese tourists insisted on taking a picture of us after we'd agreed to take one of them. But even then he just draped a friendly arm around my shoulder. Casual and matey. Absolutely nothing to worry about.

Except my reaction to it, that is. The heat of his body so close to me made my cheeks flush and I seemed to be aware of every molecule of his skin touching mine. Oh God, I wasn't falling for him, was I?

Almost decided to go back to the hotel right then, but he let his arm drop and the moment passed. As we walked on companionably, I glanced at him from time to time, aware that a lot of other females we passed were doing the same. He really was a gorgeous-looking guy so it was only natural I found him attractive. Anyone would. But he'd got Cindy and I had Chris, who was the love of my life, so there was no chance of anything happening. Anyway, why should I go back and sit in a tiny dark cell on my own when I could be here in the sunshine with Mark.

He was great company too, so easy to talk to. In fact, soon I was feeling totally relaxed and comfortable with him, as though I'd known him for years, and I found myself really opening up with him. Telling him all about me. Not the lies I'd told everyone else here. But the truth. The real me. Mostly, anyway. I even told him about my audition with the director.

'That's amazing, Kelly Ann. I've gotta see you dance sometime.'

'Yeah, I'm excited about it. Kind of nervous too, though. Probably it won't come to anything. Maybe just as well as my parents would go mental.'

'Why would they? I'm sure they'd be proud of your achievements.'

'No, they think it's daft. Just a hobby. They want me to go to uni. Get a degree and hopefully a proper job. They're probably right.'

'No, they're not, Kelly Ann. You've got to follow your dream or you'd regret it for the rest of your life.'

'Yeah, well, that's what I think but I haven't told them anything about it yet. Haven't told anyone really in case I make an arse of it.'

He smiled. 'Then I'm honoured you chose to confide in me.'

I flushed guiltily. Why had I confided in Mark, who I hardly knew, but not in my friends? Or Chris?

'So what about you?' I said, quickly changing the subject. 'Have you got a dream?'

'Sure. Who hasn't? Several, in fact.'

When he didn't say any more, I asked, 'So are they secret?'

'No secret. I want to be a lawyer.'

'Oh, that's nice.'

'But boring, right?'

'No, of course n—'

'But I don't want to be just any lawyer filing suits to make a buck,' he interrupted heatedly. 'I want to fight for justice. Defend the little guy against the multinational company who's trying to screw him. Give poor people access to proper legal advice and representation based on their need, not their bank balance.' He paused. Looked embarrassed. 'Totally naïve, right?'

'No, I think it's great. I really do.'

'My dad doesn't. You can see his point. He's a businessman and he's paying thirty thousand bucks a year so I can go to a top law school. He expects to make a return on that investment.'

'You've got to follow your dream,' I reminded him.

He laughed. 'Yeah, we're just a couple of dreamers.'

'So,' I said, happy he'd returned to the usual laid-back Mark. 'What about the rest?'

'Rest of what?'

'Your dreams. You said you had several.'

'Oh, they're secret.'

'Seriously?'

'Yeah, but I'll let you in to one more.'

'What?'

'I'm dreaming of a giant pepperoni pizza, with French fries on the side and macaroni salad – hold the mayo.' He glanced at the Pizza Hut just ahead of us. 'What do you say?'

'Sounds good – I'm starving!'

While we waited for our order Mark talked about his travels in Europe before coming to London. As well as all the usual touristy and cultural stuff, he'd done just about everything – sky-diving in Spain, mountain biking in the French Alps, and paragliding in Turkey. It sounded amazing.

'Why didn't Cindy go with you?' I asked.

He shrugged. 'Not her kind of thing. She wouldn't want to go anywhere that was more than five minutes' ride from a mall.'

'She's nuts. There's no way I would have let you wander round Europe on your own for three months if I was your girlfriend. Way too dangerous.'

He smiled. 'I'm a big boy. I can take care of myself.'

'Maybe. But I was thinking of all those hot European girls who might have tried to pull you. Your girlfriend's mad to risk it.'

His eyes stared into mine. 'I'll take that as a compliment.'

I flushed. 'Well, I mean you're safe with me, obviously. I was talking about other girls. Single ones. I've got a boyfriend in—'

'Glasgow, I know. You've mentioned it before. Chris, isn't it?'

'Yeah.'

'So how come he didn't come to London with you for the summer? Isn't he worried about all the guys in London who'd want to hit on someone as cute as you?'

'He trusts me. I love him.'

'Lucky guy.'

He looked unusually serious – almost glum – and

for a moment was silent until our waiter brought our pizzas. But soon Mark was chatting easily again, the brief awkwardness forgotten. I was glad I'd made it absolutely clear I wasn't after him and that I was totally loyal to my boyfriend. But still, it was nice to know someone as hot as Mark thought I was 'cute', even if nothing ever came of it.

After our meal it was getting dark but we wandered around Piccadilly for a while, not wanting the day to end. Couldn't help looking longingly at all the famous theatres, especially the ones doing musicals.

'We're too late now, but want to book one of these for another night?' Mark asked. 'C'mon, we can't leave London without seeing at least one show.'

'Maybe,' I said doubtfully. 'They're quite expensive.'

'My treat?' he said.

'No way.'

He shrugged. 'OK. Maybe we'll do something else then. If you want to meet up again, that is?'

'Yeah, definitely.'

And I meant it. This was maybe the happiest, most contented day I'd had since coming here. And, I just realized, the only sober one.

Mark insisted on seeing me back to the hotel even though I told him not to bother. Reminded me a bit of Chris, who always saw me home when we'd been out. So protective – even though I don't need it and can totally take care of myself. Kind of nice, though.

It was a bit awkward saying goodnight. Seemed wrong just to say, 'Cheers, see ya,' and walk away. Didn't know whether I should have given him a friendly hug, or maybe even a quick platonic kiss on the cheek. After an embarrassing pause I just kind of patted him on the arm and said, ''Night, Mark.'

He patted me back with an amused smile. ''Night, Kelly Ann.'

But he didn't move off. Just stood there, his eyes gazing into mine. God, he was gorgeous.

'Well, erm, thanks for a great day.'

'You're welcome.'

But still he didn't move away. In fact, he seemed to have moved even closer so that his face was nearly touching mine. Almost close enough to kiss. One kiss wouldn't do any harm, would it?

No way. I tore my eyes away and scrabbled nervously through my bag for my keys. Of course, I managed to spill almost the entire contents on the pavement in the process. Including the spare knickers, which Mark picked up and handed to me.

'They're for emergencies,' I said.

'A very wise precaution,' he agreed, all mock solemn.

I flushed. 'I'm not a slut. I don't sleep around or anything. It's just that after my lost luggage fiasco—'

'You don't want to have to go on any more underpants heists,' he finished, laughing. 'I understand.'

I laughed too – all tension disappearing. Mark was just a friendly guy. A friendly guy with a girlfriend back home. He'd never try to hit on me – or me on him. We were just two pals hanging out together.

'So,' I said, 'call me next week?'

'Sure.'

I waved him goodbye and went into reception. Sidebottom was on duty at the desk tonight. He frowned at me. 'Staff aren't supposed to fraternize with guests, you know.'

'He's not a guest and we're not fraternizing so mind your own business,' I snapped.

'He used to be, though. Mrs Frost wouldn't like it.'

I ignored him and headed off but he called after me, 'Kelly Ann, don't forget there's a fire drill coming up. Hope you've looked over procedure. Don't want any staff member letting us down.'

'Get a life,' I muttered under my breath.

When I got back to my room I checked the time. Ten p.m. This was the earliest I'd been in since I came here. Decided to run a nice hot bath and relax. But first I'd try out that seaweed deep-cleansing facemask that Stephanie had recommended as I'd noticed a few spots just starting to erupt on my forehead yesterday.

Got a text from Theresa: she and Suzie were at the

pub just down the road, but I wasn't tempted to join them, especially as the blue/green mask I'd just put on was supposed to be left for at least half an hour. Theresa called to try to persuade me. 'C'mon, Kelly Ann,' she shouted over the din in the bar. 'Drinks are half price all night and the band's amazing.'

But I resisted. 'Sorry, Theresa, I'm knackered. Going to have a quiet one tonight.'

'You'll regret it,' she warned.

'Have a great time,' I said and hung up.

Congratulating myself for being firm and sensible, I poured my favourite orange blossom bubble bath into a full tub of steaming hot water, put my music on, then got undressed and sank into the warm fragrant bath. Bliss.

Had only been soaking for less than a minute when I heard it. The sodding fire alarm. Damn Sidebottom! Well, there was no way I was moving from my lovely hot bath for him. And OK, I knew I'd be in trouble and that he'd grass me up to Frost Face, but I didn't care. I'd deal with that tomorrow. Nothing and no one was getting me out of this bath.

I turned up the volume on my music to drown out the alarm, then sank back into the tub, letting the warm water lap over my shoulders, and closed my eyes.

The music thankfully mostly took care of the alarm noise, but not the banging on my door and shouting, which started a minute later: 'Anyone in there?'

I didn't recognize the voice, which was male but definitely not Sidebottom's high, whiny tone. I suppose he must have sent someone to find me and make me come out. Well, he could think again. God, all this carry-on over a stupid fire drill.

'Go away!' I yelled. 'I'm not moving from here.'

Hoped that would take care of it. The door was locked, after all. I mean, what could they do? Break it down?

An axe smashed into the door just below the handle. It flew open and two firemen burst in.

Thank God I'd used bubble bath.

They wouldn't give me time to get dressed or take the facemask off, but one of them handed me a towel, which I wrapped round me before getting out. My wet feet kept slipping on the floor, so in the end one of the firemen hauled me over his shoulder and ran with me through a smoke-filled corridor, up the stairs and outside, where it seemed half of London had congregated to watch.

Including Theresa and Suzie, who were taking pictures – mostly of the firemen. Others started taking pictures of me. Hopefully no one would recognize me with the facemask on.

Theresa and Suzie did, though, and rushed over. Theresa wrapped her jacket round me while Suzie stood in front of me to hide me from gawpers.

'For God's sake,' Suzie hissed, 'why did you stay in the

bath with the place on fire? Why didn't you get out with everybody else? Have you never heard of prioritizing tasks?'

'Don't ask,' I groaned. 'Not now, anyway.'

'Your fireman was gorgeous, though,' Theresa mused. 'So it's not all bad.'

'Know what, Theresa?' I said.

'What?'

'You were right. I should have gone out with you two tonight.'

Theresa laughed. 'Told you.'

MONDAY AUGUST 12TH

Unfortunately the fire was contained to the laundry room and no serious damage done so we all had to go to work this morning and help clean up the mess in the corridors and laundry room after our shift. Even more unfortunately my tiny cell is totally undamaged, so after spending last night in a guest room Mrs Frost says I'll be able to sleep in my own place again tonight.

TUESDAY AUGUST 13TH

Hardly slept at all last night as I've been so used to the sound of washers and dryers going next door to me that the silence unnerved me and I tossed and turned all night. The lingering smell of damp, burned wood and plastic didn't help either.

Still loads of clearing up to do after our shift and haven't left the hotel all day. Was feeling homesick tonight so it was nice to get emails from Liz and Stephanie, even if they did seem to be having a much better time than me.

Email from Stephanie:
Just got back from the Caribbean. Still not pleased with my uneven tan. I mean, for God's sake, I'm practically tartan! Have been forced to book another short break in the South of France and insisted on topless beaches as well as poolside hotel lounging to try to fix things. Dave has agreed to come with me. The sacrifices he makes for love lol!

Talking of topless – where's the pic of your hot Pole? Any other hot guys there?

Stephanie x

Email from Liz:
Still in New York. Have bumped into so many famous

people! None of them hot and mostly old, though, so I didn't actually know they were celebrities until Julian told me. They all had their own psychiatrists unfortunately, and seemed totally uninterested in my offer to analyse their most secret repressed longings and desires – just kept offering to give me their autograph if I'd leave them alone. I mean, ego or what!

It's been brilliant here, though! Wish I didn't have to come back next week. How are things in London? I've heard it's a scorcher of a summer still there. Probably you'll be more tanned than any of us when you get back even though you've not been on holiday! Have you met loads of celebrities too? Email me back and let me know everything you've been up to.

Liz x

Was going to reply straight away but stopped myself. I mean, I really missed my friends but what could I say? Yeah, the weather has been great here but I almost never get out during the day to sunbathe so I'd as much chance of getting an all-over tan as a vampire. And the nearest I've come to a celebrity so far is a hotel guest who once met the second cousin of an extra on the Harry Potter film set on the train to Bognor Regis.

No, I'd wait until I'd something really cool and interesting to tell them. Like I'd been picked to join a top modern dance company in London, for instance, and so

I'd probably be famous one day. Oh God, that would be so amazing. Imagine people asking for my autograph! Mark was right. I had to follow my dream.

I really should do my dance practice too. Didn't do any yesterday because of all the extra work Frost made us do and I'm knackered today as well. Will definitely practise tomorrow. No matter what!

WEDNESDAY AUGUST 14TH

Today was just as bad as yesterday. Again we were all helping with the clean-up after work and we weren't even offered any overtime. Wasn't in our contract apparently. We didn't finish until after ten o'clock and Theresa was raging.

'That's it. I'm taking a sickie tomorrow,' she said, throwing away the day-old leftover prawn sandwich we'd been given for supper as a 'reward' for our unpaid efforts. 'I'll say I've got a migraine. Always handy for the odd day off.'

'Oh God, don't do that,' Suzie said. 'We won't get any cover for you and it will all be left to Kelly Ann and me. Anyway, the clean-up is finished. It will just be kitchen work and serving as usual.'

Theresa shook her head. 'It'll be a scorcher tomorrow, and I for one am not spending my day cooped up in a large oven being bawled at by a mad man in a stupid hat who should have been sectioned years ago.'

'Yeah, you're right,' Suzie agreed. 'But if you're not working, neither am I. I'll say I'm sick too. Bad period cramps.'

'I'm not going in on my own!' I said, panicked.

'You can be sick too, then,' Theresa said. 'We'll all skip off together. Maybe sneak off to the beach. Southend's not too far from here.'

'OK,' I agreed. 'I'll say I've got diarrhoea – nobody wants to question that too much. As soon as I learned to spell it, I used to forge it on all my sick notes at school. Erm, a couple of years ago – when I went to school.'

Suzie frowned. 'Won't Frost be suspicious when we're all sick on the same day? With different things?'

'Good point,' Theresa said.

'Yeah, we should say we've all come down with the same thing.' I threw my dodgy sandwich away too after just one nibble. 'What about food poisoning?'

'Brilliant,' Suzie said. 'And we could still use your diarrhoea idea.'

'And throw in a bit of projectile vomiting,' Theresa added.

'Done,' we chorused.

THURSDAY AUGUST 15TH

I'd 'volunteered' to tell Frost we were ill because Theresa and Suzie said I should as I'd come up with the food poisoning idea. Not sure how this was fair exactly, but didn't argue after a few vodka and Cokes provided by Theresa and an offer from Suzie to help me with make-up and 'props'. This proved to be white eyeliner applied to my lips, dark shadowing under my eyes and a bowl of fake sick (watered down cold chop suey).

Just looking at the bowl first thing this morning after too much alcohol made me feel queasy enough to decide to do without it. I dragged myself into the kitchen, still wearing my pyjamas and dressing gown, and groaned while dramatically clutching at my stomach.

Joy spotted me first. 'Where's your uniform? Go and put it on quickly or you'll be late for your shift. Mum will be here in a minute and she won't be pleased if she sees you like that.' She hurried towards the dining room with a tray of cutlery but looked back at me as she pushed the door open with her hips. 'By the way, your make-up's all over the place – didn't you take it off before you went to bed?'

The chef handed me a mop. 'You can change later,' he growled. 'Wash the floor in front of the sink first. Some idiot's spilled orange juice all over it.'

Yeah, probably him. Typical of him to blame someone else. And typical of both of them not to notice, never mind care, when their staff are ill. OK, I know I was only pretending to be ill, but still.

I let the mop fall, staggered to the sink and bent over it, making horrible retching noises.

'Kelly Ann,' Yan said, putting an arm awkwardly over my shoulder. 'What is the matter?'

I twisted my head round and looked at Yan's pale concerned face. Oh God, hated to worry him like this but there was no way I could stop now.

'I'm really sick, Yan,' I croaked. I stood up and turned round but leaned against Yan, all weak and trembly. 'So are Suzie and Theresa. Food poisoning, I think.'

The chef's face went practically purple. 'Not in my kitchen.'

'Not in whose kitchen?' Frost said, marching in briskly. She eyed me furiously. 'What on earth is going on? You'd better have a good explanation. I want to know every detail.'

However, when I mentioned 'probably food poisoning' and 'prawn sandwiches', she didn't seem to want to hear any more details after all. Just told me to go back to my room and she'd check with us tomorrow, then rushed off to try and organize cover staff. Yay, freedom!

Went back to bed and slept until ten o'clock. Bliss.

Already it felt hot and it was decided we'd definitely go to the beach. Only problem was, even though I'd packed absolutely everything else at Stephanie's insistence, I hadn't included a bikini because I was sure I wouldn't be going to a beach in London. Cursed myself. I mean, how much room would a bikini have taken up? How much weight would it have added to my suitcase, given that I was taking a foot spa pedicure?

Suzie offered to let me borrow one of hers, so I tried it on. She looked me over and shook her head wonderingly. 'Didn't think there was anyone with smaller boobs than me,' she said.

She was right. The bikini top was too big so I'd have had to stuff it with toilet paper to fill it out, which – learned after sieving toilet paper from a Spanish hotel pool one holiday – is no good if you want to swim.

'C'mon,' Theresa said impatiently. 'You can buy a cheap one when we get there.'

Tried to sneak out the fire door side exit but it was locked. I mean, what is the point of a locked fire exit? But apparently Frost insists on it for security reasons. Never mind that staff and guests get barbecued as long as no one nicks anything. She'd managed to persuade the firemen a few days ago that it was 'an aberration' and had never happened before. Hmm, serves her right if we'd all died in that fire and she got the blame. That would have shown her.

'Let's try calling Yan,' Theresa said. 'He'll probably have a key.'

I nodded. When not working in the kitchen, Yan also acted as hotel porter and security person so he'd likely have a copy.

Yan came right away. Even though he works loads more hours than we do, he didn't show any disapproval about our skiving. In fact, he was just relieved we weren't sick after all, and unlocked the door so we could make our escape.

We took the tube to Liverpool Street. The cheapest return we could get to Southend Central was nearly fifteen pounds but Theresa had an idea to save us money.

'Why don't we just get a return to the first stop?' she said. 'That's just over a fiver. We can just flash our tickets at the guard when we get to Southend and walk past. They'll be so busy they won't notice.'

'I don't know,' I said. 'What if they stop us?'

'Don't worry,' she soothed. 'They never do. I've done this before on train journeys when I've been broke and it always works. And it's not as though we're paying nothing for the trip. They're still getting a fiver.'

Felt a bit nervous about it and also guilty as it was dishonest, but my money wasn't holding out in London and I also had to buy a bikini, so in the end I agreed.

Spent practically the whole journey (after Limehouse, anyway) worrying about being caught by a ticket inspector or stopped by the guard at the end of the journey. By the time we got off at Southend Central and were approaching the gate, manned by a huge, severe-looking, black ticket collector, my stomach was churning with nerves. Suzie looked a bit anxious too.

'Don't worry,' Theresa said. 'Just flash your tickets, then walk quickly through. But remember: don't make eye contact with him. And don't run or dawdle. I'll go first. Watch me.'

She marched confidently to the gate, flashed her return ticket and swept past, no bother.

Suzie went next. She hurried to the gate, ticket in hand, and gave the guard a brief glimpse of it without even glancing at him. I thought at first she was going to get away with it, but he stopped her and made her wait as he examined her ticket closely.

I hung back a bit and watched anxiously.

'Sorry, you'll have to pay a surcharge,' he said. 'This ticket doesn't cover your journey.'

Suzie looked at him blankly, so he repeated what he said. She shook her head in a kind of puzzled and concerned way, then launched into a long spiel in Cantonese.

The collector tried a few more times, talking loudly and more slowly, but finally gave up and waved her on with a remark that sounded a lot like 'bloody foreigners'.

Now it was my turn. I walked quickly and kept my eyes averted but I just knew I'd be stopped and I was.

He examined my ticket closely. 'Excuse me, miss, but this doesn't cover your journey. You'll have to pay a surcharge.'

Was about to fess up when I had a brilliant idea. There was no way I'd get away with talking rubbish and pretending to be Chinese but I could pass for French. At last I'd found a use for all those boring French lessons at school!

'*Pardon, monsieur, mais je ne parle pas l'anglais.*'

The guard answered me in rapid, fluent French. So rapid and fluent that I couldn't follow most of what he said, but I was pretty sure he was telling me my ticket didn't cover the journey, among other things. Like the fact he was Algerian so his first language was French. When I didn't answer him he reverted to English.

'You're not French, are you?'

I stared at my toes. 'Erm, no. Not really.'

Suzie and Theresa waited patiently by the station exit, throwing me sympathetic looks while I was marched over to the ticket desk and made to pay the proper fare – a single ticket which was even more expensive than our off-peak return would have been. I mean, how fair is that? I was also given a humiliating lecture about dishonesty. Finally he laughed and waved me off with a cheeky, '*Au revoir, mademoiselle!*'

Merde. How was I going to afford a decent bikini now?

There were loads of shops in the high street but there

was no point looking in Debenhams or even Next. Was looking for a Primark when we passed a small charity shop and I saw through the window a rail of second-hand swimwear stuff all under a quid. There was a small white bikini which looked about my size – probably a kid's as it had frills on the pants and no padding in the top, but maybe it would do. Especially as it was only 50p.

I went in and examined it. There was no changing room but I put the top on over my T-shirt and it seemed to fit fine.

'What do you think?' I asked Theresa and Suzie.

Suzie eyed me critically. 'Well, it's about your size – but it looks a bit worn. The white is kind of dingy. More grey, really.'

'Of course it's worn. It's a second-hand shop,' Theresa tutted impatiently. 'The colour is fine. Sort of ecru. It's the in shade this season.'

'Do you think so?' I asked doubtfully, staring at the dirty off-white greyish colour.

'Definitely,' Theresa said, steering me to the cash desk. 'Now, c'mon. Sun, sea, sand and hopefully some fit guys are waiting.'

I paid quickly and we headed off for the beach. Although it was still early, the place was pretty crowded but we managed to find a sandy spot away from any kids and near a group of guys who were probably skiving too as one of them was on the phone explaining that he was at a meeting with the other two which was likely to last all day.

Since Theresa and Suzie had put their bikinis on before we left, they immediately peeled off their clothes and sprawled in the sun. I thought about trying to wiggle out of my shorts and T-shirt and into my bikini using a towel as cover, but the last time I'd tried this manoeuvre I'd dropped the towel before my swimsuit was on and exposed myself to the whole beach. Fortunately I was only five at the time but the memory of the little four-year-old boy who'd pointed at me and shouted, 'Look, Mummy, she's not got a willy!' still makes me blush. There was no way I would ever risk another beach embarrassment like that.

There weren't any changing rooms nearby but I spotted toilets a few minutes' walk away and headed off.

There was a queue, but I didn't have to wait too long and after I changed, I examined my reflection in the large mirrors over the sinks. The top was a bit tight but this actually made my boobs look bigger as it kind of pushed them together and out. The frilly bottoms that I'd worried might be a bit childish for me actually made my bum look good. I nodded. Yeah. Not bad for fifty pence.

When I got back, Suzie and Theresa were already in conversation with our fellow skivers. Suzie seemed keen on the oldest-looking one who'd been on the phone, so I guessed he probably had a good job, or money, or both.

Theresa was talking animatedly with the guy who looked a bit like a shorter version of Liam, the awful poet/painter, which left the skinny redhead covered in freckles and factor fifty sunscreen for me. Hmm.

He told me his name was Sam and that he'd a cousin in Scotland. Once he knew I'd a boyfriend, he didn't try to hit on me or anything and actually turned out to be quite nice and a bit of a laugh. He talked about his visit to Edinburgh one weekend for a stag do when he and his pal got so wasted they tried to climb the castle walls at midnight in their underwear and got arrested. 'Better than having boiling oil poured over us, though, like they would have done in the past,' he pointed out pragmatically.

The guys all went in for a swim early on but we lay toasting ourselves lazily in the sun for a while longer, sipping Cokes we'd brought from the hotel with us, and congratulating ourselves on not being at work.

We discussed the guys for a while. Turned out Suzie's wasn't as well off as she'd thought at first. Theresa's was 'OK, but nothing like as deep and interesting as Liam's who apparently had just texted her to suggest meeting up soon.

Actually, I wouldn't have fancied any of them even if I'd been single. They were all too pale and skinny for me. Nowhere near as gorgeous as my boyfriend Chris, with his dark, intense good looks. Or Mark – all golden tan and sun-bleached hair.

I closed my eyes and wondered what it would be like to be here with Mark today. Living in California, he'd no doubt be a strong swimmer – like a lifeguard. Probably he could swim miles out then return to shore totally unfazed as though he'd just done a length at the pool. I could just picture him now. He'd come out of the ocean smiling, the sun glistening on his tanned, wet torso and toned— Oh my God, what was I doing?

I sat up abruptly. 'Let's go swim!'

Theresa and Suzie looked up at me, startled.

'Right now?' Suzie asked. 'There's no rush. Why don't we lie in the sun for a bit longer?'

'I'm too hot!' I said, scrambling to my feet and heading for the water. 'I need to cool down. I'll just go in myself. Catch you later.'

The water was freezing. So, right, I was four hundred miles south of Glasgow but this definitely wasn't the Med. After a while it was OK, though, and it did stop me dreaming about Mark and his tanned Californian body. Decided right there and then that it would be best not to meet Mark again. He was way too hot to be a platonic pal even if that was all he saw in me.

Since I didn't know the beach, and was on my own, I decided not to go too far out even though the water was shallow, so I swam back and forth along the shoreline for a while. In the distance I could just see Theresa and Suzie making their way towards the ocean and I wanted to join them but I needed the loo first, and I was near the toilets, so I swam for shore.

As I walked across the beach I noticed that I was getting a lot of attention from guys. So much so that for a horrible panicked moment I thought my top must have fallen off in the water. But a quick check reassured me and I smiled to myself. Who would have thought such a cheap bikini would make me look so great that practically every guy on the beach was giving me admiring stares and some were even taking photos?

But I didn't have time to bask in all the attention right then as the cold water and all the Coke I'd drunk earlier had made me pretty desperate so I quickened my pace.

Got waylaid by some sleazer trying to chat me up. The whole time he was talking to me he never looked at my face once. Just offered to share his Cornetto with me while leering at my body. Gross.

Pushed past him and ran as fast as I could (whilst keeping my legs close together) for the toilets.

Fortunately there was one cubicle free. A grandmother with a young kid of around three was just about to go in but I managed to shove them both out the way and bag it.

Did feel a bit guilty as the little girl started crying that she needed a pee-pee, but accidents at three aren't nearly as embarrassing as they are at seventeen. It's a matter of priorities and the greatest need. She'd understand when she was older.

When I finished, I washed my hands, and though I was feeling wet and chilly, stepped back from the sink for a moment to admire my bikinied body in the mirror.

Oh. My. God. Now I understood why I'd got all the attention. When wet, the worn thin white material was practically transparent and I could clearly make out two dark round circles in the middle of my boobs and, oh God, a dark triangle in the front of the pants. I might as well have been naked. In fact, oddly enough, I think I might have looked less obscene if I were.

I put an arm across my chest and my other hand between my legs to cover myself. But that looked even worse – like I was fondling myself or something. Totally panicked now, I dived into the cubicle I'd just come out of, which was mercifully still empty.

What to do? Well, there was nothing else for it. I'd just have to wait here until I'd completely dried off and the material became opaque again.

Wished I'd paid more attention in science at school. If I had, I'd have known that the rate of evaporation in a cool, dampish environment is very, very slow. After half an hour the bikini was still sodden and see-through. The toilets had got busier, and judging by the number of people's feet I could see under the cubicle door, there was now a constant queue, so my permanently occupied cubicle was causing curiosity and, increasingly, resentment.

Some people were kind and concerned. 'Are you all right in there, dear? Are you ill? Have you got yourself locked in?'

'No, I'm fine, thanks for asking,' I'd murmur.

But others were suspicious and threatening, especially one really irate woman who challenged me. 'Oi, what you up to in there? You got someone else in there wif ya?'

I decided to speed things up a bit by taking off my bikini, then waving and shaking the pants and top around, which I hoped would have the same effect as a good breezy washing day. Unfortunately the bra slipped out of my fingers and sailed over the cubicle door.

'Right, that's it,' the irate queuer hissed. 'You're up to something in there and I'm not having it. Not in a decent British resort wif children and all. I'm gonna get the police. Break the bloody door down if they have to.'

A roar of applause went up as presumably she went off to contact the law.

Oh God. I stooped down and peered under the cubicle door. Spotted the bra top, which mercifully was within reach and dragged it back in. Quickly I put my damp bikini on again, stuffed toilet paper into the bra cups and down the front of the pants (which I hoped would make them more opaque), opened the door and bolted out, ignoring the queue of gawping girls and women. Once outside I sprinted across the beach to where I'd been sunbathing.

Theresa and Suzie weren't at our spot. Neither were

the guys, thank God. Gratefully I covered myself with a towel and flopped exhausted onto the sand. I heard Theresa and Suzie before I saw them. They were pacing by the shoreline, anxiously scanning the water and yelling, 'Kelly Ann, where are you?!'

I called and waved over. They didn't notice at first, but after a while I managed to get their attention and they raced over. They looked relieved. And furious.

'Where the feck were you?' Theresa said. 'We were nearly getting the coastguard out for you.'

'Yeah,' Suzie agreed. 'Thought we'd have to watch your bloated body being fished from the water, then one of us would need to identify it. Gross.'

'Sorry,' I said. 'I didn't mean to worry you. I was, erm, in the toilet. For a while. Don't ask.'

'Hmm,' Theresa said. 'As long as you're all right, I suppose. At least now we won't have to explain to Frost how you drowned in Southend-on-Sea when you were supposed to be ill. She'd definitely know we'd been skiving then.'

'Yeah,' Suzie laughed. 'She'd probably have docked our sick pay.'

Pleased they weren't annoyed any more, I laughed too. 'Do you think you could do me a favour, Theresa?'

'Yeah, what?'

'Just hold this towel around me while I get changed. I've decided I don't like this cheap bikini.'

Theresa shrugged. 'Looked all right to me, but fair enough.'

She did as I'd asked and I peeled off my wet bikini. Weighed down by wads of damp of toilet paper, the bits flumped onto the sand. Suzie and Theresa stared at them.

'Why for feck's sake do you have ruddy great lumps of sodden toilet paper stuck inside your bikini top and pants?' Theresa asked.

Oh God. Had to fill them in on my bikini disaster. Although they tried to make sympathetic noises at first, they soon gave up, and Theresa especially practically wet herself laughing. She's got a nerve, given she was the one who persuaded me to buy the stupid thing, but at least they both shut up about it when the guys came back.

It was annoying not being able to swim but I had a great time anyway. We spent the rest of the day with the guys. Kicked a ball about on the beach for a while then had a look round the fun fair. Bought candyfloss and ice-cream cones then headed out along the pier. It went on for miles but halfway out Theresa said, 'Sod this, let's find a pub.'

Had fish and chips – we had ours with cider, but the guys just ordered orange juice as they were sales reps and had brought their cars.

'So what do you sell then?' Suzie asked.

'Biscuits,' Sam answered. 'But not just any biscuits, are they, guys?'

'No,' they chorused. 'Bettie's Biscuits Take the Biscuit for Biscuits.'

'Jeezus, that's a bloody pathetic slogan,' Theresa said.

'Sold fifty million packets worldwide,' Sam countered. 'But yeah, it's embarrassing.'

'Got any free samples with you?' I asked hopefully.

'Tons, but they're crap. Wouldn't feed them to my dog.'

The others nodded in agreement.

Hmm, must be awful selling stuff you don't believe in, but I suppose it's better than slaving in a broiling kitchen and getting shouted at by a homicidal chef.

By the time we were all ready to go I was pleased to see that I was already a nice brown colour. Unlike Theresa, who'd turned bright red and burned. Sam was sympathetic. 'You should have borrowed my factor fifty. Most of us carrot tops can't take the sun. Without this' – he flashed a tube of Nivea maximum protection plus – 'I'd have to skulk in the shade like a vampire,' he laughed. 'And not because I bloody sparkle.'

'I'm not a carrot top. I'm strawberry blonde,' Theresa hissed.

Sam shrugged. 'If you say so. So, would you girls like a lift back to London? I've got to go across the City on my way home.'

'No thank—' Theresa began.

'Yeah, great,' Suzie and I chorused.

Sam's car was amazing. A cool Porsche convertible.

'Oh my God,' Suzie said. 'Reps at your biscuit company get Porsches? That's fantastic!'

Sam smiled. 'They do if their dad is the owner. But he wanted me to start as a regular employee. Get to know the business from the bottom up. All I've learned so far is we have a crap slogan and how to skive off.'

He went off to get his parking token and Suzie eyed the car admiringly. 'God, I've been chatting up the wrong one again!'

'But you don't fancy Sam,' I said.

She jumped in the front seat. 'I do now.'

But in fact we all fell asleep on the way back and Sam had to wake us up to ask directions when we got near the hotel. He dropped us off at the corner and we went around the side entrance but the fire exit wouldn't open from the outside and we couldn't contact Yan on his mobile. There was nothing else for it – we'd have to go in the front entrance and try to avoid Joy or her mum, who were usually on duty in reception at this time.

A quick peek through the window confirmed it was Frost the manageress at the desk, but she'd got her back turned to the door and was working on the computer at the side. As far as we could see the reception area, was empty. We all packed into one corner of the revolving door and pushed it gently. Once inside we crouched down so that we were lower than the reception counter top – in case Frost suddenly turned round – and silently scurried along the floor.

'Kelly Ann,' a familiar American voice called. 'There you are. I've been worried.'

I looked over in the direction of the voice and spotted Mark, who'd just got up from one of the armchairs in the far corner, making his way towards me. I frowned, shook my head and put my fingers to my mouth gesturing him to shut up, but . . . too late. Out of the corner of my eye I could see Frost had turned round and spotted us all hunkered down below the desk.

'What on earth do you think you're doing?' she said.

Theresa and I straightened up, startled and guilty, but Suzie kept her eyes on the floor, pretending to search for something. 'So, has anyone seen my contact lens yet? I suppose we'll just have to give up on it, then. I really should get the disposables.' She glanced sideways at the desk, feigned surprise at seeing Frost for the first time and stood up. 'Oh, hi there, Mrs Frost,' she said brightly.

Frost folded her arms. 'I thought you lot were supposed to be sick.'

'Oh, we are,' Suzie reassured her smoothly. 'Or were, anyway. But we felt a bit better and decided to pop out for a few minutes to get some fresh air.' She looked at us for backup. 'Didn't we?'

Theresa and I nodded mutely.

Mrs Frost eyed Theresa's red face suspiciously. 'You don't get sunburn in a few minutes.'

Theresa tried to gaze innocently at Frost but her voice shook a bit as she blustered, 'S-sunburn? God, no. It's, um, a bit of a fever I've had all day. Hasn't quite gone away yet, but I think I'm on the mend.'

Frost turned her small sharp eyes on me. 'And you've got a tan.'

'Tan?' I squeaked. 'How could I get a tan when I've been in my bed all day?'

Mrs Frost waited.

'I mean, I couldn't possibly get a tan in a few minutes, could I?'

Frost continued to wait.

'So it's, erm, not a tan – it's, erm . . . jaundice. Yeah. Jaundice. Very common with food poisoning cases actually.'

'Hmm,' Frost said. 'We'll see. Anyway, you all look perfectly healthy to me. I'll expect to see you all back at work tomorrow then.'

'Well, I'm not sure,' Theresa said. 'Think I've still got a bit of a temperature, so—'

'You *do* know that you're not entitled to sick pay for at least the first three days of absence, don't you?' Frost interrupted. 'It's in your contract.'

'So,' Theresa went on, 'I'll need to take a couple of paracetamols tonight, but I think I'll be fine for tomorrow.'

Frost's steely gaze swept over all of us. 'Good. Excellent. See you first thing tomorrow morning then. Don't be late.'

'Right,' we chorused.

'Oh, and make sure you clean the sand off your shoes before you come on duty,' she added with a nasty sneer.

Oh God, she would really have it in for us now. But she just turned back to her computer and started entering stuff on a spreadsheet – probably docking our pay.

Theresa and Suzie trailed off to their room with a whispered invitation to me to join them later and help finish off a bottle of Polish vodka that Yan had given Theresa a couple of days ago after she'd helped him fill in a driving licence application form.

I marched across to Mark, who'd retreated to the corner of the reception area again and was waiting sheepishly for me.

I scowled at him. 'What are you doing here?'

'I'm sorry, Kelly Ann. I didn't mean to get you guys in any trouble.'

'Well, you did. And you still haven't answered my question. Are you stalking me or something?'

'Jeez, no, it's just . . . well, I was trying to contact you on your mobile about some tickets I'd got, but you didn't answer so—'

'I didn't get any calls,' I snapped.

'I think you had your cell turned off.'

I pulled out my mobile. Checked it. Yeah, it was turned off. Turned it on. A couple of texts from Mark and a load from my mum. Wondered what she wanted. I'd find out later.

'So,' Mark continued, 'I called the hotel and they told me you were sick.' He spread his hands out palms up in a conciliatory gesture. 'I was worried.'

I looked at his concerned face and my annoyance evaporated. 'So you came all the way here?'

'Yeah. I asked for your room number but they wouldn't give it to me. Data protection legislation – I can't really fault them.'

I smiled. 'I suppose a future lawyer would have to go along with proper legislation.'

He smiled back. 'Exactly. But the Polish guy who works here overheard and told me he thought you'd gone out and might be back later. So I just hung around on the off chance for a while and, well, here you are.'

I sighed. 'Yeah, here I am, and now my boss knows we've all been skiving.'

'Sorry.'

''S OK, you weren't to know.'

'So, I hope I can make it up to you somehow. Maybe with these?' He took two theatre tickets out of his pocket and waved them. 'It's a modern take on *Swan Lake* by a Russian dance company. Supposed to be brilliant – getting rave reviews. Thought you might be interested.'

I looked more closely at the tickets. Sadler's Wells – probably the most famous dance theatre ever. God, how I'd love to have gone. But then I saw the price. 'I can't afford that.'

'It's OK. I—'

'And I can't let you pay for it, either.'

'I'm not paying. Got them for free.'

'How come?' I asked suspiciously.

'One of the guys I flat with. Greg. He got complimentary tickets after his company did some engineering work for the theatre.'

'So why didn't *he* use them, then?'

Mark shrugged. 'Greg's not a dance-theatre sort of guy. More a kind of beer-and-slasher-movie type.'

I laughed. 'OK then, yeah. I'd love to go. Thanks.'

When I got to Theresa and Suzie's room they were drinking vodka and cursing our luck at being caught out by Frost. Theresa handed me a glass and told me to help myself to a drink.

'Put plenty of Coke in it, though,' she advised. 'This Polish stuff can blow your head off.'

I did as she suggested and sat on Suzie's bed. 'What do you think Frost will do to us?' I asked. 'Do you think we'll get sacked?'

'No chance,' Suzie said. 'She can't do without us – and she won't find people to replace us in time.'

'Yeah,' Theresa said. 'We'll just lose a day's pay. Worth it though, wasn't it?'

'Yeah,' we agreed, clinking glasses and grinning.

'God,' Theresa said. 'Didn't we make eejits of ourselves with our stupid excuses?'

'Yeah,' Suzie said. 'Sneaking in like burglars and I'm pretending we're looking for a contact lens.'

'And me with my sunburned face and peeling nose! *Oh, it's a bit of a fever I've got!*' Theresa giggled. 'But the best was Kelly Ann. God. Jaundice! And her with a lovely golden tan. Thought I was going to wet myself.'

We all creased up then, and as I looked at Theresa and Suzie's faces, contorted and literally crying with laughter, I suddenly realized for sure that I wasn't the outsider any more. Theresa and Suzie were my friends. Real friends. Close friends.

When I went back to my room that night I felt a warm glow which, OK, was probably mostly due to all the vodka I'd drunk but also, I think, to feeling like I really belonged here. Like I was accepted. Almost like it was my home.

The thought reminded me of Mum's texts. It wasn't like her to text more than once as she's still not very good at it, and even a short message takes her ages, so I guessed it was something fairly important. To her, anyway.

I was right. Her last message said: URGENT! CALM ME.

Was puzzled for a second, but maybe she meant 'call me' rather than 'calm me'.

Called her.

'Hi, Mum.'

'Who is it?' she snapped.

'It's me, Mum. Kelly Ann. Your daughter. Obviously.'

'Don't be cheeky. I've got two daughters, so there's no *obviously* about it. And neither of them had a bloody stupid English accent last time I checked.'

'I can't help it—'

'Anyway, never mind, I've got good news for you.'

'You have? What?'

'I'm coming down to visit you. The company's paying for me to fly down to London for a training session Monday and Tuesday next week. So I thought to myself, why don't I pay a visit to my daughter? Book into your hotel Monday night so we can catch up.'

'No!' I squealed. 'You can't come here. I mean, there are loads of hotels in London. Better hotels. Much better – honestly, you wouldn't like it here.'

'It will have to do. I've already booked. Anyway, it will be easier this way for me to find out what you've been up to. Meet those new friends you've been on about.'

Oh God. I tried everything to dissuade her. Even told her there had been a recent outbreak of salmonella and Legionnaires' disease here, but there was no stopping her. And she was particularly insistent about meeting my friends while she was in London. I was doomed.

Theresa and Suzie were going to find out the truth about me. My cheeks burned at the thought of it. All the lies I'd told since I came here – about my age, Chris, my dancing career – everything would be exposed. My new friends would find out what a fraud I really was.

Considered running away, but where could I run to? All the runaways came here. To London. I'd nowhere to go.

No, I'd have to think of some other way out of this. Just had to.

MONDAY AUGUST 19TH

'That's an awful shame about your mum,' Theresa said. *'Getting dementia at such a young age.* My great-uncle Tom's got it, but he's nearly ninety.'

'I know, it's sad,' I said, trying to sound it. 'But she's OK really. It's mostly only her memory that's affected. She gets a bit confused about things. Hardly surprising when she can remember almost nothing that's happened over the last few years.'

'Sounds more like amnesia than Alzheimer's,' Suzie remarked.

Hmm, so it did. Why didn't I think of that?

'Anyway,' Suzie continued, 'it will be really interesting to meet her. You said she used to be a ballet dancer before she married your dad?'

Bloody hell, had I said that? I must have done. That's the trouble when you start lying. You can get a bit carried away with it and you can't stop. Vowed if I got away with this today I'd never lie again.

'Erm, she's got no memory of that either, so it's best not to bring it up. It might just upset her.'

'Poor thing,' Theresa said. 'By the way, I've asked Yan to take care of your mum when she arrives, since we're working then. It's his afternoon off.'

'Oh God, you shouldn't have. I mean, she'll be all right, honestly. She wouldn't want any, erm, fuss. Or to be treated like she's stupid or something. What did you say to Yan about her?'

'It's OK. I didn't tell him about the dementia. Didn't think it was my place. Just said she was new to London and to make sure she'd everything she needed and didn't wander off and get lost or anything.'

Really hoped Mum wouldn't be talking to Yan too much, telling him stuff. Thank God his English isn't too good. Probably he wouldn't understand her, anyway.

Luckily Theresa soon changed the subject away from Mum's dementia to her favourite topic these days. Liam. She saw him on Friday and Saturday night – *two nights in a row* – which apparently has never happened before and, according to Theresa, means that he is officially her boyfriend at last. She's totally over the moon about it and can't stop talking about how fantastic he is.

This is driving Suzie mental, of course, and I'm getting fed up with it too but we're trying not to show it. Don't get me wrong – I *am* pleased Theresa is happy. Just wish tosser Liam wasn't the cause of it.

Mum rang me at four to say she'd arrived and was being looked after by a nice big Polish lad. She said she'd meet me in the hotel bar once I'd finished my shift and to be sure to bring my friends with me. She was looking forward to meeting them.

It was after five before we were all ready. Mum was sitting at a corner table in the small bar, drinking her usual Bacardi and Coke, with Yan, who was smiling and appeared to be talking animatedly to her. Bloody hell – there's a first.

Mum spotted us before he did as he seemed totally absorbed in the conversation. She smiled over and pointed us out to Yan, who stood up to greet us. Mum stayed where she was like a queen on a state visit.

I stooped down to give her a quick hug but she practically ignored me as she had her eyes on Theresa and Suzie.

'So you're Kelly Ann's new friends, then?' Mum said. 'Thank God for that. I was worried she'd be a Norma nae mates again, like that time when she was expelled and had to move schools.' She turned to me. 'Remember?'

I flushed but managed to grit my teeth and nod. 'I'm fine, Mum.'

Yan interrupted at this point to say he should go now or he'd be late for his shift.

'That's fine, son,' Mum said. 'You go ahead. Enjoyed our wee chat, but you don't want to be hanging about listening to us girls' knicker talk.'

'It was a great pleasure,' Yan said. Then to my surprise he kissed Mum's hand and turned to me. 'Your mother is a wonderful woman. She has much grace and wisdom.'

Bloody hell. Then again, guys have always liked, or at the least respected, my mum. Don't know why, except that she never takes any rubbish from them.

When Yan moved off she motioned us all to sit down beside her and waved the barman over. 'Right, girls, what will you have? Don't stint yourselves now. Drinks are on me. Company's paying.' She wagged a finger at me. 'Just Coke for you, mind. You can't use your false ID when your mum's buying. Not as though I can pretend I didn't know were a minor.' She laughed. 'It's not likely I'd forget the day you were born. Bloody agony and twenty perineum stitches afterwards. Never been the same since.'

Oh God. I rolled my eyes and managed to make an I–told–you–she–was–gaga shrug without Mum noticing. I ordered a Coke. Theresa and Suzie ordered double vodka and Cokes. Felt envious. I was the one who needed the alcohol to deal with Mum, after all.

When the barman went off to get our drinks Mum turned to Suzie. 'So you're the Chinese one, then?'

'Duh, of course Suzie's Chinese, Mum.'

Mum ignored me.

'Well, yeah,' Suzie said. 'I was born in Hong Kong.'

'I've heard you lot are only allowed to have one child. Is that right? Bloody marvellous law if you ask me. Wish they'd had it in Scotland years ago – would have saved me a lot of bother.'

'Mum! I've got an older sister. I wouldn't have been born then.'

'Like I said, it would have saved me a lot of trouble.' She cackled gleefully at her own joke then turned her attention to Theresa. 'So you're the one that Januariusz fancies?'

'Who?'

'Januariusz Grzeszczuk,' Mum said, pronouncing his name perfectly. 'The nice big Polish lad.'

'No, I, erm, don't think so.'

'You're arse in parsley,' Mum said – a stupid expression that she uses when she doesn't agree with what someone's said.

'What?' Theresa asked, baffled.

'Of course he does,' Mum continued. 'Januariusz and me were having a wee chat this afternoon and your name popped up more than once. So I asked him if he fancied you and his face went as red as a ruddy postbox.'

'It still doesn't mean—' Theresa said.

'Then he said "yes".'

Theresa flushed, but she seemed pleased as well as embarrassed. I suppose it's always nice to know someone fancies you even if you're not that interested in them. 'But he's got a girlfriend,' Theresa said. 'Polish, as well, and drop-dead gorgeous like the rest of them.'

Mum shook her head. 'Agnieszka, you mean? She's his sister.'

Bloody hell, none of us knew this. How did Mum manage to find out so much about people so quickly? Probably by asking too many nosy questions.

'Oh, I didn't know that,' Theresa said. 'But anyway, I can't go out with him.'

'Pity. You could do worse. He's a plumber by trade, you know. Going to set up his own business when his brother comes over in October. You can't go wrong with a plumber, I always say. Earn a bloody fortune. 'Specially if they're grafters like Januariusz. All Poles are grafters, you know. Now if you'd take my advice—'

'Mum,' I interrupted. 'Theresa isn't interested, and anyway, she's got a boyfriend.'

Mum shrugged. 'Is he a grafter, though? What does he do?'

'He's a painter,' Theresa said proudly.

Mum nodded her approval. 'Painter and decorator's a good trade too. And you'd never have to wash your skirting boards – just tell him to give them another lick of paint when they get dirty.'

Theresa smiled. 'No, I mean Liam's an artist. He paints pictures, mainly abstracts. And he's a poet. He's very talented.'

Mum frowned. 'Don't trust these arty-farty types. Mostly good-for-nothing lazy scroungers, if you ask me.'

'Mum!' I cut in, horrified. 'That's Theresa's boyfriend you're talking about.'

'So, I'm right then?'

'No,' Theresa said. 'Liam is wonderful. Very sensitive and committed to his art.'

Mum laughed. 'Gay, then? What's a girl like you doing with one of them? Mark my words, you'd be far better off with a solid young lad like Januariusz. If I were ten years younger I'd be after him myself.'

Ten years? Bloody hell.

The waiter returned with our drinks. 'Bill them to my room,' Mum said grandly. She took a slug of her own drink, put the glass down – almost half empty – and stood up. 'Right, I'm off for a fag. Be back in a minute.'

When she'd gone I seized my chance to make sure they didn't believe any awkward facts Mum might bring up. I sighed. 'You see what I mean about Mum. Doesn't even know my age.'

They nodded sympathetically.

'Yet apart from that she seems so normal,' Theresa mused.

'She was never normal,' I said truthfully. 'And all that about changing schools. Never happened.'

'Really?' Suzie said. 'So you weren't expelled then?'

I shook my head. 'No, of course not. She's confused me with another pupil who got chucked out for accidentally wearing Winnie-the-Pooh knickers on her head when Prince Charles visited the school.'

They both laughed.

'Jeezus,' Theresa said. 'How can anyone accidentally be wearing knickers on their head, for feck's sake?'

I cringed at the memory. I'd put them on my head the night before to stop my greasy fringe from falling onto my forehead when I slept because I was told it would stop me getting spots. And as one of the few pupils chosen to meet and speak with such a famous visitor in front of the local press, I obviously wanted to look my best. But I completely forgot to take them off again when I overslept and was in a rush for school the next day.

'I've no idea,' I lied.

'Well,' Suzie said, 'I think it was totally unfair to expel her. Obviously the girl must have been mentally impaired. No one in their right mind would end up doing that.'

'Hmm,' I grunted noncommittally.

Mum came back. Ordered another round. Then proceeded to tell the full tale of how I got chucked out of school in the Winnie-the-Pooh pants incident with a lot of guffawing. Thank God I'd got my story in first.

'It's a pity I didn't get some pictures of you,' Mum said at last. 'But the school managed to keep them out of the papers.'

'Yeah,' I said. 'Shame about that. So anyway, Mum, you must be starving. Why don't we go eat something?'

'You're right, Kelly Ann, I haven't had anything since this morning. My stomach's probably thinking my throat's been cut. Don't fancy eating here, though, not with the salmonella and all that.'

'OK, Mum, we'll go out somewhere. There's a nice Chinese not too far from here.'

She nodded, swilled the rest of her drink down and stood up. 'C'mon, you lot, finish your drinks and we'll be off.'

'Mum, Theresa and Suzie are busy tonight! They've, erm, got plans. Dates. They won't be able to come.' I stared at them. 'That's right, isn't it?'

They nodded. Murmured 'Sorry'.

'That's a pity. Company would have paid for the lot. Drinks as well. Still, if you're busy . . .'

'Oh, we're not that busy,' Theresa said, slinging her bag over her shoulder and standing up.

Suzie swigged down the last of her drink and did

the same. 'Yeah, not doing anything until later on this evening. I'm sure we've got time for dinner.'

I glared at them, but they ignored me and followed Mum out to reception to call a taxi.

It was Frost on duty tonight. 'All going out again tonight, girls?' she said just as we were leaving. 'Remember, I'll expect you to report for duty five-thirty sharp.'

'Who was that?' Mum asked.

'That's our manager, Mrs Frost,' I said.

'Miserable old bag,' Mum grunted. 'Face like a constipated camel.'

Theresa and Suzie giggled and then looked at me questioningly.

'Mum's not totally confused all the time,' I whispered.

It was early, so the restaurant wasn't busy and we found a table, no bother. To my surprise Mum got the hang of chopsticks right away, expertly navigating food from plate to mouth without so much as a grain of rice dropped and nattering away between mouthfuls. Mostly 'entertaining' us with stories about my early childhood. Embarrassing stuff, of course, like how long it took me to be properly potty-trained – she'd thought she'd have to send me to school in nappies, ha ha – or the time when I was cast as a shepherd in my very first Nativity play and whacked the Virgin Mary with my crook.

Personally I thought the assault was justified. Everyone knows that the Virgin Mary is the only good role in the Nativity play, but I'd have settled for an angel, and I cried buckets when I was cast as a shepherd. Penelope, the obnoxious up-herself kid who got the Virgin Mary part, taunted me about it for weeks in the run-up to performance night. When she stuck her tongue out at me during the scene – making sure, of course, that none of the audience saw this less than holy gesture – I let her have it.

The nursery teacher was furious with me afterwards, of course, but now I think it was partly her fault. The only reason Penelope got the role was her long blonde hair, that the teacher kept going on about. I mean, really, the Virgin Mary was a Jewish girl from the Middle East. How likely was it she'd be a blonde?

When I pointed all this out to Mum at the restaurant she appeared to agree with me at first.

'Quite right, Kelly Ann, you were the victim of dis-crimination.'

'Yeah, I think so too,' I said.

'A serious miscarriage of justice,' she continued. 'A kind of abuse really.'

'Well, I don't know that I'd put it that strongly.'

'Pity you weren't cast as the donkey and you could have trampled the wee upstart to death along with the teacher,' she cackled.

Hilarious. Still, at least she was sticking to my early childhood humiliations and not exposing any of my lies.

The nice waiter who fancies Suzie was here tonight and was extremely attentive. Especially to Suzie. After we'd finished the first course and were eating our desserts – with a spoon, thank God – he and Suzie chatted in Cantonese for a while. When he left to get more drinks for us I whispered to Suzie, 'Still trying to pull you? You'd think he'd have given up by now?'

She looked embarrassed. 'Actually, I've just agreed to go out with him. Well, he *is* quite hot, and it's just a date. It's not as though I'm going to marry him.'

I smiled. 'That's great. I think he's nice and you're right – it's just a date, so where's the harm?'

'Thing is, I think I really like him. Knowing my luck, I'll probably fall for him and spend the rest of my life slaving like my parents.'

'What's this about a date?' Mum asked.

Oh God, how could I have forgotten about her bat ears? 'It's nothing, Mum.'

Mum eyed Suzie. 'So you're going to go out with our waiter, then?'

'Well. Yeah. Sort of. Maybe just the one ti—'

'Nice young lad,' Mum interrupted. 'Well-mannered, respectful. Easy on the eye. But what are his prospects?'

'Mum, it's none of your business.'

Mum ignored me. 'Not much money in waitering and the hours are bloody awful.'

'Yeah,' Suzie agreed. 'It's a lousy job.'

Our waiter came back with the drinks and Mum started to interrogate him immediately. How long was he planning to stay in hospitality? Did he intend running his own business one day? I kicked Mum gently under the table, trying to get her to stop. Suzie kicked me none too gently under the table, letting me know she wanted Mum to carry on.

It's amazing what you can find out if you ask a load of nosy questions and pretend to be interested in things you know nothing about. Like us, our waiter Alec was just working here for the summer, then he was supposed to be going to college. He was studying computer programming, but it sounded like he didn't have much to learn as he'd already invented a new console game and written all the software for it. Several companies were interested in buying it, but he'd also had an offer of funding from a rich entrepreneur to set up a company of his own and develop it himself. It was riskier but he thought he'd go for it.

'That's nice, son,' Mum said. 'Who'd have thought there would be serious money in a game? Well done, you.'

Mum asked for the bill then went to the loo.

'Your mum's amazing,' Suzie said.

'Yeah,' Theresa agreed. 'She's a great laugh too. You'd never think there was anything wrong with her brain.'

'But there is,' I insisted quickly. 'It's just not that obvious unless you know her really well.'

'That's so sad,' Theresa said, her eyes tearing up.

'Yeah,' Suzie said. 'Tragic.'

'Tragic,' I agreed' guiltily. 'Anyway, isn't it fantastic about Alec? He's probably going to be rich.'

Suzie smiled happily. 'Yeah, amazing. I wonder why he never told me before.'

'Maybe because I wanted to know if you liked me even if I wasn't going to be rich,' Alec said from behind us. He smiled, put the bill on the table. 'I've had a lot of interest from girls once they heard about the offers that I've had. But I don't want to be involved with gold-diggers.'

'God, no,' Suzie said. 'Can't stand shallow girls like that.'

Theresa and I nodded. Totally straight-faced. Suzie owed us.

When Mum got back she paid the bill by credit card, adding a hefty tip. I hoped she was right about the company paying for all this. Still, that was her problem. I was just relieved to have got the whole meet-my-London-friends thing over with without all my stupid lies being exposed.

'Right,' Mum said, as we exited the restaurant. 'Where are we off to next?'

'It's late, Mum, and we've got an early start tomorrow,' I said desperately. 'I really think we should get back.'

'Rubbish, the night's a baby.'

Oh God.

Theresa suggested going to the Bull's Head, a traditional English pub near our hotel that she took her Aunt Maureen to when she came to visit her in London last May. But Mum wasn't interested. Said she wanted to try out this new pop-up Cuban bar she'd seen advertised in the *Standard*. It was just a short tube ride from here and sounded like it might be a laugh.

Mum led the way and I must say I was impressed by how easily she managed the London tube system. She'd already bought an Oyster card so we didn't have to wait while she bought a ticket, and she navigated her way quickly down escalators and along narrow corridors to the train platform, no bother, without having to ask for directions once. When the train arrived she ignored the usual instructions to stand clear of the doors and let passengers off first. Instead, she hurled herself into the train immediately, shoving people trying to get off out of her way, like an expert London commuter.

It was the same story getting off, only in reverse. Mum made sure she was first off the train by wriggling and elbowing her way to the door ahead of everyone else, then launching herself onto the platform before anyone got a chance to block her.

'Bloody hell,' Theresa said admiringly as we trotted behind Mum, trying to catch up. 'Your mum's quick off the mark.'

'Yeah,' Suzie agreed. 'You'd never know she was a visitor. If I didn't know better I'd guess she'd been here for years.'

Theresa nodded, then whispered to me. 'You know, I'd never have thought there was anything wrong with your mum if you hadn't told me. It's so sad.'

I flushed. 'Yeah, tragic. Look, we'd better hurry up. We're losing her.'

The Cuban bar was amazing. Built on a hotel rooftop right by the river, it had a fantastic view along the Thames and across the whole city really. The live band was brilliant, the tapas snacks free and the Cuba Libres (basically rum and Cokes) were so cheap they were nearly giving them away. Of course, mine was a Virgin Cuba Libre, i.e. Coke, so not as much fun, but at least it was served with lots of ice, a slice of lime and a paper umbrella. As well as the live band, there were random performers to entertain us, like the salsa dancers, fire-eaters and a sword-swallower. But the best thing was the bar staff. All guys – black, Cuban or Spanish – and every one of them totally fit. If only Mum hadn't been there it would have been fabulous.

Not that her being here seemed to bother Theresa or

Suzie. In fact, I believe they thought she was a bit of a laugh and were well impressed by her choice of venue tonight. For a while I'd the odd sensation of actually feeling kind of proud of my mum instead of totally embarrassed. But then she suggested we all do a Conga to 'liven things up a bit' and I was mortified again. Having said that, loads of people joined in, including some of the staff and the sword-swallower. Theresa and Suzie seemed to enjoy it as well, but they were totally pissed. Unlike me. God, drunk people are so stupid.

By midnight, though, I was getting fed up with being the only sober person in the entire bar so I was glad when Mum decided to call it a night as she'd to get up 'early' tomorrow – nine o'clock, about four hours later than me – and she wondered why I wasn't more sympathetic! I went back with her, but Suzie and Theresa stayed for a bit longer.

While we waited for a taxi Mum lit up a fag and I watched her enviously. For the first time, I found myself actually fancying the idea of a cigarette. Wondered for a second whether I should ask for one but decided against it. Mum would probably be outraged – hypocrisy has never bothered her in the past, so I couldn't see it stopping her now.

'Kelly Ann,' she said suddenly, her eyes narrowed against the smoke. 'What have you been up to?'

'Nothing,' I said guiltily. 'Why would you think I've been up to anything?'

'Well,' Mum said, 'for one thing your pals were talking to me like I was dumb as a bowl of cock-a-leekie soup and about to dribble on my bib.'

'I'm sure you're imagining it, Mum.'

'Hmm. And then I was chatting with another guest earlier and she was telling me how proud I must be to have a daughter who's a professional dancer already and all set to join a famous dance company in a few months' time.'

I laughed unconvincingly. 'Must have mistaken me for someone else.'

'And Januariusz told me you had got yourself an American boyfriend.'

'He's not my boyfriend. He's just a—'

'Kelly Ann,' Mum interrupted, thrusting her arm out towards my face, palm up to indicate I should shut up, and nearly burning my nose with her fag in the process. 'I don't want to hear your excuses, but I'm telling you this. That young Chris is a fine lad and the best thing that's ever happened to you. If you cock things up with him now it will be the most stupid thing you've ever done. And by Christ, that's saying something.'

We didn't talk much on the way back, and fortunately Mum was tired so went straight to her room.

I did the same and slumped onto my bed but I was too wired to sleep. It had been a nerve-racking evening always worrying what Mum would say and whether Suzie and Theresa would find out the truth about me.

Maybe a cigarette would calm me down. I'd seen it work for Theresa and Suzie. I rummaged in my bag for the packet of Silk Cut I'd bought yesterday. Couldn't find it. I was absolutely sure it was there earlier, even though I hadn't had any cigarettes. Hmm, now I remembered Mum throwing her empty packet in the bin after we left the restaurant. And she didn't buy any more. Bloody hell, she must have nicked my fags. Typical. She'd a nerve to talk to me about honesty and call me a liar and a cheat.

Except she hadn't. No one had called me a liar. Or a cheat. Only me.

TUESDAY AUGUST 20TH

Met Mum at Piccadilly Circus after her training session and went to Pizza Hut. She didn't say anything else about last night – just talked about family stuff. Dad had finally mended the dishwasher after she made him wash up all week. My sister Angela was thinking of going back to secretarial college now that my nephew Danny was in nursery. Riveting news like that – but I was pleased to let her waffle on if it kept her from nosing into my business.

I offered to go with her to Heathrow Airport but she

said it was a long way and not to bother. She didn't need a minder and there was no point in me trailing along after her. But before she left she hugged me and whispered, 'I've missed you, Kelly Ann. So has your dad.'

'Oh thanks, Mum,' I said, surprised. 'I've missed you too.'

She thrust twenty quid into my hand. 'Get a haircut, for God's sake. You look like bloody Medusa.'

Hmm. Didn't think her sentimental mood would last long.

When I got back to the hotel I went up to Theresa and Suzie's room to see if there was anything planned for tonight.

'Hi, Kelly Ann,' Suzie said. 'Your mum get the train OK? You know, she's amazing! It's hard to believe she's got dementia.'

'Yeah, fine,' I said quickly. 'So, any plans for tonight?'

'Guess who called me today?' Theresa said.

I looked at her happy, excited face. It could only be one person. 'Liam?' I asked.

'Yeah, and guess what?'

This was getting annoying but I played along. 'What?'

'He wants to see me tonight and you'll never guess what he plans to do.'

'Go to the pub and actually buy a round of drinks?' Suzie suggested sarcastically.

Theresa ignored the wind-up. 'No, it's something amazing.'

'That *would* be amazing for *him*,' Suzie said.

'He's going to paint me!'

Suzie was unimpressed. 'What colour?'

'Stop it, Suzie,' Theresa said, but she was too happy to be really annoyed. 'He must see something beautiful in me. Something special,' she went on dreamily. 'And of course it means I'll probably be sitting for him every night this week. Every night!'

'I thought we were going to that new bar after work tonight,' I said.

'Oh sorry, Kelly Ann, but you know it's not every night a girl gets asked to pose for a talented painter. Still, I hope you and Suzie have fun . . .'

'Sorry, Kelly Ann,' Suzie said quickly, 'but I'm seeing Alec tonight. It's his evening off.'

'Oh,' I said. 'That's OK. A quiet night would probably be a good idea. I should really practise my dance routines too. Problem is, there's hardly space to turn around in my room without folding my arms, never mind dance.'

'God, you're right about that,' Suzie agreed. 'Corpses in mortuary cabinets have more space than you. Dancing would be impossible. But I think I've got an idea . . .'

It was the largest room in the hotel, a penthouse suite on the top floor, and at least ten of my rooms could have fitted into it. It had a king-sized bed as well as a sofa and armchairs, plus a huge ensuite bathroom, but, most importantly for me, acres of floor space and a huge mirror on one wall. It would be perfect for dance practice.

Because it's a lot dearer than the other rooms it's more often than not unoccupied so Suzie had checked and, sure enough, there was no booking for tonight. Theresa persuaded Yan, who has a master key, to let me in and now I was all set.

I plugged in my music and got to work. But after not practising for so long, even the warm-up seemed hard going, and when I'd launched into my dance routine I had to stop after only ten minutes – totally puffed out and sweating buckets. Oh my God, can't believe how unfit I've got in just a few weeks.

I splashed some water on my face, slugged down some more water straight from the tap and started again. This time I was better and finished a jazz dance routine without any mistakes. After another short break, I went through a whole hour of non-stop dance routine – a mixture of hip-hop, ballet and freestyle.

I turned off the music and collapsed in a sweaty heap on the bed. I'd just rest for a few moments, then go shower and change.

When I woke up it was pitch-dark and I shivered a bit in my leotard. Put the bedside light on and lay back for a moment. I'd have to move soon but I felt stiff and sore. Too late, I remembered the importance of the cool-down stretch exercises that Mrs Davies had recommended. Especially after a break in dance practice.

I should really get back to my own little room, but then again, maybe it would be an idea to stay here for the night. I could just crawl under the luxurious plump covers of this comfy kingsize bed and sleep until morning. Yeah, why not? Why shouldn't I have this huge penthouse to myself for one night? No one was using it – surely it would be stupid for it to go to waste.

I got off the bed and headed for the bathroom, but then remembered I'd no toothbrush or toothpaste. No worries – sample throwaway brush and a small tube of toothpaste were included in a welcome package, along with shampoo and shower gel. Nice and thoughtful.

Had just snuggled back into bed when I heard it – the sound of footsteps outside in the corridor and Mrs Frost's voice saying, 'I hope you'll find everything satisfactory, Mr and Mrs Black. This is our premium suite.'

A woman replied, 'I'm sure it will be fine. We're just grateful you could fit us in at short notice like this. Can't believe the Regency West doublebooked us.'

'No problem at all. Just happy we were able to help.'

Oh. My. God. What to do? Thought about rushing into the bathroom and locking the door but that was probably the first place someone would go at this time. Got up quickly, smoothed the duvet, grabbed my combats, put out the light and dived under the bed.

Not a second too soon. Peering out from underneath the bed, I saw Frost open the door and turn the room lights on. A smartly dressed couple, who looked maybe late twenties or early thirties, stood just beside her while Yan, carrying two heavy suitcases, towered over them all at the back. The woman surveyed the room and smiled tiredly. 'This looks fine.' She nodded her approval. 'Lovely.'

Her husband turned to Yan. 'Just leave the luggage at the door, mate. We'll take it from here.'

Yan did as he was asked but scanned the room anxiously. Probably checking I'd gone. Satisfied I'd disappeared, he relaxed and put the suitcases down.

At least the couple looked knackered. Hopefully they'd just go to bed and fall asleep right away, then I could sneak out.

The guy took the suitcases but didn't bring them right in. Just dropped them by the door. Then he picked up his wife and carried her into the room, kicking the door closed behind him. 'Well, how does it feel to be Mrs Black?' he asked, grinning.

'Wonderful,' she sighed, and kissed him. As he carried her towards the bed some confetti fell from her pink ruched jacket to the floor.

Oh God. Newlyweds. There was no way they were just going to fall asleep on their wedding night.

Felt her land none too gently on the bed, which creaked and sagged a bit above me. Then he joined her, the springs groaning with the extra weight. 'I love you, Mrs Black,' he whispered huskily.

'And I love you too,' she whispered. 'It's so good to be alone at last with my big snuggle bunny munchkins.'

This was followed by some wet slurpy snogging sounds. Oh God, this was awful. And wrong. I shouldn't be witnessing the most important, intimate night of a couple's life.

I put my hands over my ears and pressed my face to the floor. The not very clean floor with loads of little balls of fluff and dust, one of which went up my nose and I sneezed.

'What was that!?' the woman asked.

'Mmm? What was what?' her husband asked.

'I thought I heard someone sneeze,' she said.

'I didn't hear anything. Maybe it's someone in the next room. C'mon, babe, you're imagining things.'

I sighed as silently as possible with relief. Took a deep breath to calm myself and . . . sneezed again.

The woman poked her head down and peered under the bed. Looked straight at me and screamed.

I slid out, scrambled to my feet. They were staring at me, their faces a mixture of shock and fury.

'What the **** were you doing under the bed!' the husband shouted.

'Well, erm, dusting?' I said. 'You wouldn't believe the amount of dust and dirt that gathers underneath a bed. Honestly, people would never sleep on them if they'd any idea of how much filth they were lying on top of.' I bent down, gave the floor under the bed a swipe with my rolled-up combats. 'But that should be OK now. You'll be fine.'

I turned to go but the woman got up and barred my exit. 'Wait right there,' she said. 'Nobody cleans a room at midnight.'

'Well, we weren't expecting you. You hadn't booked, so when Mrs Frost knew you were coming she sent me to clean up. Sorry it took a bit longer than expected. But it's all finished now.'

'Why didn't you tell us you were here? You must have heard us come in.'

'Erm, no I didn't. I didn't hear you because I, erm, yeah, I must be deaf. I mean, I *am* deaf. Yeah. Stone deaf. Can't hear hardly anything. But I can lip-read. Yeah, that's how I can understand you now.'

Her gaze swept over me sceptically. 'What's with the leotard. You always put on a leotard to dust?'

'Erm, no, of course not.'

'So why are you wearing a leotard?'

'Erm, for dancing? Yeah, to dance. For you. And your new husband. It's a special additional service for honeymoon couples. But with it being so late now . . .'

'What kind of dancing?' the husband asked. 'You mean exotic stuff.'

His wife glared at me. 'Better not be.'

'No, no, of course not. It's, erm, a celebration dance. Yeah, a celebration of love and marriage for new couples. Look, let me put on some music and I'll show you.'

'Thought you were deaf,' she said.

'Oh yeah, so I am. Yeah, I'm deaf, so I wouldn't hear music, would I? No, but ... erm ... I can feel the vibrations ... ?'

It sounded lame even to me and she wasn't going to swallow it.

'This is bullshit,' she said and picked up the phone. 'I'm calling the police. You're some sort of thief or pervert or illegal.'

'No, please!' I screamed.

'Wait,' her husband said. 'Let's not get the fuzz involved. We'll be up all night answering questions, filing complaints. Sod that. Just call reception – let the hotel security handle it.'

I hid a smile of relief. Knew it was Yan on duty tonight (as usual). I was saved.

In less than two minutes he was striding into the room. He glanced at me, then fixed his eyes on the couple. 'I am very sorry you were troubled,' he said, taking my arm firmly. 'I will deal with this now.'

'Wait just a minute,' the woman said. 'I think we deserve some explanation. What the hell was this girl doing hiding underneath our bed in a leotard?'

'Yes, of course, it must have seemed very odd to you. Very . . . unusual.' Yan said slowly. He threw me a desperate look. 'But there is a simple explanation. Very simple. Yes, I assure you.'

I stretched my lips into a smile. 'Of course there is. I was just telling Mr and Mrs Black that I'm a member of staff here. Cleaning staff. And our manageress asked me to make sure the suite was cleaned thoroughly, including dusting under the bed for our last-minute guests.'

Yan nodded. 'Yes, all this is true. Mrs Frost is very strict about these things.'

'But it took longer than expected,' I continued, 'so I was still here when you turned up, but didn't hear you because I'm deaf.'

'Yes,' Yan said. 'It is very sad. The deafness. But she clean very well.'

'And I'm in a leotard in case the couple wish me to perform the wedding "Celebration of Love" dance, which is an extra service we provide for honeymoon couples to make their stay special.'

Yan's eyes widened in shocked disbelief that I'd make up such a stupid excuse. He looked down at his shoes, avoiding the couple's eyes, but he went along with it. 'Yes. The extra service.'

'I'm sorry,' the woman said, 'but I don't buy this shit.' She folded her arms and glared at me. 'Anyway, who cleans a room in the dark? The lights were off before we came in. How do you explain that?'

Oh God. 'Well, erm, I can see that must have seemed a bit weird,' I stammered. 'But there is a perfectly simple explanation, of course.' I looked desperately at Yan. 'Isn't there?'

Yan hesitated for a moment, then his grip tightened on my arm. 'Yes, there is. I think this staff member is lying. I will take her downstairs for questioning.' He marched me to the door and glanced back at the couple. 'She will be dealt with severely.'

He pushed me outside and closed the door behind us. He released my arm, but as we hurried along the corridor to the lift he kept going on at me in a loud voice so the couple would still hear him: This was not good enough. I was a troublemaker who had brought disgrace to our fine hotel. I would be shown no mercy and punished terribly for disturbing our guests on such an important night.

'Thanks, Yan,' I said once we were inside the lift. 'I'm really sorry for all the trouble I caused. I owe you one. If there's ever anything I can do for you. Just ask.'

'There is something, Kelly Ann. I hope you can do this for me.'

'Anything.'

'It is Theresa. Can you ask if she would go out with

me? She is a beautiful girl. I like her very much. But I am too shy to ask her.'

'Oh, Yan, I'm sorry. I don't think that would work. She has a boyfriend already. Sort of.'

'Liam, you mean?'

'Yeah. So you know about him?'

Yan scowled. 'Yes, he is no good. He does not treat her with respect. He is *dupek*. I would treat her nice. Make her happy.'

I sighed. 'I know you would, Yan. But I'm still not sure she'd see it that way.'

'But you will ask?'

'Yeah, I'll ask.'

When we got back to the reception desk I apologized again for all the carry-on. 'I'm really sorry, Yan. You must have thought I'd gone nuts making up those stupid stories but I had to say something.'

'Why not tell the truth?'

'Because Frost would have fired me. She's just looking for any pretext now.'

Yan shook his head. 'Kelly Ann, you are a good person but please be careful. Lies could get you into big trouble one day.'

I went off to my room thinking about what Yan had said and hoping he was wrong. Since I'd got here I'd lied to just about everyone: my friends, family, boyfriend – everyone. Except Mark. Mark was the only person I'd been almost completely honest with from the start. I could be myself with him. Yet I didn't feel easy about our theatre 'date' on Saturday. Had a horrible feeling that being honest with Mark could cause me more trouble than all my stupid lies put together.

WEDNESDAY AUGUST 21ST

'Sorry, Kelly Ann. I mean, Yan is very nice and all but he's just not my type. Anyway' – Theresa smiled dreamily – 'things are going great with Liam.'

I nodded glumly. It was what I'd expected but I was disappointed for Yan, anyway. And for Theresa too, sort of. Yan was so much nicer than tosser Liam. Still, there was no point in saying it. Theresa wouldn't listen and would probably just slag me off.

'So how's the painting coming along?' I asked politely.

'Don't know,' she giggled. 'He won't let me see it until it's finished. But he's determined to complete the whole thing by Saturday.' She smiled happily. 'Go on, ask me why.'

'Why?' I asked dutifully.

'Because they're going to give him an exhibition on Sunday!' she said excitedly. 'Well, him and some other young artists. They've got funding from the council.'

'That's great,' I said, impressed.

'Yeah, so in a few days my portrait will be hanging in a public gallery. I could be famous!'

'Cool. That's brilliant, Theresa.' Then I had a thought. 'Erm, what kind of portrait is it? I mean, is it just your face?'

'No, it's all of me,' she said gleefully.

'Right. But it's, erm, not a nude, is it?'

She flushed. 'Yeah, well, it is. But it won't be sleazy. It's Art.'

'But it *will* be displayed in public,' I said. 'Won't that be a bit embarrassing?'

'Oh, Kelly Ann, don't be such a prude. It's not like it will be porn or anything. Liam's an artist. Deep and sensitive. I'm sure it will be lovely.'

I wasn't. Neither was Suzie when I told her. Still, what could we do?

'Can I have a word with you, Kelly Ann?' Joy said, just as I was passing the reception desk on my way out to get some Silk Cuts.

'Erm, I'm actually in a bit of a hurry.'

'It won't take a moment. Do you think you could come into the office at the back, though? I really wanted to talk to you in private.'

Oh God, what had I done now? This sounded serious. I opened the flap at the side and followed her through to the small back office.

'Look, if this is about the broken vase, OK, it was me, but it shouldn't have been on the edge of the table, and anyway, it was really ugly. I—'

'No, nothing like that,' Joy interrupted. 'Actually, I wanted to ask your advice about something.'

'You want to ask *me* for advice?' I said incredulously.

'Well, yes. But it's sort of personal so I hope I can rely on you to keep it confidential.'

'Personal? Yeah, OK then.'

'Good. You see, it's about David. I wanted some tips on how to, well . . . I don't know . . . make him keener on me, I suppose.'

'Why would you want to do that?' I blurted.

'Why? Of course I want to. In fact, I was hoping that one day we might, you know, get engaged.'

'Oh right, yeah, I get it but, erm, what's this got to do with me?'

She sighed. 'It's just that you seem to be so successful with guys. I mean, you've got a doctor boyfriend at home and you're dating a nice-looking American law student here—'

'I'm not dating him. He's just a friend.'

'Whatever. So I thought you might have some tips for me.'

This was something new. Someone actually asking me for advice about guys. I mean, me! Mostly my involvement with boys has been a series of embarrassing disasters, but hey, maybe that's all behind me now and I've matured into a person other people turn to for guidance. Must say I felt kind of flattered. Even if it was Joy.

'OK, well, what's the problem? I thought you two got on fine.'

'We do. Or we did, anyway. The thing is, David's a very attractive guy.'

I stifled a guffaw. I mean, for God's sake.

She frowned. 'What's wrong?'

'Nothing. I just, I, erm, almost sneezed. Hay fever acting up again. So go on, you were saying . . .'

'Yes, well, David is a very good-looking guy and, you know, working in a hotel there's a lot of temptation. Attractive female guests and, erm, staff. I'm up against a lot of competition.'

Jeezus. 'You've absolutely no worries about the staff,' I assured her. 'None of us would touch him with a barge—I mean, erm, we'd never betray you like that.'

'Thanks, Kelly Ann. But still, I know his eyes have started to wander. I think he's losing interest in me.'

I shrugged. 'Dump him, then. It's always better to get in first.'

Her eyes teared up. 'But I don't want to. David and I have been together for nearly two years now.' She dabbed at her eyes with a tissue. 'In fact, Friday is our anniversary and we're going out for dinner. I'd been hoping that he might, you know, want to talk about *us* then, even . . . well . . . it isn't going to happen, is it? I'm just kidding myself.'

'You're too good for him,' I said sincerely. 'Forget about him.'

'But I can't,' she sniffed. 'What would I do without him?'

Celebrate, I thought. *Oh, and get a life as well, that would be an idea.* 'You'll get over it.'

'I'll never get over it,' she said dramatically. 'Please, Kelly Ann, have you any suggestions on how I can keep his eyes from wandering elsewhere? Get his attention back on me?'

I sighed. 'Well, I still think you should forget about him, but if you're really sure—'

'Please.'

I looked at her. The way she dressed reminded me a bit of my boring older sister – black skirt down to her knees and white blouse buttoned up to her neck. OK, they were her working clothes, but even when she went out she never wore anything even remotely sexy: just flat pumps, baggy tops and smart trousers.

'Hmm, OK then. Maybe you should think about dressing a bit sexier – you know, high heels, short skirt, tight top, that kind of thing. Pulling clothes.'

'Oh, I don't know.' She chewed her lip. 'Do you think that would work with David?'

I shrugged. 'He's a guy, isn't he?'

Joy grinned. 'Yeah, you're right. I'll do it. So, erm, what were you saying about a vase? Not the eighteenth-century antique one that cost a fortune, I hope?'

'God, no. Definitely not. Why would you think that?'

FRIDAY AUGUST 23RD

Got a call from the temp who's doing reception tonight saying that someone called Sam wanted to see me. God, wonder what he wants.

He was waiting at the desk with my whiteish bikini in his hand. 'Hi, Kelly Ann. Nice to see you again.' He held the bikini up and swung it about a bit. 'You left this in my car.'

'Oh, you shouldn't have bothered coming all this way to return it. It's just a cheap second-hand thing. You could just have kept it.'

He grinned. 'Don't think it would have suited me.'

'Thanks,' I said, smiling, and took it from him.

'Who's that?' he said suddenly, looking over my shoulder. 'Christ, didn't know you provided that kind of service at the hotel.'

I turned and looked in the same direction. Saw a girl along the corridor by the lift wearing a halter top, tiny leather shorts so high you could see each bum cheek, and thigh-length high-heeled boots. Oh my God. Joy. Had no idea she'd such an amazing figure, but for God's sake, she'd definitely taken the pulling clothes thing too far.

She spotted me, smiled and twirled around – nearly falling over in the process – then teetered towards me.

'She's not what you think,' I whispered to Sam. 'She's normally all sensible and proper.'

'Even better,' he said, not taking his eyes off her.

'Oh God, I've got to get her out of those clothes before David sees her.'

'Need any help?' Sam offered.

'Shut up,' I hissed as Joy finally drew up in front of us.

'What do you think, Kelly Ann?' she said, smiling.

'Well, I—'

'You haven't introduced us, Kelly Ann,' Sam said, his eyes still fixed on Joy. 'I'm Sam, and you are . . . ?'

'Joy. I'm the assistant manager here.'

'Nice to meet you, Joy.' He shook her hand. Didn't release it. 'Maybe since you're the manager here you could tell me a better place to park my Porsche? It's sitting on a double yellow at the mo—'

'Look, Joy,' I interrupted. 'Do you think I could have a word with you in private?'

'Sorry, Kelly Ann,' she said. 'I don't have time right now. David is supposed to be meeting me here about now. In fact, here he is now.'

Oh God.

Sidebottom's eyes bulged and his mouth hung open. He stared at Joy in disbelief for a moment like a grouper fish in shock. Then he said, 'I'm going nowhere with you dressed like that. You look like a tart.'

Then he stomped off.

Joy's lips trembled and her eyes started to tear up. 'I don't think he liked my new look, Kelly Ann.'

Oh God. This was all my fault. I apologized and tried my best to console her, but Sam seemed to be doing a better job than me. He'd put his arms around her shoulders, told her she looked great and that she was way too good for a prat like David who didn't appreciate her. She didn't seem to be objecting at all, so I left them to it.

Seems like I'd given good advice, after all. Even if accidentally.

SATURDAY AUGUST 24TH

As soon as I put on the red strappy dress I felt guilty. This was Chris's favourite and the one I wore the night we finally made love for the first time. It seemed disloyal to wear it tonight, but I didn't have anything else good enough for such a classy venue. I stepped into the matching high heels and surveyed myself in the mirror. My tanned legs looked good in the heels and the dress clung tightly to my body. I frowned. Would Mark think

I was trying to come on to him tonight? Maybe I should wipe off the scarlet lipstick.

But my phone buzzed, telling me that Mark was in reception and the taxi he'd come in was waiting outside. I'd told Mark we could get a number 38 bus from Piccadilly which would drop us right at the theatre door but he wouldn't hear of it. Our tickets were free so we could afford to splash out on a cab. Do things in style. Panicked at the thought of the taxi meter running, I grabbed my velvet clutch bag and hurried out.

When I first caught sight of him he literally took my breath away. He was standing casually by the desk, dressed in an obviously expensive black suit with a crisp white shirt that accentuated his tan, and the overhead lights were shining on his gleaming blond hair. He looked impossibly handsome – like an airbrushed film star. I just stood and gawped. Fortunately, by the time he noticed me I'd managed to put my tongue back in my mouth, but my next move was almost as uncool. 'You look amazing,' I blurted.

He smiled. 'Hey, you just stole my line.'

I blushed. 'No, well, I mean, your suit looks great. It, erm, suits you.'

'Thanks. And you look stunning in that dress – like an exotic princess. So' – he bowed elaborately – 'your carriage awaits, my lady. But please shift your butt as the meter is ticking.'

I laughed and we hurried out. But on the journey I couldn't stop myself sneaking a peek out of the corner of my eye at his handsome profile every few minutes. But most times I tried, I found he was already looking at me with an amused expression, as though he knew what I was up to. I supposed he was used to girls reacting to him like this. Of course he would be. Well, there was no harm in looking, was there?

When we got to the theatre he paid the driver and gave him an enormous tip. 'That's way too much,' I said.

He shrugged. 'About average in the US. Anyway, I don't want to look cheap when I take a cute girl to the theatre.'

'It isn't average here. Trust me. And the girl is paying half, so she wouldn't have minded you looking cheap.'

'Kelly Ann, relax. I can afford it and I'm not going to let you pay half. Not after finding out what you earn.'

I rummaged in my purse, pulled out a twenty-pound note. 'No, really, take it.'

He shook his head. 'My treat tonight. And don't worry. I won't expect any other kind of payment from you if that's what you're thinking. Believe it or not, I don't need to buy girls, you know.'

'Oh, I didn't mean—'

'Cool. Now, c'mon. We don't want to miss the start.'

The theatre was packed. Some people were all formally

dressed like us but a lot were in casual clothes so I realized we hadn't needed to dress up after all. But I'm glad we did. Made it seem even more special somehow.

The show was the most amazing performance I've ever seen. Edgier and more exciting than conventional ballet: the dancers were fluid, fast, flawless. Especially the lead male and female dancers. I hadn't thought it was possible for anyone to leap as high, bend as far, or twist as often in mid-air as they did. They were totally awesome. It was the most exhilarating thing I'd ever seen in real life.

And also the most depressing. How could I ever compete with people as talented as they were? These dancers were real professionals. Superbly fit, talented, perfect. I wasn't in the same league. I was kidding myself thinking I could ever be as good as that. I shouldn't go to the audition – I simply wasn't good enough. I'd just make a fool of myself.

After the show Mark suggested a drink but the theatre bar was too crowded so we wandered out to find somewhere else. On the way he talked about the show, saying how much he'd loved it, and I nodded in agreement, but didn't say much as I was still thinking about my own dancing ambitions and whether I should call off my audition even though Mrs Davies would be disappointed in me.

'What's up, Kelly Ann?' he said at last. 'You've hardly said a word since we left the theatre.'

'Nothing. I'm fine. The show was brilliant – thanks so much for taking me.'

'So what's the matter?'

'Really, nothing. I've had a fantastic time.'

'But?'

I sighed. Mark obviously wasn't going to be put off. In some ways he seemed to know me better than anyone else here, even though we hadn't spent much time together. Better than Theresa or Suzie even – maybe because I'd been more honest with him. 'I'm nowhere near as good as any of the dancers we saw tonight. I'm thinking my audition with this director will just be a waste of time. I'm thinking of cancelling.'

He didn't answer right away. Took time to think about what I'd said. 'So why did your dance teacher suggest it?' he asked at last.

'Well, she says I've got talent, but I think maybe she just likes me.'

'Right. And this director who saw your demo? I guess he's just being charitable? Yeah, I suppose he auditions talentless dancers all the time, out of the kindness of his heart. Probably he's got too much time on his hands so, hey, what the heck.'

I smiled. 'Well, when you put it that way . . . But what happens if I go there and fail? What if he says I'm just not good enough?'

Mark shrugged. 'Then you're no worse off, are you? But, hey, at least you tried.'

'I suppose, but it's scary.'

'You know what scares me?' he said.

'No, I can't imagine you ever being scared.'

'Zombies.'

'Really?'

'Yeah. But I reckon I could probably outrun them. They're pretty slow, you know.' He put his arms out and made slow shambling movements.

I laughed. 'Idiot! Stop it, everyone is looking at us.'

'So, let them look.' But he stopped it anyway and became quite serious again. 'I'm not really afraid of zombies. Know what I'm really afraid of?'

'No. What?'

'Of the things I never did in life. The important experiences I missed. The things I should have tried and didn't.'

'OK, I get it. You've persuaded me. I'll go to the audition.'

'It wasn't just the audition I was talking about.'

Wondered what he could mean, but he didn't explain his comment when I asked him to. Just shrugged and said he'd tell me one day. I suppose he must have meant the things *he* hadn't done, though judging by all the stuff he'd got up to in Europe already, I don't think he could have left much out.

We found a really nice piano bar which had some seats left but I thought it looked too posh and sophisticated. Mark wasn't fazed, though. Walked in like he owned the place, even though he'd told me before that he'd almost never gone to bars in the States as you had to be twenty-one and they were really strict about ID. Wished I'd his confidence but I think you have to be rich, gorgeous-looking and American to get away with it.

Mark ordered a beer and I had a vodka and Coke. No one carded us, maybe because we looked grown-up and classy in our outfits. We chatted about the show some more and I was happier to do this now because, thanks to Mark, I didn't feel so envious and inferior.

'You know, I've never seen you dance, Kelly Ann. I'd really love to see that.'

'I could let you have a copy of my demo,' I offered.

'I'd like that but it would be great to see you for real.'

'Well,' I laughed, 'not here. I think people might freak if I started leaping about.'

He shrugged. 'I don't know, they might enjoy it.' He looked around. 'Some of them look kinda bored. Maybe it would liven the place up a little.'

I smiled. 'Don't think so.'

'Well then, what about a dance just with me? Nothing fancy – I don't do pirouettes and pliés usually, and I've forgotten my tights.'

I shook my head. 'They don't have a dance floor.'

'We don't need one. There's plenty of space between the piano and the bar.'

'It's probably not allowed.'

'Who says? Last time I checked there was no law against it. C'mon.' He stood up and took hold of my hand. Smiled at me. 'Screw it, let's do it.'

At first I was a bit embarrassed even though we just sort of waltzed sedately. But nobody minded our getting up to dance. Instead, they smiled encouragement, and a few other couples got up as well so I could relax and enjoy myself. Mark was a total gentleman too. He didn't try to hold me too close, or grab my bum and grind his groin into mine the way a lot of guys do if you do a slow dance with them. Instead, he just held my hand to his chest and put his other on my waist as we swayed to the music.

But he kept his eyes on my face the whole time, as though I was the most important, fascinating person in the world. And as I gazed back at him I felt myself melting. Wanting to draw him closer. I rested my cheek on his shoulder. Touched my lips to his neck.

The music stopped. People applauded. I broke away from him guiltily. What was I thinking? This was all wrong. And I wasn't even drunk.

'I'm knackered,' I said.

'It's only ten o'clock,' he protested. 'Even Cinderella didn't have to be back until midnight.'

'Yeah, well, Cinderella didn't have to contend with

a homicidal chef plus five kilos of liver and devilled kidneys to defrost and serve before lunch.'

He laughed. 'Fair point.'

We walked to the taxi rank and waited in the queue. I hadn't thought to bring a jacket as it had been so warm when we left, but it was cooler now and I shivered a bit in my strappy dress, although my cheeks were burning with shame. My relationship with Chris hadn't always gone smoothly: we'd split up several times and dated other people afterwards. But I'd never cheated on Chris. Never. Now here I was, just four weeks apart, and I'd nearly snogged another guy.

I glanced sideways at Mark. God, he was gorgeous, though. Why did I have to meet someone as hot as him?

He looked at me and frowned. 'You're shivering, Kelly Ann.' Hooked off his jacket and draped it tenderly over my shoulders. 'That better?'

I nodded glumly. And why did he have to be so nice too? Oh God – this must be the last time I ever see him. The temptation to cheat was just too much.

When the taxi came I tried to give Mark his jacket back, but he insisted I keep it – the cab might be cold. He'd collect it later. It was no problem.

OK, after he collected his jacket I'd never see him again. Before I could stop him, he'd handed the driver money for my fare and waved goodbye.

I slumped back in my seat, relieved to be away

from temptation but somehow also depressed I couldn't have spent longer with him. Why did life have to be so complicated?

My phone buzzed. Mark. 'Hey, Kelly Ann, how are you?'

'Erm, about the same as I was a minute ago?'

He laughed. 'Yeah, missing you already! No, really, don't panic, I'm not a crazy – just forgot to tell you something tonight.'

'What?'

'Flatmates found someone who wants to lease the place long-term – some hot chick – so I'll be moving out next week.'

'Oh, that's a shame. Where will you go?'

'No worries, I've booked into a nice hotel I know. Staff are great.'

Oh God.

SUNDAY AUGUST 25TH

Theresa was really keen for us all to go see her portrait at the art exhibition, but it hadn't been easy to get Frost to agree to Suzie and me going at the same time - especially as it was the holiday weekend, with the Notting Hill Carnival tomorrow, so like every other hotel in London we were mobbed.

Suzie invented a grandmother's funeral. I stuck with diarrhoea and had to sneak out. I think Frost had her suspicions, but since she wasn't paying us any money for being absent (she made that totally clear) and the evening shift agreed to cover, she didn't argue too much.

It wasn't in a proper gallery like the Tate but a community hall in Willesden. There were loads of people there, though, probably because of the free sandwiches and cakes on offer. Couldn't see Liam at first but Theresa spotted him at the far end in the corner and we made our way along, glancing at the exhibits on the way.

There was some nice normal stuff but most of it was rubbish, like the Lego construction which looked like a mangled washing machine but was called 'Torment', some brown Plasticine lumps which looked like dog turds and were in fact called 'Dog Turds', and a toilet with a placard saying 'My Life' which a little boy was putting to its original use.

There was a small crowd around Liam's painting so we couldn't see it at first, but Theresa shoved her way eagerly in front of them and we followed.

It was called 'Nude Girl Sitting on Plastic Chair' and it did look a bit like that, but nothing like Theresa. For a start the girl in the painting, if she'd been real, would have weighed about twenty stone. Her enormous arse hung over the completely inadequate chair. She had a huge bloated belly and breasts the size and shape of large buckets. Her face was upside down and was missing one eye and an ear. These had been placed on her left elbow and right shoulder. Only the hair looked like Theresa's as it was long, wavy and red, but with her upside-down head, it looked more like a beard.

'So what do you think?' Liam asked.

Grotesque, I thought. 'Great,' I said.

'Hmm,' Suzie said. 'It's, well, it's erm ... indescribable.'

Liam nodded. Pleased. Looked at Theresa, who had said nothing yet. Just stared at the painting like she was mesmerized. 'It's my best yet,' Liam said proudly. 'And you made it possible.'

Theresa shook her head wonderingly, then finally seemed to wake from her trance. She stared at Liam. 'It's ... it's ... '

'I know, amazing,' Liam crowed smugly.

'Shite.'

'It's what? What do you mean?'

'I mean, it's shite,' she repeated, louder this time. 'Rubbish. I wouldn't wipe my arse with it,' she shouted.

Everyone was looking in our direction, wondering what the commotion was about, and people started to crowd around us, probably thinking this was part of the art show.

Theresa removed the painting from the wall, reached up her arms and slammed it on Liam's head. Probably cheap canvas as his head went right through it, leaving the frame resting on his shoulders. He stood in shock for a moment. Everyone did. Except for Theresa, who pointed to him and said, 'Man with Head Through Canvas.'

MONDAY AUGUST 26TH

Can't believe it. It's the Notting Hill Carnival and practically the whole of London is erupting with music and dance, yet I'm stuck in a boiling greasy kitchen all day and most of the evening too. Frost is giving us overtime money, but it no way makes up for missing just about the most fun festival in the world even though I'm living almost right in the middle of it.

We were reduced to watching snatches of the carnival on TV, which just made it worse somehow. Like Cinderella given a glimpse of the royal ball while she was cleaning out the ashes so she'd know exactly what she was missing. Swore if I was still in London next year I'd make sure I was on one of those fantastic OTT floats dressed in a gorgeous feathery costume and dancing all day with thousands of other revellers, having the time of my life. It was nearly ten o'clock by the time we finished our late shift. Suzie, Theresa and I hurriedly got changed to go out and enjoy the after-carnival partying Suzie assured me would be everywhere. But just as we were leaving, Liam turned up at the hotel. He was raging. Demanded Theresa pay him for materials and time – though what she had destroyed was priceless, of course. Called her a philistine, incapable of recognizing true art when she saw it. Then called her a crazy tart.

Theresa was going to go for him then, but Joy had already called security.

Yan 'escorted' Liam from the premises so forcefully he ended up sprawled on the street outside. Don't think he'll be back. Theresa offered to buy Yan a drink to thank him, but he refused. 'I am just doing my job,' he said.

Theresa looked disappointed. So was I. I suppose she must have left things too late.

Or maybe not. 'OK,' Theresa said. 'If you won't accept a drink as thanks, I'm just going to have to kiss you instead. Last chance. What's it to be?'

I thought Yan would probably ruin it by going all shy and hurrying off red-faced. But I was dead wrong. Without waiting a second he swept her up into his arms and kissed her full on the mouth. When he set her down it was Theresa who was blushing furiously. But in a nice way. Kind of pleasantly surprised and excited.

And there were more surprises. Joy insisted Yan take time off and go out with us. He shouldn't be on call twenty-four seven at the hotel – everyone needed a break sometimes. Hmm. Maybe Joy wasn't as bad as I'd thought.

Suzie was right about the after-carnival partying. Music blasted out everywhere – reggae, calypso, samba, R&B, hip-hop, just about every type you can imagine – as people spilled out onto the streets, laughing and dancing. Even the police were smiling and swaying to the beat of whatever sounds they passed. Tonight London just seemed the friendliest, most fun city in whole world. And I so wanted to stay here. But not working in a crap hotel. I needed to do well in this audition. I just *had* to.

It was nearly three in the morning by the time we all got back to the hotel. Exhausted, but happy. Especially Yan and Theresa, who'd hardly taken their eyes off each other all night. Mum was right about Yan. Theresa was going to be much happier with him.

TUESDAY AUGUST 27TH

Mark checked in this afternoon but he didn't text me until after my shift about five o'clock: HEY HOW R U? I'M IN ROOM 12A. CAN U COME UP? BRING JACKET?

Would have looked weird to refuse so I said I'd be there soon. But first I rehearsed what I'd say if he asked me to go anywhere with him tonight: *No, I'm sorry. It's just I've got a lot on tonight.*

233

Of course, he'd probably plead with me for a bit, though: *C'mon, I'm sure you could spare a few hours.*

But I'd my answer all ready: *I've promised to go with Suzie to visit her sick grandmother. She hasn't got much time left.*

Sorted.

I hoped he'd look less gorgeous in ordinary clothes but unfortunately he didn't. When he answered my knock, he appeared at the door dressed in loose jeans and a black T-shirt and he still looked bloody fantastic.

'Hi, Kelly Ann, come on in.' He opened the door wide and swept an arm towards the room, inviting me in.

He hadn't finished unpacking so there were still piles of clothes on the bed. I put his jacket beside them.

'Sorry about the mess,' he apologized. 'Hey, take a seat if you can find a space.'

He swept some piles together, making more room on the bed, and I perched uneasily on the edge. He didn't sit beside me but busied himself putting stuff away while he chatted effortlessly the whole time, obviously not feeling any awkwardness about us being alone together in his bedroom. Unlike me.

When he offered me a drink from the minibar I refused at first as I know how stupidly expensive they are. But when he waved my objection aside – 'one won't do too much damage' – I agreed in the hope it would make me feel a bit more relaxed.

He pointed to the minibar. 'Pick something for yourself and can you get me a beer?' he said as he picked up some toiletry stuff and made his way to the ensuite bathroom.

'OK.'

'At least it'll be cold,' he called through the open door. 'What's with you Brits and warm beer?'

Beer seemed to be the cheapest alcoholic drink available, so although I don't like it I picked out two cans. One for each of us. I'd just hold my nose and knock it back.

When he came out I handed him the can and opened my own. Or tried to, anyway, but the ring pull was being awkward and broke off in my hand.

'Can I help you with that?' Mark said after popping his can open, no bother.

'No I'm fine,' I said. 'It's nearly there. I'll just push it in with my finger. Like this . . . Oh shit, I'm sorry.'

Mark jumped back, but too late to stop the foaming beer soaking his shirt.

'I'll get a towel,' I said, heading to the bathroom with some stupid idea of drying it off, I suppose.

'Hey, no worries,' Mark said. He stripped off the shirt and tossed it in the bin. 'Never liked that one much, anyway.'

I stopped. Stared at him. His chest was tanned, toned and smooth, the low-cut jeans showing off an athletic six-pack. Taken by surprise like that, it was impossible not to ogle. Forced myself to look away in case I started to drool.

If he noticed my reaction, he gave no sign of it. Just continued talking as though nothing had happened. 'Hey, let me get you another beer. He smiled. 'I'll open it this time.' He got another can, popped it open, handed it to me. Picked up his own. 'Cheers.'

'Cheers,' I said, still not looking at him. I took a few sips of the beer. God, it was vile.

He slugged some down, then put his can down on the table and extracted a red T-shirt from a drawer. 'So, I was wondering if you're doing anything tonight? Thought maybe we could get something to eat. Take in a movie later . . . ?'

I shook my head. Gave the spiel I'd practised. 'No, I'm sorry. It's just I've got a lot to do tonight.

'Sure, that's cool.' He pulled on his T-shirt. 'I'll catch you some other time then.'

'I'm sorry, I really can't,' I ploughed on with my prepared speech. 'I've promised to go with Suzie to visit her sick grandmother. She hasn't got much time left.'

'Excuse me?'

'Right, so I'm glad you understand.'

'Like I said, it's cool.'

'Yeah, cool with me too. Totally.'

'OK. It's a shame about Suzie's grandmother, though.'

'Yeah, shame. Right, I'd better go then.'

'Aren't you going to finish your beer?'

Oh God, I supposed I'd have to drink it since it was so dear and I'd already ruined the first one. Hmm, maybe if I drank it really quickly I wouldn't taste it much.

I put my head back, tipped the can into my mouth and glugged it down in a single swallow. Then gave a massive belch.

He laughed. 'Hey, you really do like your beer. Don't think I've ever seen a girl do that before. You want another?'

I flushed. Totally mortified. 'God, no.' I got up. 'I have to go.'

'Right now?'

'Best not to keep Suzie's gran waiting. You, erm, never know.'

'That bad? Yeah, you'd better go now then.' He got up and walked with me to the door. Shook his head sadly. 'She isn't expected to last the night?'

Hmm, I might need Suzie's gran to last a bit longer. 'Well, she could linger for a while. I might have to visit again. To support Suzie.'

Once back in my room I replayed the whole embarrassing encounter in my head again. Oh God, what must he think of me? Acting like a sex-starved bonobo ape just because a nice-looking guy takes his shirt off in front of me.

Knocking back a can of beer in one go, then belching. Gross. I might as well have picked my nose and scratched my arse.

Hmm. I might not need Suzie's gran to linger after all. Chances are he won't want anything more to do with me now, anyway. The thought should have relieved me but it didn't. Was beginning to wish I'd never met him.

I'd planned to practise my dance routines but Suzie begged me to go to the pub with her. Theresa was going out to dinner with Yan tonight and she was bored. Decided to go, but not drink much so I could practise when I got back. But after polishing off half a bottle of vodka in Suzie's room beforehand 'because the drinks at the wine bar are so dear', I abandoned any hope of rehearsing tonight.

Maybe it was just as well. Mrs Davies had told me that what impressed the company director about my demo was my originality. The fact that I hadn't been properly conventionally trained so my style was 'raw and un-restrained' was actually an advantage. So perhaps it was best I didn't practise too much? Be spontaneous?

Felt a bit less guilty, but only for a second. Knew that Mrs Davies had told me people had to practise till they were perfect, then it looked spontaneous. I'd practise tomorrow. Definitely.

Despite being so expensive, the posh wine bar was

really crowded as usual so there was no hope of us getting a seat. Had to fight our way through to the bar as well and, since there were no guys serving, would probably have had to wait for ages for a drink. But luckily the red-headed guy in front of us turned out to be Sam and he offered to buy a round.

He was with Joy, who wasn't dressed like a prostitute this time but was not looking all dowdy and proper either. She'd on a short flared skirt and strappy top and looked good. Normal. Chatting with her and Sam afterwards, thought she seemed much less stuffy and annoying too. Quite nice, in fact. Maybe Sam was good for her.

Sam bought another round, and though Suzie and I had offered to pay we didn't object too much when he waved our offer aside since he was loaded anyway.

Was having a nice – and for once in London – cheap evening, so was quite enjoying myself when I saw him making his way through the crowd towards the bar. He spotted me too and waved. Mark. Looking fantastic in the red T-shirt, but not as great as he'd looked without it. I flushed at the memory. God, he really was gorgeous. But how was I going to explain our absence from Suzie's grandmother's deathbed?

He joined us, said 'hi' and was introduced to Sam. He asked if we were all OK for drinks. We nodded. He got served right away by a barmaid who'd had her eye on him and ordered two Millers.

'So, Suzie,' he said, 'Kelly Ann told me about your grandmother. I'm really sorry.'

Suzie shot me a questioning look but just nodded solemnly.

'Oh yes,' Joy said, looking at Suzie. 'Such a shame about your grandmother dying. I'm so sorry, Suzie. I didn't get the chance to ask you how the funeral went.' She sighed. 'I suppose as well as these things can ever—'

'It's not her dead gran Mark's talking about,' I interrupted quickly, staring hard at Suzie. 'It's your *sick* gran.'

'Oh, that,' Suzie said, relaxing. 'I don't remember telling you about her, Kelly Ann. But yeah, she's doing fine now after her hip operation in Hong Kong. Almost fully recovered.'

I squirmed. 'Not your gran in Hong Kong. The other one. In Hackney. The one who's really ill who we visited tonight.'

'You've got *three* grandmothers, Suzie?' Mark asked, puzzled.

Oh God.

Suzie looked from me to Mark and back again. 'Erm, yeah. Three grandmothers. How could I possibly have three grandmothers?' She paused. Looked at me hopefully for some explanation. I shook my head. 'Because people can only have two grandmothers, can't they?' she stalled. 'Normally. Unless . . . oh yeah . . . unless one of them is a *step*gran, of course!'

'Of course she is,' I said, smiling and nearly laughing out loud with relief. Good for Suzie! 'Yeah, the seriously ill one in Hackney is a *step*gran.'

Everyone stared at me. And no wonder – grinning like a maniac while talking about a woman at death's door. I frowned, tried to look appropriately glum but probably too late.

'Anyway, I'm sorry, Suzie,' Mark said. 'How did it go tonight?'

'Oh, not too bad,' Suzie said. 'She's a lot better. Hopefully she'll—'

'But still terminal, of course,' I said.

'Oh, erm, yeah,' Suzie agreed, glaring at me. 'She's a bit better *temporarily*, but of course she's going to die eventually.'

'Sorry,' Mark said again.

Sam and Joy made comforting murmurs too.

The atmosphere was getting a bit sombre so I tried to lighten it a bit. 'Well, she's very old, anyway. And Chinese, so probably a Buddhist. If they're right she'll be back soon – maybe reincarnated as a caterpillar or something.'

Suzie rolled her eyes at me. Knocked back the rest of her vodka and Coke then handed me the glass. 'Your turn to buy the drinks. I've earned it. I mean, I need one to help me cope with the stress of my dying stepgrandmother.'

'Hey, let me,' Mark said.

'No,' Suzie insisted. 'Kelly Ann will get mine.'

'OK. If you're sure? I should be going now, anyway, or Amy will start feeling neglected.' He looked across the bar. Nodded and smiled to the leggy sporty girl I'd seen him talking to when he last stayed at the hotel. 'See you all later.'

I watched him walk across to her. Hand her the beer. She kissed his cheek. Sipped the beer in a normal fashion – no explosive belching. Smiled at him. Laughed from time to time. Happy, relaxed.

I hated her. Oh God, there was no doubt about it, I was jealous. And not just a bit jealous. I wanted to punch her and wipe that satisfied happy grin off her face. It wasn't fair. He asked me first. If I'd said yes I'd be where she is now. Getting all Mark's attention. Enjoying the envious glances of other girls.

But I'd blown it. She'd got him now and I'd probably never have another chance. And OK, yeah, I know I've got a boyfriend, but he's in Glasgow and Mark's here. Not that I'd ever betray Chris, of course. And Mark's got a girlfriend too. But while he's in London he should have been *my* friend. Not hers.

By the time I got back to our hotel and talked with Suzie, though, I was calmer. Luckily she wasn't pissed off with me any more when I told her why I'd made up the dying gran lie and just thought it was a bit of a laugh. Probably the last double vodka I'd bought her helped.

But she was serious when she said, 'Kelly Ann, I know I've mentioned this before, but your boyfriend must be something else. Not many girls would knock back the chance to go out with a guy like Mark.'

'Yeah, he is,' I said. 'Chris is amazing. I love him so much.'

It was true. As for Mark, the problem was I fancied him way too much for a friend as my jealous feelings had proved. I needed to stay away. I'd made the right decision. Definitely. But maybe the wrong excuse. Thank God for Suzie's quick thinking. Stepgran! Brilliant.

THURSDAY AUGUST 29TH

Only four days to go to until my audition and I don't feel nearly ready. With everyone all loved up lately, I've had time to practise in the evening these last two days, but it won't make up for all I should have been doing since I got here. Ever since the fire I've used the corridor outside my room, as no one goes there any more now that the launderette doesn't work, although yesterday David reported me. But Joy didn't show the report to her mum. She gave it back to me and told me to just ignore that prat

David. Joy is a lot nicer now she's going out with Sam instead of him. David, on the other hand, is more of a pain than ever.

But the corridor isn't exactly ideal and I really miss having a proper dance studio to practise in – like Mrs Davies's – or even my bedroom back home which has enough space and a large full-length mirror. Still, it would have to do.

Instead of wearing my leotard tonight I opted for a dress rehearsal and put on the outfit I'd worn for the demo and the one I'd audition in. Very low-cut black micro shorts and high-necked crop top with long sleeves. Stephanie had helped me pick it out. She said it emphasized my best points – washboard abs and good bum – while minimizing my worst. No boobs.

Mrs Davies said it was simple, allowed free movement and that the long sleeves and bare midriff added drama. I thought I looked nice in it too, plus it was really comfortable to dance in. I hoped it would give me confidence on the day.

After checking to see that David wasn't patrolling the corridor, I put my music on low – so no one upstairs could hear it hopefully – and prepared to warm up. Had just finished with a splits when I heard the lift open. Shit. Probably David again.

But it was Mark. This was the last thing I needed. What was he doing here? Felt kind of stupid and a bit naked posed like this in a corridor so I scrambled to my feet. Turned off the music.

'Hey, don't stop! Sorry, I didn't mean to disturb you.'

'What are you doing here? How did you know where to find me?'

He frowned. 'I asked Joy. You haven't been answering my calls or texts. I was just wondering what was wrong. If I'd offended you somehow.'

'No. I've been busy, that's all. Can't you take a hint?'

As soon as the words were out I felt awful. Mark had done nothing wrong. In fact he'd been lovely to me since we first met. Kind, helpful, generous. He didn't deserve this reaction from me.

Mark looked surprised. And hurt. Couldn't blame him. 'Look, I can see this was a mistake,' he said. 'I think it's better if I go now.'

'No, wait. I . . . I'm sorry if I sounded annoyed. It's just, I really have been busy. Mostly practising for my audition. As you can see.'

'Sure, no worries. That's cool. I'll leave you to it.'

'No, don't go! Not right now, anyway. I mean, we're still friends, aren't we?'

'Do you want to be?'

'Of course I do.' And I meant it. He'd been a good friend to me since I got here. It wasn't his fault he happened to be gorgeous too. And he'd never so much as made a pass at me.

'Then we're friends.' He smiled. 'So, when exactly is your audition?'

'Monday. Three o'clock.'

'As soon as that? OK, then you'd better carry on. Mind if I hang around and watch? I'd love to see you dance.'

'God, no. Sorry, but I'd feel kind of stupid doing that here with you watching. Self-conscious.'

'A pity. But OK, I understand.'

'Thanks.'

'So, I was wondering, what about after your audition? You got time to meet up then?'

'Well, I don't know.'

'I thought you said you wanted to be a friend?'

'Yeah, I do, but—'

'And the thing is, we don't have much time to hang out together. I've booked my flight home. I go a week today.'

'Oh.'

He heard the disappointment in my voice. I did too. I was surprised in a way. I mean, I always knew he'd be going back so I didn't expect to be this sad about it. But I was. He'd been really nice to me ever since the very first day. I'd miss him.

'So, how about it, Kelly Ann? You want to do something next week?'

'Yeah, OK. That would be nice.'

'Cool. In fact, why don't I take you to dinner Monday night to celebrate?'

'What if I don't get it?'

He shrugged. 'Then we can drown your sorrows.'

'OK.'

'Good, it's a date. Just promise me two things.'

'What?'

'You'll let me see me see you dance once in that outfit – even if it's just the demo clip.'

'OK.'

'And you won't drink beer.'

MONDAY SEPTEMBER 2ND

Woke up with a humungous hangover but fear kind of scared it away. Once I'd dragged my aching body out of bed and showered I felt nervous and wired rather than totally drained, but still had a thumping headache. Wish I hadn't decided last night that a few drinks at the pub would help me relax, that a few more would do me no harm, and that one last bright blue aftershock would be a really brilliant idea. Still, at least I wasn't feeling sick – probably because I'd already thrown up last night. Bright blue barf. Not easy to clean up!

Just as well my audition wasn't until three o'clock. I'd be fully recovered before then, but first there was my morning shift to get through. I'd hoped to get out of that, but Frost couldn't spare me so now I'd have at least sixty greasy English breakfasts to prepare and clean up before heading off.

Mark turned up for breakfast about eight, but it was too hectic to talk to him, so after throwing me a few encouraging looks he left. Suzie and Theresa were too busy to notice how nervous I was, which was just as well. Although they knew I was meeting with Darling today, they thought the offer was more or less already in the bag and it was just a matter of me making up my mind whether to join the company or not. Like I was kind of auditioning him. Wish I hadn't made up that stupid lie but it was too late to change it now.

The last guests to finish were at one of my tables – a hugely pregnant woman and her small skinny husband – but they were taking ages as they were doing more arguing than eating. Mostly about him boozing the whole time when they were supposed to be on a break to celebrate their wedding anniversary.

'You're welcome to come with me to the pub,' he said. 'It's not as though you're not invited.'

'Sod that. Like I'm going to sit drinking orange juice all night while you get rat-arsed. You think that's my idea of a good time?'

'I'm not the one who's pregnant. Why shouldn't I have a pint?'

'Oh, you're not the one who's pregnant! Well, thanks for pointing that out. I'd never have worked it out for myself. Pregnant, who'd have thought? Full marks for observation. And I wonder whose fault that is? Or did I just get pregnant on my own like that sodding komodo dragon at Chester Zoo.'

'It's not the only thing you'd have in common with a poisonous big reptile!' he spat.

On and on while their breakfasts congealed and I'd to bring them another. But at last he stormed off and she waddled after him.

I thought I'd finish late and be a bit pushed for time, but Theresa and Suzie told me to go early while the chef wasn't looking – they would take care of the clean-up.

I went back to my room, showered again to wash away the smell of fried food and sweat which always clings to me after working in the sizzling hot kitchens. I dressed in combats and T-shirt, then I carefully packed and re-packed my rucksack: dance costume, music, hairbrush, battery charger, straighteners, make-up, bottled water, sports isotonic drinks and towel. Then I put my fully charged mobile and purse in the zipped pockets of my combats. All ready.

I was a bit early, even allowing for the fact I wanted to get there with at a least half an hour to spare, but I was too nervous to sit around any longer so I headed off upstairs.

Mark was in reception pretending to read some tourist bumph.

'Hi, Kelly Ann. You're a bit early, aren't you?'

'Hi. Yeah, a little bit.'

'I kinda figured you would be. I've been waiting here for a while hoping to catch you before you left. Are you nervous?'

I nodded, my jaw clenched. 'Yeah, a lot.'

'You shouldn't be. You're gonna be fine. I know it. Is it bad luck to say good luck at these things?'

'I think so. Yeah, definitely.'

'So what do I say? Is break a leg just for actors? Doesn't seem right for a dance audition. What's the right thing to say?'

'Erm, *merde*, I think.'

He laughed. 'Hey, no shit.'

I smiled weakly, my stomach twisting. 'I've got to go.'

'Wait.' Mark took my hands in his. 'Remember what your dance teacher told you. You've got real talent. So trust me – you're gonna be great. Now promise me you'll call when it's over and then we'll celebrate. OK?'

I nodded. Smiled. Some of Mark's confidence seemed to rub off on me and I felt better. Hopeful. Yes, this was my day of destiny. I'd been given this chance and I was going to make the most of it.

Waved goodbye to him and set out. Got to Euston, no bother, but I'd nearly an hour before my appointment and the dance studio where I'd be auditioned was only about ten minutes' walk away. I'd probably look too desperate if I turned up that early.

Anyway, I was thirsty – partly the hangover and partly because it was another scorching hot afternoon – so I decided to go to the station café and get a Coke. If I sipped it slowly it would be just about time to head off.

The place was crowded – mainly travellers with loads of luggage – but I managed to find a seat and gratefully shrugged off my rucksack then sipped my (very expensive) Coke slowly to make it last. Too late I remembered the drinks in my bag, but they'd probably not have let me sit in the café without buying something, anyway.

I tried to go over in my mind the routine I'd be performing in less than an hour, a kind of mental rehearsal that Mrs Davies said she always used to do before auditions, but was put off by the annoying guy beside me who was playing crap rap music on his iPod loud enough for me to hear clearly, but just in case I didn't he sang the lyrics – all about giving his bitch what she deserved and telling it like it is.

I glared at him. Despite the heat he was wearing a black hoodie and jeans so low the crotch was around his knees. Probably trying to give the impression that he was some cool black gangsta type. But he was just a lanky yob with greasy fair hair and pale spotty skin pretending to be a brother. Pathetic.

If he noticed my disapproving glowers he gave no sign of it and just continued his tuneless droning. I turned away from him, closed my eyes and tried to concentrate on my audition, without much success, so I was relieved when I realized he'd got up and headed for the door. I watched his retreating back move off among the station crowds and heaved a sigh of satisfaction. Until I realized that the grey rucksack with the blue stripe strapped to him was mine.

Oh my God! He must have just nicked it when my back was turned and, calm as anything, walked off with it. Shit! It wasn't any use to him – I'd my money and mobile in my pocket – but he wasn't to know that. But it had my dance stuff and music. And he was disappearing off to the underground escalator with it.

I sprang up, ran out the door and screamed, 'Stop, thief!' but no one paid any attention. I shouted again but still no one reacted.

Oh, what was the use? He'd disappeared from view so I decided to save my breath and run after him. But it isn't easy to race after someone in a crowed train station. People are just so bloody slow and really rude when you try to barge past them. By the time I got to the escalators he was gone but I ran down them two at a time anyway, shoving dawdlers out of my way, and when I got to the bottom I spotted him just going through the ticket barrier.

Lost some time scrambling in my purse for my travel card. Once through the barriers and down more escalators I thought I'd lost him again at first. But luckily, although the underground was mobbed, he was tall so I was able to see his greasy head bobbing above the crowds to my right.

He wasn't dawdling but he wasn't hurrying either, so he probably had no idea I was after him. I raced on and soon caught up. I grabbed at my bag but couldn't pull it off his shoulders. 'Give me that!' I panted.

But he just glared at me. 'Sod off!' And pushed me away.

I fell over but quickly scrambled up again. However, he'd already headed off. 'Stop,' I shouted, running after him again. He glanced back briefly, saw me gaining on him and broke into a run.

He was headed in the direction of the northbound, Northern line and I chased him as fast as I could but he was getting further away from me all the time. By the time I got to the platform he was nowhere in sight, but a north-bound train was about to close its doors so maybe he was on it. I managed to jump on and looked around frantically. He wasn't in this carriage, anyway. Maybe he was in one of the ones further up? Hmm, or maybe he wasn't on this train at all.

Pushed my way from crowded carriage to crowded carriage but didn't see him. Oh God, he was gone. I'd lost him along with all my stuff.

But then I saw a lanky guy in a hoodie get off at Camden. And yeah, he'd my rucksack strapped to his back. It was him!

I managed to scramble off and speed after him but he spotted me, and after shouting 'Sod off, I told you,' he loped away. I kept him in sight until I reached the bottom of the escalators, where I got trapped behind a group of tourists with loads of heavy luggage who obviously must have been foreign or totally illiterate because they seemed to be incapable of reading 'stand on the right'.

By the time I got to the exit I thought I'd lost him completely, but looking frantically right and left down the high street I could just make out his head bobbing in the distance across the road and saw him turn into a side street.

I flew after him, terrified I'd lose his trail if he changed direction again without me seeing him. But I was in luck. He must have thought he'd lost me as he was strolling along, still singing awful rap lyrics out of tune, totally unaware I'd managed to follow him here. The street was a dead end and I caught up with him just outside a launderette.

Without warning, I rugby tackled him to the ground, tore my rucksack out of his arms, scrambled to my feet and ran for it. Heard him shouting behind me and looked over my shoulder to see he'd got up and was chasing after me.

Raced back to the main road, spotted an empty taxi and shoved out my arm. It drew in to the kerb so I got in and gave the address of the dance studio. As we took off, I saw my thief shake his fist at me. Bloody nerve. He's lucky I didn't report him to the police, but there was no time for that. I checked my mobile. Oh God, ten to three. I wasn't sure exactly where the studios were from here but reckoned they couldn't be too far away. Hoped not, anyway.

The driver told me it was just four miles so I sat back, tried to catch my breath and calm down. But four miles in London traffic took nearly half an hour and it was twenty past three when he finally dropped me off at the dance studio building.

It looked amazing – all windows and glass that sparkled in the sunshine. Inside was even better. Light and space everywhere: tall arched windows, smoky blue-grey glass walls, polished wood, shiny tiled floors, mirrors and a spiral staircase that soared up through the middle of the floor. Contemporary but totally classy.

Unlike me. Caught sight of my reflection in the mirror. Dirty T-shirt and ripped combats from tackling my lanky bag thief. And huge sweat stains under my arms. Nice. Oh God.

But the beautiful blonde receptionist made no comment about my appearance when I told her about my audition appointment. Just smiled and said I was lucky they were running late. She invited me to take a seat while she found out when I was scheduled now.

Wanted to kiss her. But stopped myself and paced about while she called Darling.

I had to wait an excruciating fifteen minutes at reception before a slim, dark-haired woman dressed all in black came down the spiral staircase towards me.

'Sorry to have kept you waiting, Kelly Ann. I'm Kate, the company's choreographer.'

Close up, she was older than I'd thought at first. There were fine wrinkles at the corners of her eyes and a few silvery hairs among the black. She must have been nearly forty but you could see she'd been a dancer by the way she moved and stood. If I ever got old I wouldn't mind looking kind of like her.

She chatted as she escorted me upstairs, mostly asking me questions about myself. Trying to put me at ease, I suppose, but I could barely answer her as my throat had gone all dry and my tongue seemed to have attached itself to the roof of my mouth.

We stopped at the changing rooms and she opened the door. It was empty.

'You're our last candidate, Kelly Ann. The others have already left. Your audition is in the studio just along the corridor.' She looked at her watch. 'Martyn is on the phone right now but he shouldn't be long. I'll come back for you when we're ready. Probably about ten minutes. Does that give you enough time?'

I nodded and she left.

I went in. There were loads of lockers, benches and showers. I'd have loved to have a shower after all my running around but there was no time. I'd just have to splash water on my face and spray deodorant everywhere else. Hopefully I'd be able to redo my make-up and straighten my hair. Thank God I'd come prepared.

Tore open my rucksack. First thing I noticed was the smell. A mixture of sweaty socks and mouldering underwear. Who'd put those there? Stupidly, I plunged my arm into the contents of the bag looking for my stuff. Nothing but unwashed clothes, a tin of tobacco and roll ups, a tube of athlete's foot cream and a packet of condoms.

Shit. He hadn't stolen my bag after all. His must have been the same brand as mine.

I threw the rucksack on the floor, spilling a lot of its disgusting contents. Oh God, what was I going to do? I couldn't audition in my combats, could I?

Well, why not? I thought desperately. After all, this was contemporary dance. Not ballet. I didn't need a tutu exactly. Yeah. Maybe I could say it's a kind of urban grunge style or something. And maybe they would have the music I needed? Or I'd dance without it. Might impress them more. Anyway, what else could I do?

Was interrupted by a knock on the door. Surely they were a bit early?

I got up, took a deep breath to steady myself, pasted on a smile and opened the door.

Recognized the lanky guy from Euston, but not the much more solidly built muscular policeman and the sturdy no-nonsense policewoman who flanked him on either side, blocking the exit.

'Is this the girl who assaulted you and stole your bag, Mr Langley?' the policeman asked, looking over my shoulder at the rucksack.

Langely nodded. 'That's her.'

'What are you doing here?' I blurted. 'I mean, how did you find me?' Too late I realized how dodgy I must have sounded. Shit.

'Mr Langley had the presence of mind to note the registration of the taxi you made your getaway in and contacted us immediately,' the policeman said.

'Getaway? Bollocks. Erm, I mean, this has all been a stupid misunderstanding,' I stammered. 'You can't really believe I'd want to mug anyone for the minging stuff in *his* bag. Honestly, there's a totally innocent explanation for all this.'

'Good.' The policeman nodded. 'We'll hear it down at the station.'

Explained to them that I couldn't possibly do that right then as I'd an important audition which could affect the future happiness of my entire life. But they didn't seem to understand and kept insisting I'd to go with them and make a statement right away.

Put my foot down and told them that I was going nowhere until I'd done my audition.

Thought the handcuffs were totally over the top.

And very embarrassing. Especially as Kate and a distinguished-looking man – who I guessed must have been Martyn Darling – appeared just as I was being led off down the stairs. I stretched my head back. 'Do you think we could reschedule?'

Neither of them answered.

The police kept me ages at the station. They offered me a solicitor, which I refused, but wouldn't let me use my mobile to call Darling, saying they'd have to make the call for me, which was the last thing I wanted. As was calling my parents, which they also suggested – I'd rather have beaten myself senseless with a baton and tasered my tongue before I'd tell Mum and Dad where I was right then.

Meantime they kept going over with me Langley's explanation of events, which they'd said sounded plausible to them.

According to Langley, he'd been at a pop festival over the weekend and was on his way home when a girl he recognized from the café at Euston earlier grabbed his bag. He managed to foil this first attempted robbery and remonstrated with me. However, I refused to listen and continued to pursue him so he'd had to flee in fear for his property and safety. He'd thought he'd shaken me off in Camden, but I appeared out of nowhere, assaulted him and made off with his bag.

I mean, how believable was that rubbish! Why would anyone in their right mind go to those lengths for the disgusting contents of his bag? But the police insisted it was a credible account consistent with the facts and refused to let me go until they'd checked out my 'story'. Hmm.

They did get a bit nicer to me, though, once they knew I'd been telling the truth. Or maybe it was after idiot Langley started singing along to the lyrics of 'F*** the Police' while he was checking to see if any of his belongings were missing. All there, he'd said, except his wallet with a hundred and fifty quid in it. Yeah, right.

They finally let me go around nine o'clock when they located my bag, which had been handed in to lost property, and even offered me a lift home. On the way back I called the director but he didn't answer. There were worried texts and voice messages from Mrs Davies, who'd obviously heard about my arrest. I called her back, told her it had all been a mistake, and asked her if Darling would give me another chance.

'I'm so sorry, Kelly Ann, but I'm afraid candidates have already been selected and offers made. He won't be taking on any more new clients this year at least.'

Her voice sounded very final and I knew then that that was it. I'd blown my chances for ever. I ended the call, crouched into the corner of the police car and covered my face with my hands. All my hopes and dreams were over and I hadn't even been given a chance to audition. This was the worst day of my entire life.

My phone buzzed. For a second I'd a crazy, stupid idea it might be Darling saying he'd changed his mind and was going to give me another chance, but it was a text from Mark. One of quite a few he'd sent me asking how things had gone and why I hadn't been in touch. Texted him back: NOT PICKED. NOTHING TO CELEBRATE. Then I turned off my mobile.

When they dropped me off – a bit away from the hotel like I'd asked – the policewoman turned to me and said, 'Sorry, love, but if it's any consolation we've arrested Langley for possession – found some hash in his bag he must have forgotten about.'

It was. But not much, because he'd totally ruined my life, anyway.

TUESDAY SEPTEMBER 3RD

Thought I'd spend the whole of last night crying my eyes out but I didn't. The fact is, I was too disappointed and depressed to cry. Couldn't sleep, either. Mark had texted and called me a few times but I didn't answer. Just didn't want to talk about it with anyone. That was the only good thing about practically no one knowing about the audition. At least I didn't have to deal with people feeling sorry for me.

But it was hard to act normal at work today. Of course Suzie and Theresa asked how the meeting had gone. I just told them that I wasn't sure whether I'd take up the company's offer as I felt the stuff they do is a bit too commercialized. Said I wanted something more cutting edge and experimental. Rubbish like that which they swallowed, I think, because they don't know anything about dance. They were disappointed, though, that now I definitely wouldn't be sharing a flat with them this year like we'd talked about. I was too.

Mark turned up at breakfast and tried to catch my eye but I pretended not to notice. However, as I was about to clear the table next to his he reached over and caught my wrist. 'Waitress, why is there a dead fly in my coffee?'

'What?'

He grinned. 'You're supposed to say, *I guess because the hot water killed it.*'

I forced a smile. 'Sorry, yeah, I'm kind of slow this morning.'

'You OK?'

'Yeah, fine,' I lied.

He studied my face. 'You don't look fine. What happened yesterday at the audition? Want to talk about it?'

'Not really. Anyway, it's a long story and I'm busy

right now,' I said, glancing towards the table I was supposed to be clearing.

He let go of my wrist. 'What about after work then? We could maybe go out for a drink. Drown your sorrows.'

I sighed. 'Thanks, but actually I think I'll just stay in tonight. I'm kind of tired.'

'OK. But if you change your mind just let me know.'

I nodded and got back to work, but as I was about to head for the kitchen Mark called after me, 'Hey, Kelly Ann!'

I turned back. 'Yeah?'

'You never did let me see your dance demo.'

'Oh, sorry. I forgot.'

'Is it on a disc? Could I drop by your room and pick it up tonight maybe? Or you could email me it to me. I'd really like to see it.'

'OK, I'll email it to you.'

'Promise?'

'Yeah, I promise. Text me your address and I'll do it on my break.'

Suzie and Theresa were both going out with their boyfriends after work so I'd be alone tonight, but I was glad. The effort to appear as though nothing had happened when I was practically suicidal was exhausting.

I went back to my room and lay down on the bed, hoping to doze off for a while. No such luck. Kept going over and over in my mind what might have been if that tosser hadn't contacted the police.

Too restless to relax, I got up and paced the room. Well, I got up *meaning* to pace the room, but who was I kidding? Opened the door and paced up and down the corridor.

Felt better to be moving, but still the thought of what had almost been tormented me. I'd missed out on realizing my life's ambition just because I'd mistaken someone else's rucksack for my own.

But wait a minute, had I really? I mean, there was no guarantee I'd have passed the audition. After all, I've had hardly any training and all the other candidates probably had years of intensive instruction at top dance schools. Yeah, most likely I'd never have got in anyway.

Felt much better somehow. Sort of comforting to know I just wasn't good enough rather than totally arsed it up.

Went back into my room and lay down on the bed again. Finally exhausted, I was just about slipping off to sleep when I heard a knock on my door. Probably Theresa or Suzie, wanting to borrow some cigarettes or just have a bit of a chat before going out. Hoped it was for cigarettes as I didn't want to talk to anyone now.

But when I opened the door it was Mark. 'Hi, I know you said you didn't want to go out but I thought you might need a friend tonight.'

'Oh well, thanks but—'

'Jeezus,' he said, glancing over my head at the room behind me. 'Is this where you actually live? I'm not sure this is even legal!'

'Yeah, it is kind of small,' I said, embarrassed.

'You think? So anyway, can I come in?'

'Well, I'm not sure—'

'Me neither.'

'What?'

'I'm not sure if there's enough space. But maybe if I breathe in we'll just about fit. Want to give it a try?'

I smiled despite myself. 'Very funny. OK, c'mon in, but you can't stay long. I really am knackered.'

He had to bend his head to get through the door. Once inside, he looked so out of place in my tiny room. And not just because his tall frame was obviously unsuited to the size of the place. He was too classy for it somehow. Like Prince Charming in a slum.

He glanced at the bed. 'Can I sit down?'

There was nowhere else to sit since I didn't have a chair, so I nodded. He lowered himself onto the end of the bed, his long legs touching the wall opposite, and looked around.

'Cute giraffe,' he said, eyeing Gerry, who was lying on my pillow. But' – he peered at him more closely – 'what are the pink stains on its neck and mouth?'

'No idea,' I lied.

'Looks like lipstick.'

I flushed. Unlike with most people, I'd been fairly honest with Mark since I'd been here, if you don't count Suzie's dying-granny story. But there was no way I was going to confess to coming home from the pub and snogging a large stuffed animal because I was drunk and missing my boyfriend. Mark might think I was mental. Or worse – just very sad.

'Yeah, it does look a lot like lipstick. But it isn't. Obviously. In fact, erm, now I come to think of it, I remember he got stained when I put him in a hot wash along with a pink skirt.' I picked Gerry up and tossed him into a corner of the room. 'Hopefully it will come out if I wash him again.'

Mark shrugged and patted the bed beside him. 'Hey, why don't you sit down?'

I shook my head. 'I'm fine, thanks.'

'OK, I'll stand too. It doesn't feel right trying to talk to you from down here.' He stood up and smiled down at me. 'That's better.'

Not for me it wasn't. Trapped in this small space, he loomed over me and it was impossible not to be aware of everything about him. Even the fresh scent of the shower gel he used and the slow steady rhythm of his breathing. It didn't help either that he didn't make any attempt to continue chatting but just stared at me, as though waiting for something, smiling slightly but with a serious look in his eyes.

It was probably only for a few seconds, but while he seemed calm, patient even, I was beginning to feel really awkward as the silence stretched on. Yet I couldn't think of a thing to say.

'It's a bit cooler today,' I said eventually. 'Not nearly as hot, anyway. Doesn't look like rain, though.'

'Hmm,' he said non-committally.

Oh God, surely I could think of something better to talk about than the weather.

'Would you like a Jaffa Cake?' I asked. 'Frost gave all of us a packet today for nothing. They're past their sell-by date but they're still OK to eat.'

He smiled. 'No thanks.'

God, he'd a gorgeous smile. 'Are you sure? They're my favourite biscuit,' I babbled on desperately. 'Or you'd probably call them cookies, but then again maybe not. They're kind of in-between a biscuit and a cake. Not crunchy but soft and—'

'Kelly Ann,' he interrupted, 'I've a present for you.' He took a small pink box from his jeans pocket and handed it to me. 'I meant to give it to you yesterday to celebrate.' He shrugged. 'But anyway, maybe it will make you feel a little better. Go on. Open it.'

It was a silver locket with an engraved ballerina on the front. 'I'm sorry, Mark, I don't think I can accept this. Isn't it the kind of thing you should be buying for your girlfriend?'

'Cindy only wears gold – says she allergic to anything else. C'mon, please put it on. Otherwise I'll just have to wear it and I don't think it's gonna look good on me.'

I smiled. 'OK, but you really shouldn't have.'

I tried to put it on but fumbled with the delicate catch and Mark had to help me. The touch of his cool fingers on my neck and warm breath on my cheek felt way too close. Like a kiss almost. And for a second I imagined he was going to do just that. I held my breath and tensed. But once he'd fastened the chain he pulled away from me and looked at the locket. 'It suits you. As soon as I saw the ballerina engraving I knew it would. A graceful dancer just like you.'

'Thanks,' I said, breathing out again. 'But I'm not sure you should call me a dancer any more. It's not like I'm ever going to be a proper professional doing perform-ances and stuff like that.'

He frowned. 'Kelly Ann, I just finished watching the demo you sent me before I came down here.'

'Oh, right. Yeah. So did you like it?'

'No.'

'Oh . . . right . . . well, I suppose it's not really—'

'I didn't *like* it. I *loved* it.'

I smiled. 'Thanks. So you thought I was good then.'

'No. I thought you were brilliant. Amazing. You took my breath away.'

I flushed and looked away. He couldn't mean that

really. He was probably exaggerating to make me feel better about the audition disaster. 'Thanks, but you don't need to say stuff like that just because you feel sorry for me.'

He moved even closer to me and took my hands in his. 'Look at me, Kelly Ann. I don't know why this company turned you down but I do know this. You've got talent. And one day you're going to make it. Just so long as you keep believing in yourself.'

At first I tried to blink back the tears but it was useless. Finally all the disappointment and despair I felt spilled out and I cried. Sobbed my heart out as Mark held me. And kept holding me as he stroked my hair and made reassuring noises. Didn't let me go even though his T-shirt was getting damp from all my blubbery tears.

It was such a relief to finally pour out all my disappointment and frustration without pretending I was OK. And to have someone there to hold me and comfort me. He didn't seem to mind at all. Mark was the nicest, most supportive friend a girl could ever have.

When I finally stopped crying he reached over and took a tissue from the box on my table. He dabbed my eyes and cheeks, tenderly drying the wet tears from my face, then handed me another tissue to finish the job.

'Oh God, I must look awful,' I said, wiping my eyes furiously then tossing the damp tissue in the bin.

'You look beautiful, Kelly Ann,' he murmured. He put

his arms around me and kissed the top of my head. 'Beautiful.'

I pushed away from him. What was happening? This was all wrong. Opened my mouth to tell him. Really meant to. But he pressed his lips on mine and kissed me. A long slow kiss. Then he drew back. Gazed at my face. 'I've wanted to do that for so long,' he murmured.

I shook my head. 'No, this isn't right. I can't do this.'

'Sure you can,' he said. 'You want to just as much as me. I know you do.'

God, he was right but I couldn't. Mustn't. 'But I've got a boyfriend and you've got—'

'A girlfriend. I know. But they're not here.' He moved towards me. Pulled me into his arms again and brought his beautiful face close to mine so that our lips were nearly touching again. 'It's just you and me. Here. Now. This moment in time is for us. And if we don't take it we'll never know what we missed.'

I forced myself to look away from him. 'I'm sorry, Mark, I can't. I love Chris. I could never hurt him.'

'No one need ever know.'

'I'd know.' I slipped out of his arms and twisted away from him. 'You have to go.'

'Kelly Ann, listen to me,' he begged.

'Please go. Now!'

'Look, I'm sorry. Just hear me out.'

He pleaded with me some more but I forced myself

not to listen to him. Instead I pulled on a sweater and my trainers, grabbed my bag and ran out.

He followed me. Called my name.

I glanced back at him and yelled, 'Go away. Leave me alone!'

He stopped dead, his expression worried and hurt. But I couldn't risk feeling sorry for him. Not now. I turned and sped along the corridors then raced upstairs. No idea where I was going. All I knew was I needed to get away from this hotel. And from Mark.

Must have wandered around London for hours as it was starting to get dark and I was beginning to feel cold by the time I got back to the hotel. But the walking and the break worked. I felt calmer now. I'd done the right thing, I was sure of it. Yeah, Mark was a gorgeous-looking guy. And fun. But I didn't love him. I loved Chris. No matter what Mark said about regretting the things you don't do, he was wrong about this. If I'd cheated on Chris with him I'd have regretted it for the rest of my life.

Didn't notice him at first, even though he was standing right by the reception desk – I suppose because it was the last thing I expected. But then he walked towards me, arms out, and smiled.

'Kelly Ann,' Chris said. 'I've missed you so much.'

I froze. Stared at him. 'What are you doing here!'

He stopped and dropped his arms. His smile faded a

bit but then returned. 'This isn't quite the welcome I was hoping for.'

'It's – it's j-just such a shock,' I stammered. 'I mean, shouldn't you be working in Glasgow?'

'Pleasant surprise is what I was aiming for.' He held out his arms again and I moved into them automatically. He wrapped me in a bear hug and immediately I relaxed – feeling totally safe and loved just like I used to when we were together at home. But it didn't last. Out of the corner of my eye I saw Joy watching us curiously. Had Chris said anything to her about us? Had he seen Theresa or Suzie? Talked to them?

I moved out of his embrace. 'Let's go outside for a bit.' I frowned at Joy. 'Where we can talk in private, maybe get a drink or something.'

I turned to make for the exit just as Mark came in the door. Shit. He hurried towards me and took both my hands in his. 'Kelly Ann, where have you been? I've been looking everywhere for you. Wanted to explain. Apologize.'

'Who are you?' Chris asked, his voice hostile.

Mark dropped my hands. Looked at Chris. Then at me and raised an eyebrow questioningly.

'This is Mark, a friend of mine,' I said. 'Mark, this is my boyfriend Chris. The one I've been telling you about. He's come down from Glasgow to see me.'

'Cool,' Mark said. 'I guess you guys will want to catch up then. We can talk later.'

'Great,' I said brightly. 'See you.'

I hurried to the door, forcing Chris to follow me, but once outside he stopped walking and turned me to face him. 'Who was that?'

'I told you – he's a friend. That's all.'

'He didn't act like just a friend.'

'Well, he is. He was just worried I'd got lost, that's all. I've done it a few times.'

'So what did he need to apologize for?'

'Oh yeah, that. Well, it was, erm, nothing really. He, erm, spilled a drink on my good T-shirt last night and, er, didn't realize he'd done it until today.'

Chris looked at me sceptically. 'Sounded a bit dramatic for something so trivial.'

'I really liked that T-shirt.' But I could see that Chris wasn't convinced. I sighed. 'Look, Chris, fact is, Mark is a friend. That's all. Maybe he hoped he would be more than that, but he wasn't. You know I'd never cheat on you. I couldn't. I love you.'

His shoulders, which had been all tense and stiff, suddenly relaxed. 'I'm sorry, Kelly Ann. I never should have doubted you.'

'It's OK.'

'No, it's not OK. You're an honest person. Straight-forward and direct. I should have known better than to think you'd lie to me – or anyone else, come to that – about important stuff. Forgive me?'

I flushed guiltily. 'Of course. Yeah, of course I do.' I steered him down a side street away from our hotel. 'So,' I said, 'how come you're here? Is something wrong?'

'No, nothing wrong. My work finished – guy I was covering for came back from holiday. So I thought, I could hang around Glasgow for a week waiting for my girl to come home. Or I could get in my car, floor the accelerator all the way and be with her in less than eight hours. It was a no-brainer.'

'How long have you been here?' I asked anxiously.

'Not long. Got here about an hour ago. Told the girl at reception that I was a friend of yours and asked where you were. She said you were out. Didn't know when you'd be back, so I just waited.'

'Is that all you said?'

'Yeah. What else would I say?'

'Good,' I said, relieved. 'Where are you staying?'

'At the hotel, of course.'

'You can't stay there!'

'Why not?'

'It's, well, it's way too dear.'

'Yeah, it is a bit expensive but I've only booked for one night.'

'Just one night?'

'For now. I was hoping I could maybe stay with you afterwards.'

'No, you can't. It's not allowed.'

He smiled. 'I guessed that but I could always sneak in. Climb in through your window. Like Romeo and Juliet. Or the *Twilight* vampire. Wouldn't just watch you sleeping, though.'

'I'm on the basement floor.'

'I could tunnel in then.'

'My room's too small.'

'Small is good. Cosy. We'd have to stay close all night.'

'No! You can't stay.'

Chris stopped, turned me towards him and cupped my face gently in his hands. 'Look at me, Kelly Ann. What's wrong?'

'Nothing. I don't know.' I looked away from him. 'It's just not allowed, that's all. Look, here's a wine bar. It's a bit expensive usually, but they do a two drinks for one on Tuesdays.'

Despite it being a cheap night the place wasn't too crowded so we found a table near the bar easily enough and Chris went off to order our drinks.

'What's that?' I asked when he returned with what looked like a fizzy white wine. 'I didn't ask for a sparkling wine.'

'It isn't,' he said, smiling. 'I asked them to put some lemonade in it. The way you like it.'

'Oh God, what did you do that for? They'll think I'm some idiot who doesn't know anything about wine.'

Chris frowned. 'Does it matter what they think?'

I took a sip of the wine. Actually it did taste better. Nice and sweet, although I know I'm not supposed to like that. 'Suppose not. Did you check your change? Some of the staff here are a bit dodgy. Especially if they think you're a tourist.'

'You think I can't count?'

'No, it's just that, well, you're not used to London and—'

'And so a country yokel like me won't be able to cope in a sophisticated metropolis like London.' He took a swig of his Miller beer then put the bottle on the table. 'Not used to these fancy foreign beers. Think I'll just away home to my croft and have a wee dram with my haggis and tatties. Then it's an early night for me. Got some sheep shearing to do at dawn.'

I giggled. 'Sorry, Chris.'

'It's nice to hear you laugh. I've missed that. I've missed you,' he said, smiling.

'Oh God, I've missed you too.'

'Have you?' he asked, his expression serious again.

'Of course I have. What do you mean?'

'Well, since you've been down here you hardly ever returned my calls or texts.'

'That's not true. Well, maybe sometimes. I . . . I've just been busy, that's all. Working. Mostly.'

'Are you sure that's all?'

'Yeah, what else would there be?'

'I don't know. Even when we *have* talked on the phone you seemed different somehow.'

I sighed. 'The English accent, you mean? I can't help that. I pick up accents easily.'

'No, not just that. You seemed distant. Preoccupied. I thought I was losing you.' He stretched out his arm, stroked my cheek with his hand and stared at me intently. 'Did I lose you?'

I leaned over and kissed him. 'You could never lose me. I love you.'

'Let's go back to the hotel,' Chris murmured. 'We've got a nice room waiting for us. We can have a drink there. If we want. No climbing or tunnelling necessary.'

I nodded. Smiled. 'OK.'

But just as we were about to leave I spotted Theresa and Yan coming in. I kept my head down and tried to sidle past but it was hopeless.

'Hi, Kelly Ann,' Theresa said, but looked pointedly at Chris.

There was no way out. I'd have to introduce him to her. 'Hi, this is Chris. My boyfriend from home. He just came down today. Sorry we can't stop to chat but we were just going.'

Yan nodded politely but Theresa had her nosy face on. She'd be more difficult to shake off.

'Hi,' she said with a friendly smile. 'It's great to meet you.'

'You too,' Chris said.

'We've heard a lot about you.' She laughed. 'All good stuff so no worries.' She peered at him more closely. 'God, you look a bit younger than I imagined, though.'

Chris shrugged. Made no comment.

Theresa looked at me, puzzled. 'So how come you didn't tell us Chris was coming down?'

'I didn't know. He wanted to surprise me.'

'Oh, that's lovely,' Theresa gushed. 'So romantic.'

'Yeah, it is. So we kind of wanted to, you know, catch up.'

'Oh, right.' Theresa laughed. 'We'll see you two later then.'

'Yeah, hope so,' I lied brightly.

Oh God, how was I going to keep Chris hidden away from anyone who knew me for nearly a week? But somehow I'd have to. Just couldn't face everyone finding out about all my lies. Especially Chris.

Once outside Chris pulled me into his arms again and pressed his lips to mine. He stroked my hair, kissed my neck, and soon I forgot about everything except how wonderful it was to be together again. Felt myself melting. Oh God, it had been so long. Heard someone moan. Think it was me.

We broke apart and hurried back to the hotel. Joy was still on duty and eyed us both curiously. Chris asked for the key. She handed it to him. 'Have a nice evening,' she said to us both with a smirk.

Chris nodded. 'Thanks.'

I ignored her and set off in the direction of the lifts.

His room was on the second floor. He kissed me lightly on the mouth, then opened the door with a flourish and invited me in. On the double bed lay a bouquet of long-stemmed red roses. A tray with two tall slim glasses and an ice bucket containing real champagne rested on the bedside table. Oh my God, how much had this cost him? Felt tears prick the corner of my eyes. OK, I might be an utter failure in some things, but none of this mattered to Chris. I'd found an amazing boyfriend. In this, at least, I was a huge success.

'Oh God, Chris, you shouldn't have.'

'Yeah, maybe you're right,' he said, his expression all serious.

'What?'

'Well, judging by how you snogged me outside earlier I could probably have pulled you with a bunch of daffs and a bottle of cider.'

I laughed, moved to mock slap him, but he dodged me, pulled my arm over and we both landed on the bed. I winced. Roses are gorgeous and my favourite flower – just a pity about the thorns.

But soon I forgot all about the slight scratches they'd given me. Forgot about everything really except how good it was to feel the weight of Chris's body on top of me again, his hands stroking my thighs, lips exploring mine.

We were interrupted by the phone ringing.

'Ignore it,' I whispered.

'I wasn't planning on answering it.' He smiled as he stretched over and unplugged it.

I unbuttoned his shirt, pulled it off. He helped me peel off my sweater and T-shirt and tossed them on the floor. At last we were touching skin on skin. Someone moaned. Chris, this time. He kissed my throat, but my pendant got in the way so he unclasped it. He was about to put it on the bedside table when he stopped.

'This new?'

I flushed. 'Oh, yeah. I, erm, bought it yesterday at a sale in Covent Garden. Usually I wear the one you got me but just this once . . .'

I trailed off because he'd turned it over and was reading the inscription on the back out loud.

'*To KA, love from M*. With two kisses.'

I sat up. 'It's not what it seems like.'

Chris stood up and tossed the pendant at me. 'What's going on, Kelly Ann?'

'Nothing. I promise you. I just thought you'd be annoyed if I told you Mark had given it to me. And I didn't know about the inscription. Honestly, Chris, I wouldn't lie to you. Not about anything important, anyway.'

He sighed. Ran a hand through his hair. 'I want to

believe you. It's just that you seem to have changed since you left Glasgow. I'm not sure I really know you any more.'

'I love you, Chris. That won't ever change.'

Someone knocked loudly on the door. For God's sake. If this was Theresa I'd kill her.

'Go away!' I shouted.

'Kelly Ann, is that you?' Joy asked. 'Is your boyfriend there?'

'No, go away,' I said again.

'Kelly Ann, it *is* you. Open up, please. It's an emergency.'

Shit. This had better be good. We dressed quickly. I opened the door but Joy ignored me. Looked right past me and spoke to Chris.

'Doctor, there's a woman gone into labour on the third floor, room three-oh-five. We've called an ambulance but it's caught up in traffic. Please come quickly. I think she's going to have the thing before the paramedics get here.'

'I think there's been some mistake—' Chris said.

But Joy wasn't listening. Instead, she turned to me and rattled on. 'You show him where it is, Kelly Ann. David is with her but you know what a useless prat he is. I'm off downstairs to wait for the ambulance and make sure no one blocks the entrance.'

She sped off before either of us could say anything.

'I don't understand. Why would she think I'm a

doctor? Has she got me mixed up with someone else?'

'Don't know,' I lied, 'but we'd better go and see if we can help David. He's meant to be the first-aid guy but he's a tosser. Couldn't deliver a self-addressed letter, never mind a baby.'

We dashed off upstairs. The door of room 305 was partially open and we could hear a woman screaming and swearing.

When we went in the woman who'd been arguing with her husband yesterday at breakfast was crouched on the floor at the foot of the bed groaning, her large pink dressing gown not quite covering her enormous belly. David was standing in the corner of the room with his back to the wall, as far away from her as possible. He was holding a mobile phone. 'You'll be all right, Mrs Kennedy,' he said. 'Ambulance won't be too long.' He spotted us. Ran over and handed the phone to Chris. 'Thank God you've come, Doctor. The paramedics are on the line now. They want to talk to you.'

'I'm not a doctor,' Chris said. 'I'm a medical student.'

'Shit. Kelly Ann told everyone you were a doctor.'

Chris glared at me. 'Well, I'm not.'

'Well, you'll have to do for now. I'll go see if any of the other guests are doctors.'

Then he opened the door and ran off. Wanted to follow him, but the woman gave another scream and shouted, 'Somebody help me!'

We both hurried over to her. Chris knelt in front of her and put his hands on her shoulders. 'Mrs Kennedy, I'm not a doctor, I'm a medical student, but I think I can help you. Do you want me to help you?'

'Yeeees,' she panted. 'For God's sake.'

'Where is your husband? Has someone contacted him?'

'Out on the piss, as usual, and not answering his bloody mobile!'

Chris nodded, identified himself to the paramedics on the phone then strode into the bathroom and returned with two towels.

'Kelly Ann, put this one underneath her to deliver the baby on. Leave the other until later.'

'You want me to stay?'

'Yes, you helped with your sister's baby, didn't you? So you'll know what happens.'

'Well, I was there,' I whispered, 'but I didn't see anything.'

'What?'

'I closed my eyes. I mean, I wasn't going to look at my sister's private bits, was I?'

Chris rolled his eyes. 'Just do what I tell you then and try to keep her calm. And pay attention this time. I might need you.'

He went back into the bathroom and washed his hands quickly but thoroughly, right up to the elbows, while I tried to manoeuvre the towel underneath the woman's hips. She started to slip forward so I held her shoulders to support her and muttered something stupid like, 'So are you hoping for a boy or a girl then?'

'One or the other,' she snapped, then groaned again as another contraction gripped her.

When Chris came back he was talking to someone on the phone. He knelt down in front of the woman and asked if this was her first baby.

'No, but it will be the bloody last,' she said. 'I've learned my lesson this time.'

He relayed this information to whoever was on the phone. Asked some more questions, which she tried to answer between groans and screams.

Chris was amazing. He stayed dead calm the whole time. Reassuring her everything would be all right while relaying information quickly and concisely to the paramedic and taking instructions. A lot of it I didn't understand, like: 'Cervix fully dilated, head crowning.' Other bits I did. 'No time, baby's head is coming through.'

At this the woman bellowed like cattle being tortured as she squeezed the baby's head out. Gross. Wouldn't have blamed Chris if he'd freaked out then and run for it, but he stayed where he was and supported the head gently with his hand.

'Well done,' he said. 'You're nearly there.'

He was right too. With a couple more pushes the

shoulders came through, then the whole baby slipped out onto the towel.

The woman sighed with relief and slumped back exhausted, resting her head on the floor. 'What is it?' she asked.

When Chris didn't reply right away she asked again, 'Look, I know you're just a medical student, not a doctor, but surely you can tell if it's a girl or a boy.'

'It's a girl,' Chris said. But there was no relief or joy in his tone. I looked at his face, which for the first time seemed worried rather than calm. I glanced again at the baby. It was covered in blood and gunk and its face was a bit bashed in – just like my nephew had looked when he came out. But this baby was a bluish colour and was completely still and silent like a doll. Oh God, it wasn't breathing!

Noticed that the umbilical cord was round its neck but Chris had already slipped his fingers underneath and was easing it off. Still the baby didn't breathe. The guy on the phone was asking questions, but Chris didn't answer. Instead he cleared some gunge from the baby's mouth and nose. Still no movement at all from the baby. Chris, his face pale and grim, tilted its body so its head was a bit lower than the rest of it, then started rubbing its chest and feet. At last it gave a little gasp, then another. Then it screwed up its face and bawled.

Yay! Have never been so happy to hear a baby crying in my life.

Chris slumped forward with a sigh of relief and closed his eyes for a second.

I wrapped the baby in the spare towel and handed it to its mum. 'Don't worry, it will look a lot better once it's been washed,' I soothed.

But she wasn't listening to me – just gazing adoringly at her baby's red, bad-tempered face. 'She's beautiful.'

Chris went off to wash his hands again and splash water on his face. Noticed that his fingers, which had been so steady all this time, were shaking a bit now. He must have been near to panic when the baby didn't breathe, but he'd held himself in check until the emergency was over. He was going to make a fabulous doctor. Don't think I've ever been so proud of him. Or fancied him so much.

When he came back the woman thanked him.

'That's all right, Mrs Kennedy. I'm just glad everything went OK.'

'I think you could call me Maggie,' she said. 'Now that we've got to know each other a bit.'

'You're welcome, Maggie.'

'What's your name?'

'Chris.'

'If it were a boy, I'd have called him after you, but—'

'I understand,' he said.

She turned to me and smiled. 'What's your name, love?'

'Kelly Ann,' I said.

'Kelly Ann,' she repeated. 'Hmm, Kelly Ann.'

'Yeah.' I smiled. 'Are you going to name your baby after me?'

She shook her head. 'Sorry, love, I would have, but the fact is, I'm not that keen on your name. No offence, but I think I'll call her Coral. It's a nice name.'

Thanks a bunch!

Next thing I knew, the door burst open and the ambulance crew piled in, followed by Joy, David and a middle-aged bearded guy in a bathrobe and slippers holding a doctor's bag. Brilliant. Would have appreciated them a lot more ten minutes ago.

The crew immediately surrounded the new mum and baby, but after a quick check they relaxed, shook Chris's hand and said they would take them both to hospital but everything would be fine.

Chris and I went back to his room and sat on the bed – both drained. After a minute he got up, ignored the champagne but opened the minibar and downed a miniature bottle of whisky in one go. He took out another bottle and offered it to me but I refused. Don't like to seem unpatriotic but I'd rather drink toilet cleaner than Scotch – even the smell of the stuff makes me want to retch. Chris slugged back the second bottle, leaned against the wall and stared at me, his expression grim.

'Why did you lie about me being a doctor?'

'It's not really a lie. Not much of one, anyway. You will be a doctor one day.'

'Why did you lie, Kelly Ann?' he insisted.

'I don't know. It's just that saying you were a doctor sounded, well, more interesting. More mature, somehow. Anyway, it was just a little lie. There's no harm done.'

'It wasn't a little lie. Because of you, the hotel staff came looking for me, a first-year medical student, instead of searching the guest list for a properly qualified doctor. You could have put that woman's life at risk. And her baby's.'

'But they're fine.'

'No thanks to you.'

'But you were great. I mean, you're way smarter than most ordinary doctors, anyway. Everyone at uni says you're brilliant.'

'It's not a matter of how smart I am, Kelly Ann. It's a matter of experience. I haven't done practical obstetrics on the ward. There are some things you just can't learn from books.' He sighed. 'Now, I'm going to ask you one more time and this time I want an answer. Why did you lie?'

'I don't know. I just wanted to pretend I was older. More sophisticated, more exciting, I suppose. So I had to have an older, more mature, experienced boyfriend as well.'

'And what else have you lied about?'

'Nothing.'

'Are you sure?'

'Yeah.'

'Thing is, while I was waiting for you earlier I talked to your other friend, Suzie. She told me you had an agent who'd set up a meeting between you and some dance company director and that you had been planning, up until yesterday, to stay in London permanently.'

'Oh God.'

'I reckoned she must have picked things up wrong. Maybe you'd started taking some dance lessons here. Perhaps you might think of coming to London after we've both finished uni. Something like that.'

I flushed. 'Yeah, something like that.'

'Because I didn't believe you'd keep something as important as this from me. But now I'm not so sure.'

'I don't have an agent,' I said. 'I just wish I did. So I made it up.'

'And what about this guy? The one who gave you the locket.'

'I told you, he's a friend. Just a friend. That's all. You have to believe me.'

'Why should I believe you? You've lied about everything else.'

'Not about that. Look, I just wanted to be someone else for a while. Someone interesting and exciting. That's all.'

'Yeah? Well, the Kelly Ann I knew and loved never pretended to be something she wasn't. The girl I knew was honest, authentic, the real deal. Not some phoney with a put-on English accent playacting.'

'Chris, don't! That's not true. Please try to understand.'

'I don't understand much any more, but I do know that the Kelly Ann I loved has changed into someone else in just six short weeks. And I don't think I like her.'

'You don't mean that.'

'Every word.'

Felt tears stinging my eyes. 'Maybe I should just go.'

'Maybe you should.'

I sprang up and made for the door, turned the handle and opened it. He didn't try to stop me like I'd hoped. I turned round. 'That's me going then.'

He nodded. Turned his back on me.

Damn Coral. Why, oh why, did she have to be born tonight?

WEDNESDAY SEPTEMBER 4TH

'So,' Theresa said, 'let me get this straight. You're seventeen, not nineteen. Your boyfriend is a first-year medical student, not a doctor. Oh, and you've never danced in any proper theatres or shows. Is that it?'

I hung my head. 'Yeah, pretty much. Except I don't think he's my boyfriend any more.'

'But your name *is* Kelly Ann?' Suzie said.

'Of course.'

'And you do come from Glasgow?' she continued.

'Yeah.'

'And I know you can break a mugger's nose with your high heel and do the splits. But not at the same time.'

Despite everything, I grinned. 'All true.'

Theresa laughed. 'You're a mad eejit most of the time too. But why all the lies?'

'I don't know. I suppose I just wanted to impress you. It was stupid. I'm really sorry.'

'Don't worry, Kelly Ann,' Theresa said. 'We've all told a few porkies at times.'

'Yeah,' Suzie agreed. 'And mostly for the same idiotic reasons.'

'I wish Chris was as laid back about it as you two,' I said.

Theresa frowned. 'You mean he'll really finish with you just over a few white lies? That's a bit harsh.'

'You don't know Chris. He's really, I don't know, *moral* about some things. And my pretending he was a doctor already really got to him. I got a text from him last night. Said he was going back home today and not to bother coming to say goodbye.'

Theresa folded her arms. 'You've got to speak to him before he goes. I'll tell Joy to let us know when he's checking out and to stall him until we get there. She owes you one for helping her get shot of Sidebottom and for the intro to Sam.'

'We?' I said.

'Yeah. Me and Suzie will come with you. Make him see sense.'

'Hmm, I don't know if that's a good idea.'

'Trust us,' Theresa said.

Oh God.

Chris was standing by the desk at reception with his rucksack on the floor, and even from the back he looked impatient and frustrated by the extremely slow check-out procedure Joy was putting him through. She spotted us and nodded. Completed the process at last with her usual efficiency. Chris picked up his bag and swung round.

'Hi,' I said.

'You didn't need to come say goodbye,' he said. 'I told you that.'

'I wanted to. So did my friends Suzie and Theresa.'

He nodded politely.

'Yeah,' Theresa said. 'We're Kelly Ann's friends. And we think she's OK – even if she does tell the odd little lie now and then. Doesn't everyone?'

Chris raised an eyebrow. 'Little lie?'

'Yeah,' Suzie chimed in. 'Everybody does.'

'Look, I appreciate you're Kelly Ann's friends but this really has nothing to do with you.'

'Especially when you're away from home for the first time,' Suzie continued, ignoring him. 'When I started uni I was living in halls and everyone's family seemed so much richer and classier than mine. So I pretended my dad was a wealthy businessman in Hong Kong instead of a failed Chinese takeaway owner in Hackney.'

'Same thing with me, sort of,' Theresa added. 'When I first came to London to study English Literature, I thought everyone was smarter and more interesting than me. So I pretended I lived right next door to Marian Keyes and that she was best pals with my mum and me. Even forged her signature and dedication on one of her books. *For Theresa, my inspiration and best mate.*'

Chris sighed and his stern expression seemed to soften. He brushed a hand through his hair. 'OK, right, I get what you're saying. I'll think about it.'

'Good.' Theresa beamed. 'And, you know, you shouldn't be so harsh on Kelly Ann. Especially given her mother's Alzheimer's at such a young age. It's bound to put a terrible strain on a daughter.'

Chris threw me a look of contempt, slung his rucksack over his back and strode out.

Knew for sure now that it was over. For ever.

THURSDAY SEPTEMBER 5TH

Saw Mark kiss the leggy, sporty girl goodbye this morning as I was passing reception on my way to get more cleaning stuff from supplies. It was only eight-thirty so it was totally obvious they had spent the night together. He caught me staring. I looked away quickly and hurried off.

'Kelly Ann, wait!' he called and jogged after me. He caught up with me just by the stairs. 'Hey, I'm glad I caught you. Can we talk?'

I stopped. Turned round. 'Hi,' I said reluctantly. 'I'm actually kind of busy right now.'

'I won't take long. I heard you and your boyfriend split. I'm sorry.'

I shrugged. 'Not your fault.'

'I'm sorry, anyway.'

'Yeah, me too.'

'I saw you looking over at me. I guess you think I'm pretty shallow. Right?'

'Not my business.'

'You know, my relationship with Cindy isn't exclusive – we both see other people when we want.'

'You don't need to explain anything to me. Like I said, it's not really my business.'

'But I want to. Truth is, I really care what you think of me, Kelly Ann.'

I shrugged. 'OK then.'

'Well, the way I see it is we've got one life, right? One shot at the game. And I want to play it. Live life to the max. I don't want to regret a bunch of stuff I never tried. I want to experience everything. Have it all, I suppose. Can you understand that?'

I stared at him. 'Have you ever loved anyone so much that even though you fancied someone else like mad, you would never want to sleep with them?'

He hesitated for a moment. 'No,' he said slowly, 'I've never felt that way about anyone.'

'Then you haven't experienced everything, have you?'

'I guess not,' he conceded.

'So you can't actually have it all, can you?'

'You're right, I can't argue with that.' He smiled wryly. 'Ever thought of studying law?'

I smiled back. 'No.'

'You know, Kelly Ann, I do regret one thing.'

'What's that?'

'That I didn't meet you before you fell for your boyfriend. Yeah, I really regret that.'

Thought about it. Would Mark have fancied me when I was, say, thirteen or fourteen? A tomboy covered in spots and happier about winning a spitting competition with Gary and his pals (five metres twenty-nine centimetres – a record with the help of a mouthful of Irn Bru) than dating the class hottie?

'No, you don't. Trust me.'

But Mark did give me, Suzie and Theresa a nice going-away present just before he left for the airport. He'd been looking into UK employment law, and apparently Frost wasn't allowed to make most of the deductions to our pay that she did, no matter what we'd signed up for in our contracts. Something to do with statutory rights, he'd said, which Suzie seemed to understand right away, but not me or Theresa. We all understood, though, when he said, 'Bottom line is, your employer owes you guys a shitload of money or you could haul her ass to a tribunal.'

Frost understood too when we told her! Yay!

We won't be paid until Saturday though, and I'm completely broke. Went upstairs after work to see if I could cadge a cigarette from Theresa or Suzie as I'd none left. And I really, really wanted one. I suppose I must have started inhaling after all and got really into in it somehow, rather than just pretending to smoke to fit in. Come to think of it, I've been leaving much smaller fag ends too, and one tramp who'd practically stalked me before to nab my discarded butts had got really grumpy then disappeared. Oh God, I *had* changed on this holiday. I'd become a smoker!

'Sorry, Kelly Ann, I've given up,' Theresa said. 'Yan worries that they're not good for me.' She smiled. 'And he says the smell spoils my beautiful red hair.'

Bloody hell. First time she's admitted to having red hair. But I didn't say anything.

Asked Suzie.

'I'm sorry, Kelly Ann, but I've given up too. Or I'm

trying to, anyway. Alec says successful business people don't smoke. It's the wrong image.'

'Oh, right. Well, good for you.'

'It's not easy, though.' Suzie grimaced and showed me her Nicorette patch. 'Wish I'd never started. It was peer pressure, really. Some girls I started to hang out with smoked and I didn't want to look different. Wanted to fit in, you know. God, I was stupid.'

Theresa nodded. 'Same thing happened with me. Got to know some girls who were a couple of years older than me who smoked. I thought they were pretty cool. So when they offered me a cigarette I took it. How stupid can you get?' She popped a piece of Nicorette gum in her mouth. 'What about you, Kelly Ann? How come you started smoking?'

'Same,' I sighed.

'Never mind. Guess what I've got to cheer us up before payday?' She took a bottle of vodka from a cupboard and brandished it about. 'It's Polish. Another present from Yan. Because we don't want to be giving up too many bad habits all at once.'

Spent the rest of the night with Suzie and Theresa drinking vodka, congratulating ourselves again on our triumph over Frost, and slagging off Sidebottom as well as the mean guest who tipped Suzie five pence this afternoon. When I got back to my room around midnight I realized how much I was going to miss them when I left.

They'd been really great friends to me – loyal and fun. But I'd no reason to stay now. I'd have to go home on Monday. But go home to what?

SATURDAY SEPTEMBER 7TH

Payday – and much more cash than usual due to Frost giving us back nearly all the deductions she owed us. Normally I'd be happy but I'm not. Totally miserable, in fact. But it's a bit better to be miserable and have money than miserable with none, I suppose, so I went to the shops straight after work to buy stuff to cheer myself up.

I splashed out on a red T-shirt, purple skirt and yellow canvas shoes because I thought the bright colours might make me look and feel less depressed. When I got back, I tried them all on and examined my solemn-faced reflection in the mirror. Hmm. Didn't look any happier. In fact, I looked more like a large budgie who'd given up the will to live and was seconds from throwing its multi-coloured body under a steamroller.

I took them off, pulled on black jeans and a grey jumper which were more in keeping with my mood. And the weather, which had turned a bit chilly. Seems like my scorching summer in London was well and truly over already. Went to the newsagent's, where I bought chocolate and crisps. Noticed they had Irn Bru in stock for the first time too. Hmm, just as I was due to go back home. Typical. Bought six cans of Irn Bru as well. Almost bought cigarettes too. But hesitated. They were expensive and none of my friends now smoked. If I carried on any longer with this I'd probably get really addicted like Theresa and Suzie and one day have to wear stupid patches and chew bad-tasting gum while still wanting to gnaw my knuckles off.

Decided not to buy them, after all. Hmm. Probably one of the few good decisions I'd made since coming to here. That and the decision not to cheat on Chris with Mark. But where had it got me? Chris had finished with me anyway.

It's hard to believe it's only two days until I go back to Glasgow. Feels like I've been here for ever and it seems weird to be leaving. But I've booked my ticket: Euston to Glasgow single one-way direct for Monday, and that will be it. Not only leaving the hotel and the friends I've made here but London too. For good.

I suppose I had uni to look forward to. I won't be going back to school, and uni will be different. No teachers taking registers and handing out punishment exercises for not doing homework. Student bars, clubs and parties instead of school dinners and netball practice. But still, it was depressing. Another three or four years of studying and sitting exams, which I'd probably pass, but not that well, and then what?

It's different for Chris, who wants to be a doctor more than anything and is brilliant at exams. He has his future all mapped out. But me? The best thing about Glasgow and uni was I'd be with Chris. Well, not any more.

Of course, I'd called, texted and emailed Chris loads of times over the last few days. Made more grovelling apologies. Swore to him that I'd never cheated on him with Mark. Begged him to forgive me. But the only answer I got was that he needed time to think things over and I shouldn't contact him again until then.

At least I'd still have my best friends Stephanie and Liz. Or maybe not. Realized guiltily that I'd been so caught up in my new life in London and all the new people I'd met that I'd hardly answered any of their texts or emails lately. Probably they'd want nothing to do with me either. Couldn't blame them.

Texted them, anyway: HI, COMING HOME MONDAY. SORRY I'VE NOT BEEN IN TOUCH FOR A WHILE. U WERE RIGHT. HAVE MADE A TOTAL ARSE OF EVERYTHING. KA X

Liz called first – about thirty seconds after I pressed the SEND button. 'Right, tell me everything. Don't worry – anything you say is completely confidential. I won't tell another living soul.'

Oh God.

Stephanie called next. 'Liz told me everything. For God's sake! Only you could get dumped by your boyfriend and not even get to shag the fit American guy who's been drooling after you. Will you never learn!'

But both of them promised to be there for me when I got back and help me sort out this latest mess. Whatever else I'd lost, at least it wasn't my two best friends.

SUNDAY SEPTEMBER 8TH

Went to Madame Tussauds for my last full day in London. Suzie's idea, since I hadn't met any famous people here like I'd hoped. Got photographs taken with Robert Pattinson, Johnny Depp and loads of other famous people. Not quite the same, though, and really annoying as I've heard Liz and Stephanie spotted Brad Pitt when he was filming in Glasgow and got his autograph. Just my luck.

Still, I bet they didn't manage to get a sneaky snog with him the way I did with Robert and Johnny. Well, those figures are very lifelike and if you use your imagination . . . Better than a mobile phone or a giraffe, anyway.

MONDAY SEPTEMBER 9TH

Said a tearful goodbye to Suzie and Theresa this morning. They will stay another week at the hotel, then move out to share a flat in Camden with another girl Suzie knows. We made promises to keep in touch, but it won't be the same with them in London and me four hundred miles away in Glasgow.

Picked up my final payslip, then Yan went with me to the station and helped me get my luggage on the train. Then he took a pink-wrapped box from his pocket and handed it to me.

'Oh my God, you shouldn't have,' I said. 'That was so nice of you.'

His big face flushed. 'It is for your mother. She is a very gracious and wise lady.'

'Oh, right. Well, thanks, anyway.'

I hugged him goodbye and he hurried off. As the train pulled out of the station I made a vow. One day I'd be back. Maybe not for a long time, but I *would* come back to live and work in London. I'd be older then. More sophisticated. Smarter. Next time I wouldn't make an arse of everything.

Mum and Dad were at the station to meet me. So were Liz and Stephanie. But no Chris, of course. Well, I really hadn't expected him to be there, had I? So how come I felt heavy and sick with disappointment?

It was nice to be home and back in my own room. Stephanie and Liz wanted to stay and catch up on all that had been happening, but even though I'd missed them, I just couldn't face talking about anything right then. Especially not about Chris. For once even Liz understood and they left me alone.

Couldn't be bothered to unpack either, even with the luxury of having drawers to put things in, so I just slumped down on my bed and cried.

Must have fallen asleep as it was dark by the time Mum came up with a cup of tea and a square sausage sandwich with brown sauce. My favourite supper. But it might as well have been sandpaper filled with sawdust – it tasted of nothing and chewing was just a chore.

Oh, Chris, I'm back home but nothing is the same any more. I clasped Chris's pendant to my heart, remembering when he'd given it to me in the train. *'If you love someone, let them go. If they come back they're yours. If they don't they never were.'* It was so true. But what I didn't realize then was that it wasn't just Chris letting *me* go. I was letting Chris go too. And he was never coming back.

SUNDAY SEPTEMBER 15TH

I was in my room listening to sad love songs Chris and I used to like. Well, actually, OK, *I* used to like – Chris was more into R&B instrumentals and rock – when Liz and Stephanie burst into my room.

'What are you doing here?' I said. 'I told you I didn't feel like doing anything today.'

Liz folded her arms and glared at me. 'This has gone

on long enough, Kelly Ann. It's been nearly a week now. You're going over to Chris's to sort this out.'

I shook my head. 'Look, I know you mean well, but it's hopeless.'

'Rubbish,' Liz said. 'C'mon, stop wasting time. You're going over there right now.'

'No way,' Stephanie said.

'Thanks, Stephanie,' I said gratefully. 'At least one of my friends understands how—'

'No way are you going anywhere looking like that!' Stephanie continued, opening a large tote bag she'd brought with her. She spilled the contents onto my bed: pots of creams and powders, make-up brushes and sponges, lipsticks, lip-liners, lip-glosses, plumpers, eye-shadow pallets, blushers, bronzers, concealers, as well as other stuff I'd never heard of like primers and ceramides.

She picked out two tubs and handed them to Liz, along with some circular cotton pads. 'I'll go through her stuff and see if I can pick out a decent outfit. Or maybe an indecent one. Ha ha. You take her into the bathroom and exfoliate her face – should get rid of the worst of those blotches. Oh, and put the cucumber eye-mask on for at least ten minutes. Let's hope that takes some of the redness and puffiness away. Then I'll see if I can do some-thing about her hair. I mean, has she even brushed it since she got back? She can't very well go and see her ex looking like Mr Rochester's mad wife.'

'Wait a minute,' I said. '*She's* here and she's already told you she's not going anywhere.'

Liz scowled at me. 'We can do this the easy way or the hard way, Kelly Ann. Which is it to be?'

'I'm not going.'

'The easy way,' Liz continued, 'is you let us make you look nice then you go with us to Chris's.'

'And the hard way?' I couldn't help asking.

'You have intensive counselling by me. For as long as it takes. All night. All week. All month. Fine by me. Then you go with us to Chris's.'

I headed for the bathroom.

When Stephanie was satisfied with my appearance – 'You'll have to do, I suppose' – they marched me off to Chris's, holding me between them with their arms locked round my elbows like prison warders escorting an inmate. All that was missing was the handcuffs and leg chains.

But the closer we got, the more my stomach twisted and churned. This just felt wrong.

'Stop! I can't do this. It's going to end in disaster. I just know it.'

'Well, it's already a disaster,' Stephanie pointed out. 'Chris has finished with you. I mean, how much worse could it get?'

'Yeah, that's true, I suppose,' I said, oddly comforted.

'Not strictly true,' Liz argued. ''Cos if this afternoon

goes badly you could be humiliated on top of being dumped, which *would* be worse.'

'That's it,' I said, trying but failing to break free of my captors. 'Liz is right. I'm not going.'

Stephanie scowled at Liz. 'Yeah, great point. Well done. You'd make a fantastic psychologist.'

'But it could go well, probably it will go brilliantly,' – Liz soothed unconvincingly.

'Anyway, it's all his fault,' Stephanie added.

'It is?' I said.

'Yeah,' they both chorused emphatically.

'How?' I asked.

Stephanie shrugged. 'He's a guy, isn't he? Must be his fault. We'll think of something.'

'Yeah, of course it's his fault,' Liz agreed. 'You just remember that. You're the victim here.'

'I am?'

'Definitely,' Stephanie said. 'But you're not going to take any more crap from him. Why should you?'

'No,' I agreed doubtfully. 'Why should I?'

'It's not as though Chris is perfect, you know,' Liz continued. 'I called him three days ago and offered couples' counselling and you'll never guess what he said to me?'

'No,' I lied. 'I've no idea.'

'He told me to mind my own business.'

'Tosser,' Stephanie said. 'Much the same thing happened

to me. I called him yesterday. Told him how stupid he was. I mean, you've both been without sex for over six weeks and what has he done about it? It's not natural.'

'And what did Chris say?' I asked, knowing I was supposed to.

'Told me he'd no intention of discussing his sex life with me or anyone else and hung up.'

'He didn't!' Liz said. 'God, he's so repressed. We're definitely going to have to do something about your boyfriend.'

'Ex-boyfriend,' I corrected.

But no one was listening to me.

For the rest of the way Stephanie and Liz kept on about how wrong Chris had been to dump me, and how he needed to be told straight and made to pay for his bad behaviour. Started to believe it myself. Maybe they were right. Chris had been horrible to me and I didn't deserve it. Felt better. It hurt a lot less to be mad at him than just desperately longing for him.

But when we got to his house I hesitated. 'Oh God, I don't know if I can face him now. Not today, anyway.'

But Liz and Stephanie totally ignored me and practically dragged me, toes scraping along the garden path, to the porch. Liz was about to rap on the door when it opened. But it wasn't Chris. It was his dad. He had his jacket on and his car keys in his hands.

'Hello, girls,' he said. 'This is a surprise. Haven't seen you in a long time. How are you?'

'Never mind that,' Liz said. 'Where is he?'

'You mean Chris?' his dad asked.

'If you want to call him that!' Liz snapped. 'We can think of other words.'

His dad looked puzzled. 'Yes, well, that *is* his name. He's upstairs. Come on in. I'll tell him you're here, then I'll have to go. Meeting the wife in town for sales shopping. For my sins.'

'You just go on,' Stephanie said. 'You don't want to miss the best bargains. We'll go up and confront Chris ourselves.'

'Confront him?'

'Have a bit of a chat. Catch up,' Liz said, pushing past him and pulling me inside. Stephanie followed and we all headed for the stairs.

Chris's dad cast a worried glance in our direction. Mouthed what I thought was, 'Sorry, son. Good luck,' then hurried off.

We barged into Chris's bedroom. He was sitting on the bed listening to music with headphones in, bouncing a football rhythmically on the floor with one hand while reading an anatomy book he held with the other – unlike most guys Chris could always definitely multitask. He looked perfectly relaxed and happy. Well, until he saw us, anyway. Hated him. And loved him too. So much.

Chris stood up, startled, and removed his headphones.

He glanced at me first, and for a moment I thought I saw an expression of relief. Love, even. But it was too fleeting for me to be sure – probably just my wishful thinking.

He turned his attention to Stephanie and Liz. 'What are you doing here?'

'We could ask you the same question,' Liz snapped.

Chris looked puzzled. 'Well, it *is* my bedroom.'

'Never mind that. Don't try to change the subject. Why aren't you at Kelly Ann's begging forgiveness for how you've treated her?' Liz asked.

Chris frowned at Liz. 'This is none of your business.'

'None of my business!' Liz fumed. 'You've got some nerve. Kelly Ann is my best friend in the whole world. The most loyal and wonderful friend anyone could ever have. Of course it's my business! And you've dumped her. Cast her aside like yesterday's fish and chip wrapping.

'Yeah,' Stephanie agreed. 'Kelly Ann is my best friend too. A fantastic, wonderful person even if she has no fashion sense whatsoever and once bought custard yellow eye shadow plus has insisted on wearing a pendant today that looks like a tampon—' Liz elbowed her in the ribs. 'Erm, but anyway, she didn't deserve to be dumped. Thrown away like a used condom. And for what? Because she told one tiny little lie—'

'More than one,' Chris corrected calmly.

'OK,' Stephanie conceded. 'Two tiny little lies—'

'More than two,' Chris said.

'Oh, for God's sake!' Stephanie snapped. 'Who's counting? This isn't about maths. But OK. All right. A few tiny little lies. Everyone tells lies. It's completely normal. Isn't it, Liz?'

'Yes, of course it is,' Liz agreed. 'Well, unless you're a compulsive liar and just can't stop yourself telling lies all the time. Or an autistic person who can't tell a lie at all. Not even, "Of course your bum doesn't look fat in that size twenty pencil skirt" or—'

'Get to the point, Liz,' Stephanie hissed.

'Oh right, well, the point is Kelly Ann didn't deserve to be chucked for a few little tiny white lies. I mean, some doctor you're going to be, Chris, if you won't treat patients just because they once told a fib. *I'm sorry, Mrs Brown, but you said you were two years younger than you really are on your consent form so I'm afraid you can't have the life-saving heart surgery and will just have to die. Serves you right for telling lies ...*' Liz ranted on but Chris had stopped listening. Instead, his gaze focused on me. 'Did you read the text I sent you this morning, Kelly Ann?'

'You sent me a text?'

He nodded. 'Yes.'

'Oh well, I haven't checked. Haven't even turned my mobile on this morning.' I took it from my pocket and switched it on. One message unread.

Stephanie snatched the mobile from me, pulled me out to the landing, put her mouth to my ear and whispered urgently, 'What have I told you about playing hard to get? Just keep quiet and let me handle this.'

We went back in. Liz had finally shut up, ending with, 'What's all this about a text?'

Stephanie ignored her and glared at Chris. 'Kelly Ann will read your message when she gets time, but she's likely to be busy for the next week or so. Lots of shopping and clubbing to do, not to mention dealing with all the requests for dates she's had from guys who've heard she's now single again. Had to fight them off with sticks.'

Liz snatched the phone from Stephanie. 'Probably better if I read it first. Just to make sure there is nothing in it which might be damaging to her sense of self-worth. She might need counselling before she can deal with it.'

But Chris prised the phone from Liz and handed it back to me. 'This is your mobile, Kelly Ann. And your text. What you do about it is your decision.'

I opened the message and read it, with Stephanie and Liz peering over my shoulder of course.

I WAS ANGRY AND JEALOUS. SAID THINGS I DIDN'T MEAN. I CAN'T LIVE WITHOUT YOU. FORGIVE ME? LOVE ALWAYS. CHRIS XX

'Remember what I said about playing it cool?' Stephanie hissed.

'We need to analyse this,' Liz cautioned. 'Deconstruct the meaning and implications.'

But they were too late because I'd already flung

myself at Chris, nearly knocking him over, but he caught me and whirled me up off my feet, then we were hugging and kissing and kissing and hugging and . . . well, you get the idea.

'For God's sake,' Liz said. 'Get a room!'

Chris put me down but kept an arm tight around my waist, holding me close as though he were worried I'd run off. *As if.*

'We've got a room,' he said, smiling. 'It's just a bit overcrowded right now.'

'Hmm,' Liz huffed. 'We wouldn't have had all this bother, Kelly Ann, if you'd just checked your bloody mobile this morning.'

'Yeah, sorry. But you know, in a way I'm glad I didn't,' I said.

'How come?' Liz asked.

'Yeah,' Stephanie said. 'How come? This has been a bloody waste of time. Especially since Ted Baker's got an end-of-summer sale on this afternoon.'

'Well,' I said. 'If I'd checked, then you wouldn't have needed to speak up for me today. And then I'd never have known you thought I was such a wonderful person and fantastic friend.'

Stephanie blushed – a thing I've almost never seen her do. 'Obviously I was exaggerating. Totally. Except the bit about your having no taste or fashion sense whatsoever, of course.'

'Me too,' Liz said, her face scarlet. 'Didn't mean any of it. I was just being ironic. In fact, now I come to think of it, we probably need to discuss your dysfunctional behaviour in the friend-relationship paradigm and—'

Chris unwound his arm from my waist, kissed me and whispered, 'Don't go away.' He moved over to Liz and Stephanie, put an arm round each of their shoulders and firmly guided them out of the bedroom and down the stairs.

Heard the front door close and Chris bounding back up. He crossed the room quickly again and we kissed for a long time until I could hardly breathe. When we eventually broke apart, Chris held both my hands in his and gazed at my face. 'I'm sorry for putting you through all this these last couple of weeks, Kelly Ann.'

I shook my head. 'No, it was my fault. I shouldn't have lied to you.'

'But I completely overreacted. The thing is, for most of the time you were away I was worried and suspicious.'

'Why?'

He shrugged. 'Like I told you in London, you seemed so distant sometimes on the phone. Different. I thought I was losing you.'

'Well, you weren't. And nothing happened between me and Mark. Honest.'

'I know.' He pulled me close and kissed me. 'You came back, Kelly Ann.'

'So did you,' I said.

'But I'm never going to let you go again.'

'I don't want you to.'

My phone buzzed. I ignored it, but then it went another twice. Three new messages.

'May as well check them, Kelly Ann, in case there is anything important. We've got all night to ourselves.'

Stephanie: REMEMBER – PLAY IT COOL. TREAT EM MEAN KEEP EM KEEN.

Liz: ARE U SURE U DON'T WANT COUPLES' COUNSELLING?

I smiled. They were great friends who really cared about me even if I'd no intention of taking their advice.

I opened the third message.

Mrs Davies: AUDITION FOR CHORUS DANCER – LONDON WEST END THEATRE ONE MONTH TIME. INTERESTED?

My smile vanished. Oh my God, another chance. What should I do?

'What is it, Kelly Ann? Anything important?' Chris asked.

I hesitated, then pressed DELETE ALL MESSAGES. 'No, nothing. Nothing important at all.'